Praise for Kerry Greenwood's Phryne Fisher series

'Phryne Fisher is gutsy and adventurous, and also well endowed with plenty of grey matter. She has it over Robicheaux and Poirot because she's drop-dead gorgeous.' *West Australian*

'Fisher is a sexy, sassy and singularly modish character. Her 1920s Melbourne is racy, liberal and a city where crime occurs on its shadowy, largely unlit streets.' *Canberra Times*

'Greenwood is the class act of local crime writing.' *Weekend Australian*

'A joy to read.' *Newcastle Herald*

'Snappy one-liners and the ability to fight like a wildcat are appealing in a central character.' *City Weekly*

'Greenwood's prose has a dagger in its garter; her hero is raunchy and promiscuous in the best sense.' *Weekend Australian*

'Manners and attitude maketh the PI, and Phryne is, as always, perfect.' *The Book Bulletin*

'Greenwood is a gifted storyteller with a light, sharp touch.' *Australian Book Review*

'Smart, sharp, incredibly stylish, fearless individual and completely the heroine!' *The Geelong*

KERRY GREENWOOD is the author of nineteen novels and the editor of two collections. Previous novels in the Phryne Fisher series are *Cocaine Blues, Flying too High, Murder on the Ballarat Train, Death at Victoria Dock, The Green Mill Murder, Blood and Circuses, Ruddy Gore, Urn Burial, Raisins and Almonds, Death Before Wicket, Away with the Fairies* and *Murder in Montparnasse*. She is also the author of several books for young adults and the Delphic Women series.

When she is not writing she is an advocate in Magistrates' Courts for the Legal Aid Commission. She is not married, has no children and lives with a registered Wizard.

THE
CASTLEMAINE
MURDERS

A Phryne Fisher
Mystery

Kerry Greenwood

ALLEN&UNWIN

Allen & Unwin
83 Alexander Street
Crows Nest NSW 2065
Australia
Phone: (61 2) 8425 0100
Fax: (61 2) 9906 2218
Email: info@allenandunwin.com
Web: www.allenandunwin.com

Cataloguing-in-Publication details are available from
the National Library of Australia
www.trove.nla.gov.au

ISBN 978 1 74114 074 3

Set in 11.5 pt Adobe Garamond by Midland Typesetters
Printed and bound in Australia by Griffin Press.

MIX
Paper from
responsible sources
FSC® C009448

The paper in this book is FSC® certified.
FSC® promotes environmentally responsible,
socially beneficial and economically viable
management of the world's forests.

20   19   18   17

This book is dedicated to
my dear cousin Muriel Wright.
Whose relatives would like to say that if EK has finished
with the ploughshare, they'd quite like it back . . .

And with many thanks to the usual cast, David
Greagg, Dennis Pryor, geologist Lesley Greagg,
cocktail concocter Mark Pryor, sinologist
Wendy Tolhurst, plus the remarkable and
ingenious researchers Graeme Duke and Jean
Greenwood, who between them found and
named Constable Thomas Cooke. Profound
gratitude to Anne Doggett and the energetic
and learned Hilary Griffiths of the Castlemaine Historical Society and to Sunshine
Library, which never ceases to surprise me . . .

The love of money is the root of all evil.

The Holy Bible, 1 Timothy 6:10

CHAPTER ONE

The only people who are disgustingly idle are the
children of those who have just become rich . . .

George Bernard Shaw
The Intelligent Woman's Guide
to Socialism and Capitalism

Phryne Fisher was watching an unprecedented spectacle. She leaned back in her cushioned chair in her sea-green parlour and took a sip of one of Mr Butler's most impressive cocktails.

Lin Chung, Phryne's Chinese lover, was in a rage. He was pacing. He was shouting. Phryne had never seen the sense in intervening in a really good rage. Better, she thought, to pay attention and allow the enraged one to expel it from his system. She listened.

'It is outrageous! After handing over the family to me—she said that was what she was doing—after retiring, she still wishes to keep all the reins in her own hands! She will not let loose one iota of her power unless I force her to do so, and even then she objects to every decision I make!'

'Indeed,' Phryne murmured. He had been ramping for

about ten minutes and surely must cool down soon. Admittedly, Lin Chung's formidable grandmother was enough to ruffle the calmest. She had been the sole ruler of the Lin family in Victoria for more than twenty years, ever since her meek husband had died as the only way to remove himself from her benevolent but extremely firm rule. She had only agreed to step down after her judgment had proved to be faulty, and clearly she was not going quietly.

'Since our sister Su-Niang's marriage to their son, we are no longer at variance with the Hu family! I wish to visit, and Grandmother has forbidden me! As though I was ten years old!'

'Yes, but that does not mean that you have to stay forbidden,' said Phryne. 'You are the head of the family, you know.'

'I cannot disobey her,' said Lin, lowering the volume a trifle. 'That would shame her. She is terribly venerable and what she will tell the ancestors about me if I cause her to have an apoplexy doesn't bear thinking about. We would all come down with leprosy. Or typhoid. At the very least, bad luck unto the fiftieth generation.' Lin Chung finally managed a smile. Phryne felt encouraged to continue.

'Oh. I see. Yes, this needs consideration. Mr Butler? Could you concoct a couple of considering cocktails?'

'Certainly, Miss Fisher. Miss Eliza was inquiring, Miss? About the . . . noise?'

'Tell Miss Eliza,' began Phryne, and bit her tongue. The Hon. Eliza Fisher, Phryne's younger sister, had arrived two days before, filled the small house with a hundred trunks, and had immediately made her presence felt by loudly disapproving of the climate, the house, the staff, Phryne's two adoptive daughters, the shops, the manners of these appalling colonials and even the sea, which was far too blue and not to be compared to Skegness. Phryne had once been close to Eliza, but it was amazing what a few years and a county education could do for a girl. Render her unbearable, for instance.

'Tell Miss Eliza that all is well and suggest that she might find a sherry soothing. Where is she?'

'In the smaller parlour, Miss Fisher. She is reading *Vogue*.'

'Give her a sherry, Mr B, and send Dot to talk to her. She can bear all that huntin' shootin' fishin' talk better than I can.'

'As you wish,' said the butler, and dematerialised in that special butlerine manner which Maskelyne would have paid thousands of pounds to learn. He was back, far faster than was actually possible, with two glasses, which he bestowed upon the recipients with the air of a bishop sprinkling holy water over the devout.

Lin Chung, finding himself on his feet, sat down, abashed.

'I'm sorry. I have been making a scene.'

'No, really, it was fascinating. I've never seen you so enraged. I wonder what's in this cocktail? It's delicious.'

'Cointreau, I think, maybe orange juice. How does he do that so quickly?'

'He moves in mysterious ways,' said Phryne. 'I've an idea. Can you meet Mr Hu by accident? Say, in the street?'

'What do you mean? I'd have to wait outside his office all day.'

'No, what I meant was that you should ask Su-Niang to tell Mr Hu that if he wanted to meet you he should, as it might be, pass by the front of the Lin family mansion at eleven o'clock, where he would encounter you, entirely by accident. He would then invite you to his house for tea, and you could not properly refuse as you are no longer having a feud with the Hus. That way you preserve Grandmother's authority and you get to talk to Mr Hu.'

'And if he invites me to his house, then I must invite him to my house.' Lin Chung was delighted. 'After which all the cousins and family will be able to mix freely and we may at last find out what happened to the Lin cousin who ran away with that Hu man.'

'You mean that you have lost a female relative and haven't been able to find her? That seems careless.'

'Not at all. We haven't tried to find her. She was cut off, of course, from the Lin family by her disgrace. The Hu man might also have been exiled. Great Grandfather Hu was in charge then; a very unbending person. You think Grandmother is strict? Compared to Old Man Hu, Grandmother is the voice of complaisance and the epitome of democracy.'

'Formidable,' commented Phryne, fascinated by the mechanisms of a real feud. 'How long ago did you lose this Lin lady?'

'1911, I believe. I was a child but I remember the fuss. Slammed doors. Lin Wan's mother screaming. Hysterics. I was kept out of it, being a boy. But we have always wondered what happened to Lin Wan. Her mother is still alive and not well. She was one of the reasons why I wanted to talk to Mr Hu. Plus, of course, the gold they stole from us in 1857. With compound interest it ought to be a tidy sum by now. Excellent solution, Phryne. I shall telephone Su-Niang immediately, if I may?'

'Certainly, and get a move on. We're taking the whole merry family to Luna Park this afternoon, you know.'

'Including . . .' Lin paused. Inflexible courtesy stopped him from saying what he thought of Phryne's sister Eliza, but even inflexible courtesy can develop cracks under such vehement disapproval as Miss Eliza showed for Lin Chung.

'Yes, her too. Perhaps we can push her off the Big Dipper. And Luna Park will, of course, be a garish colonial imitation which is not a patch on Sunday Bank Holiday at Brighton. Courage,' she said. 'We can lose her, and the girls are really looking forward to this expedition.'

'Very well,' replied Lin Chung, and went into the hall to telephone his sister.

'Did you say gold?' Phryne asked when he came back, having arranged to meet Mr Hu entirely by coincidence at eleven the following morning.

'What?' Phryne's conversation sometimes had the effect on Lin Chung of two of Mr Butler's cocktails before lunch. 'Gold? Oh, yes, the Hu robbery. It was in 1857—I have the exact date somewhere—at Castlemaine. Four Lin couriers were carrying quite a lot of gold from the diggings at Forest Creek to the bank at Castlemaine when they disappeared. They were ambushed by Hu robbers. Their bodies were never found, which is of course very serious. They should have been properly buried. We have been making offerings for them at the Festival of Hungry Ghosts ever since.'

'This feud,' commented Phryne, 'has antique value if it has been going on since 1857.'

'1854,' corrected Lin Chung. 'The Lin and the Hu families have both been in Australia since 1851. We came out from the Sze Yup, the Four Provinces, in search of the Second Gold Mountain. That was when it started. Hu jumped a Lin claim, then Lin jumped a Hu claim, and it rather went downhill from there. Of course, the goldfields were lawless places.'

'Eureka Stockade and so on?' Phryne had a very low opinion of the Eureka Stockade. Any revolutionary movement which was easily crushed by twenty-five soldiers in one afternoon did not deserve the name.

'And the pogroms against the Chinese. They massacred us at Lambing Flat in New South Wales when the gold started to run out. In fact, a perfectly promising anti-Chinese riot was stopped at Golden Point, I am told. By a lone policeman. We remember him, even if no one else does. His name was Constable Thomas Cooke. A very brave man.'

'He must have been. How much gold are we talking about here?'

'Four hundred ounces troy weight. That is, let's see, at goldfield prices that was two pounds six shillings the ounce . . . well, about nine hundred pounds. That was real money in those days.'

'That's real money in these days,' said Phryne, startled. 'And you haven't seen it since then?'

'No. And because we were at feud with the Hu family, we couldn't ask about it in order to find the bodies and bury them. Several Hus have attributed their bad luck in Castlemaine to their avenging ghosts.'

'Yes, I can see that the couriers might have been quite cross about being robbed and murdered.'

'In any case, I am not the one to ask. I don't know much about that time. I must speak to Great Great Uncle Lin Gan about this before I go to Castlemaine.'

'Great Great Uncle?'

'Yes, he's very venerable, very sleepy, and might not remember anything about it, but he was born on the goldfields. Now, what about this outing?'

'Lunch,' said Phryne. 'Then Luna Park. Just,' she sighed, 'for fun.'

The weather was perfect for a trip through Mister Moon's laughing mouth into Luna Park. Phryne loved carnivals, circuses and funfairs, and once she had donned her walking shoes and gathered her family about her she led them into the park with an expectation of pleasure. Ruth and Jane, her adopted daughters, were wearing their new cotton dresses: the darker Ruth in fuchsia, the paler Jane in lobelia blue, with matching ribbons on their straw hats. Phryne had persuaded Lin Chung into a casual suit of exquisite shantung. She herself wore a neat dark red suit and a small cloche hat which could not be blown off, even by the hurricane which always raged over the Scenic Railway. Dot, Phryne's confidential maid and companion, wore a terracotta jacket and an immovable hat jammed down onto her twined plaits. She was privately swearing an oath that no one was going to get her onto that Scenic Railway again, not if it were ever so. Last time she had nearly lost her hat and her lunch had striven to follow.

The Hon. Miss Eliza Fisher wore full English Lady Mayoress Opening the Fair panoply, flowered dress to mid calf, wide straw hat and an unwise pair of high-heeled shoes. Phryne, who was not, as she freely admitted, a nice woman, smiled privately. If Eliza's ankles survived the day, her heels probably wouldn't. Miss Eliza was fully four inches taller than Phryne, taking after her big, florid father rather than her thin dark mother. She was large-boned, blonde and imposing, with a high colour and bright blue eyes. Phryne could imagine her dominating a dinner party. But not Phryne's dinner party, except over Phryne's dead body. She could not understand what had happened to Eliza. When she had been called Beth, she had been Phryne's little sister, to be protected and fought for. Now she was not only not little, but she was combative enough for two. Three, even. She seemed to have landed in Australia determined to loathe the place where she was born, and she had made her point with such force that even the sound of the county drawl which she now affected made Phryne's teeth ache.

Phryne, who had been looking forward to seeing Beth again, could not wait to get rid of Eliza.

She sneered as she passed under the Coney Island image: 'How common! But I suppose you enjoy these vulgar amusements.'

Ruth and Jane bridled. Dot said quickly, 'The carousel! Let's go on the carousel!'

Phryne bought tickets and distributed them freely. Eliza condescended so far as to seat herself gingerly in a chariot and the girls threw themselves onto their favourite steeds. Jane loved a black horse called Barbary and Ruth doted on a white stallion called Winter. Phryne mounted the step with Lin Chung behind her and found a horse with fiery nostrils and a golden mane. The carousel began to move to 'Moonlight in Vienna' and all was gilt and dust and music. Phryne caught scents as they whirled around: chips frying in old fat, a gust of Turkey lolly, pure spun sugar, then machine oil, saddle soap, and finally ice cream. The calliope music was loud and simple and jolly. Damn Eliza! She was not going to be allowed to spoil Phryne's innocent amusements.

Phryne settled down to enjoy herself. She loved carousels. She had ridden on them in Paris, she had ridden on them in Blackpool, and for her money this Luna Park carousel was the best in the world. Not a creak or a thump from the engine, not a bump from whatever it was that made it go round—gears, perhaps? Ruth turned and laughed, and Phryne laughed with her. All the fun of the fair.

When the music stopped she handed over another ticket and Luna Park whirled around her again like the aftermath of Mr Butler's very special cocktails. The ones for resurrecting the dead, perhaps. She was sure that Mr Butler would have a cocktail for that. He had one for all other situations. She should ask him to concoct a special for Miss Eliza. With cyanide as a base and a little sprinkle of strychnine for that tingle on the tongue. And now the horses were slowing down again.

Phryne reluctantly left the carousel and the girls tugged at her hands, one in each direction.

'The River Caves!' cried Jane.

'The Scenic Railway!' cried Ruth.

'Both,' said Phryne. 'I will go on the Scenic Railway with you, Ruth dear, and Lin, Dot and Jane will enjoy the damp delights of the River Caves. Which will you have, Eliza?'

'They both sound disagreeable,' drawled Eliza, patting her hat on which the entire Chelsea Flower Show waved and bloomed. 'One is wet and the other's windy, don't you know.'

The 'don'tcherknow' settled events for Phryne. 'Then you shall sit here, breathe the sweet St Kilda air, and wait for us to come back,' she announced, taking Ruth's hand. 'And perhaps buy yourself an ice cream. Back in a jiff,' she said, and they ran away from Miss Eliza and her disapproval.

As they climbed the wooden steps to the Scenic Railway, Ruth remarked, 'I never had a sister, so of course I could be wrong, but are sisters usually so different? From each other, I mean.'

Ruth was a little afraid that she might have been making a personal remark—Miss Joseph was really firm about how making personal remarks was the height of impoliteness. But Phryne smiled.

'People change, grow apart. She wasn't like that when we were children. But she stayed in England and did the flowers and became a baronet's daughter and I—well, I did a lot of other things. And they were most enjoyable too. I'm intending to do some of them again. Come along, Ruth. This looks like a nice little car.'

They climbed into the car and the bar which restrained the unwise or merely drunken from doing handstands on the railway clicked down across their laps. Phryne just had time to hear Ruth say thoughtfully, 'It won't be like that with me and Jane, but then, she isn't my sister at all, really,' before they were off in a swoop like a gull's, down the slope and round the corner at neck-breaking speed.

Speed! Phryne had never had enough of it. Faster than a car on a road, faster even than her Gypsy Moth lolloping up into the sky with that heart-lifting leap as the ground releases the plane and the law of gravity is, for a little time, repealed. Down again into an intoxicating gulf, then a whisk along the highest rail, the carriage running flat and fast. Phryne could see right out to sea, as blue as washing day, with white birds flying and boats like toys etching little trails in the watery silk. Then down, down, levitating, hair lifting, Ruth screaming with delight, Phryne joining her. Only making love with a really worthwhile lover was as exhilarating as the Scenic Railway. And Lin, the lover in question, poor man, would now be enduring the Japanese Scenes, Arizona Cowboys and Tropic Dances of the mannequins in the River Caves. Despite their popularity with courting couples, to whom any dark could be usefully employed, Phryne considered them a waste of a good penny. Besides, the water smelt faintly of bleach. She had dark enough in her own bedroom and no one to forbid her to lie down with whomsoever she wished.

Except Eliza, of course, who would be carrying home to Father overheated tales of Phryne's intrigue with a Chinaman. And what could Father do about it? She reflected further. Forbid her the house? He was welcome to it.

On that defiant note, the Scenic Railway went down, climactically, for the third time.

Phryne and Ruth, a little dishevelled but very happy, met the rest of the party at the entrance to the River Caves. A mob of children swept them apart for a moment. They were all dressed alike, small mommets with grey serge tunics and round felt hats, led by one nun from the front and herded by another two from behind. Phryne caught up a straying midget and returned her to her insecure grasp on the rope which they were all holding.

'Oh, thank you,' gasped a small plump nun. 'Hang on, Keziah, do! It's their annual treat,' she explained as the whole string halted while the head nun hunted for their ticket to the River Caves.

'Are they a school class?' asked Phryne.

'No, they're orphans,' said the nun. 'The Board has an arrangement with Luna Park. We can have five rides, and this is the last, thank God.'

'And ice cream?' asked Jane. She and Ruth had been as poor as these children, and badly treated as well. They had keen sensitivities when it came to poverty.

'I'm afraid we don't run to ice cream,' said the nun. 'But we've a pound of mixed lollies for the train home.'

'You now have funds,' said Phryne, reaching into her purse. 'Ice cream and Turkey lolly. It will take days to get them unstuck, but we can't have everything.'

'Thank you, but . . .' The nun hesitated. Her sister nun gave her shoulder a quick push.

'Take the money, Sister Immaculata, and say thank you,' she urged. 'It's only once a year for the poor little mites. God won't mind them having a treat.'

'Thank you,' said Sister Immaculata, unable to resist the lure of the ten-shilling banknote. 'God bless you. May we know which name to remember in our prayers tonight?'

'Jane,' said Phryne. 'And Ruth. They were orphans themselves.'

'Not any more,' said Ruth, taking Phryne's hand.

The young nun smiled.

'God bless you, Jane and Ruth. Sister! Sister Benedict! We're having ice cream!' called Sister Immaculata to the leading nun. The orphans, to a girl, heard and understood.

The entire group, dragging their rope, descended on the ice-cream stall.

It was unfortunate that Miss Eliza was in the way, and that she got so smeared by grimy little hands before Phryne, fighting down an urge to laugh, could unwind the orphans and release her. The orphans, single-mindedly determined upon ice cream, a delicacy which few of them had ever tasted, were not cooperative.

Finally Eliza was extracted in no very pleasant frame of mind. She brushed at her dress, settled her hat, and scowled freely at all bystanders. She announced that she was going home.

'One more ride,' said Phryne. 'We haven't been to the Ghost Train yet. You can come along or find a seat somewhere away from the orphans and their ice cream. That was a good deed, girls.'

'Did you give them the money for the ice cream?' demanded Miss Eliza. 'But, Phryne, they're . . .'—she lowered her voice—'Catholics.'

'Really?' asked Phryne, who was losing control of her patience. She had never had a great stock to call upon anyway. 'How did you work it out? The ladies dressed as penguins, was it?'

'You're making fun of me,' diagnosed Eliza. 'You don't have any standards, do you?'

'Yes, but they're different from yours,' retorted Phryne. 'Come along.'

Something of the elder sister in her voice compelled even Miss Eliza to fall in behind as Phryne handed over her tickets to the Ghost Train attendant, who wore a gorilla suit. He grunted acknowledgement, which was probably all he could do through that mask. They settled themselves in two connected carriages.

With a jerk, the little train slid into the dark.

Phryne liked the Ghost Train even though it was palpably fraudulent, being unsupplied with ghosts. In fact, any ghost who wanted a quiet place to rattle his chains in peace would have chosen an unadjacent area. Any real supernatural moaning would not have been heard over the shrieks, screams, growling noises and rattlings which emanated from behind the scenes, produced by enthusiastic Luna Park employees. Cobwebs made of cotton thread trailed pleasurably over the face. A ghost draped in a rotting shroud groped for them as the train clattered past. Phryne held on to her hat as a furry arm swiped for her head and the werewolf's shriek of disappointed rage followed them down the dark passage.

'All right, Lin dear?' she asked the beautiful young man beside her.

'I could do you a genuinely frightening Ghost Train, you know,' he answered. He had been trained as a magician in China. 'With mirrors and luminous paint and a few tricks, I could give you a journey into madness and nightmare.'

'I know you could,' said Phryne affectionately. 'But I've seen real nightmares and I prefer horrors which are really, really unreal. Like that cowboy dummy. One could never imagine that he was a real corpse, could one?'

The train stopped. The dummy hung from the low ceiling.

Phryne reached up and grabbed the foot, trying to turn the papier-mâché mask towards her. The boot came off in her grasp.

'Drat, I've broken it,' she commented. Then she made a small noise like a kitten's mew. Only Lin Chung saw how she froze while examining the broken-off boot. All the colour leached out of her face, leaving her the colour of the moon.

'What is it?' he asked with sudden concern.

She showed him. Inside the dummy's boot were the leathery ragged skin and the darkened bones of a real human foot.

In the thirteenth year of the reign of the glorious Emperor Lord of the Dragon Throne Kwong Sui of the Ching Dynasty, seventh day of the seventh month, festival of the Bridge of Birds.

Esteemed Uncle

The unworthy nephew Sung Ma reports that he has joined the Lin Family from the Four Provinces who are going to the Second Gold Mountain to seek gold. They have employed me because I am literate and have some knowledge of medicine and divination. I am leaving on the ship Kate Hooper *in the morning.*

I know that your justifiable wrath will be measureless at this rebellion, honoured Uncle, but once I failed the second literary examinations and you informed me that I could no longer stay idle in your house, I must have money, and where to find it? I must become a merchant, to do that I must have capital, and they say that in this place there is gold in the streets.

My little capital should be sufficient to maintain my mother and sisters until I return. I know that to descend from scholar to gold grubber is a disgrace. But I have failed as a scholar. Perhaps

I will succeed as a ku'li. My strength is certainly bitter enough. Please convey my respectful love to my aunt and cousins. I enclose a letter for my mother which, if you would be so kind, you might allow your steward to read to her.

The disgraced younger nephew Sung Ma kowtows three times and begs forgiveness.

CHAPTER TWO

Then consider the police: the friends of the honest woman and the enemy and hunter of thieves, tramps, swindlers, rioters, confidence tricksters, drunkards and prostitutes.

George Bernard Shaw
*The Intelligent Woman's Guide
to Socialism and Capitalism*

After that there was no hurry to get home. While waiting for the police to arrive, Dot, Phryne and Lin Chung ate ice cream, Ruth and Jane ate Turkey lolly, and Miss Eliza did her best to have hysterics.

'Give it up,' said Phryne dispassionately as her sister choked, gasped and sobbed. 'You didn't do that when we found that old man who had crept in under the bushes in the park and died there. I know you didn't. You were fascinated when you were ten. This is what you have trained yourself to think a lady does under the circumstances, isn't it? You were mis-informed. Have some ice cream. It's very good.'

The one requirement for a really satisfying fit of hysterics is a sympathetic audience and as Miss Eliza's troubled gaze wandered over her immediate family, she couldn't find any sympathy. Jane was interested because she wanted to specialise in morbid psychology after she completed her medical training. Lin Chung had averted his eyes from this distressing spectacle. Dot was looking prim. Ruth was eagerly asking the ice-cream man if he had some cold water she could throw over a lady who was having the vapours.

The cold water decided it. Miss Eliza sat up and announced that she was going to bear up. It did not do to give way. Letting down the Empire and so on. Phryne bought her an ice cream as a reward.

It really was surprisingly good on her stiff upper lip, rich and creamy, with bits of genuine strawberry in it. She ate it all.

'You don't need to wait, girls,' said Phryne. 'Go and use up those tickets.'

Miss Eliza felt so much better that when Jane and Ruth wanted to go to Neptune's Kingdom and consult the mermaid fortune-teller, she offered to escort them and was warmed to hear their acceptance. Perhaps they weren't such bad children.

Phryne eyed her daughters and said, 'I'm sure you'll be good,' in a tone which warned them that they had better be good, and they nodded a little sadly. It seemed like a waste of nice water not to allow Miss Eliza to slip into the waxwork mermaid's deepish little pond. The edge was always slippery.

But good it was and they walked across the hot dusty park to the brightly painted pavilion of Neptune. There was the old gentleman, looking cheerful, trident in hand, surrounded by some rather buxom mermaids. There on her rock was the mechanical mermaid who told fortunes. She was life-size, made of wax, or perhaps porcelain. She had sapphire blue eyes and a glittering silvery blue tail, and her ample bosom was decorously concealed behind a curtain of blonde hair. There was the deepish small pool, with real goldfish flickering among the weed. The mermaid had a series of little scrolls in a box before her. When Jane put in her penny, the delicate hand moved, the mermaid's seaweed-crowned head bowed, and she picked up a scroll and dropped it into a chute.

'It will be "You will go on a journey and meet a mysterious dark-haired man",' she said. 'Same as always.' She unrolled the little scroll. 'No, it says "Beware. Death in the dark". How curious! What about you, Ruth?'

Ruth inserted her penny and the mechanical hand hovered and pounced.

'Men are fools that wish to die,' she read. 'Is't not fine to dance and sing, while the bells of death do ring?'

'That's unusual,' commented Jane. 'I think it's from a poem. I'll look it up when we get home. Do you want to try, Miss Eliza?'

Eliza put in her penny and unrolled her scroll.

'There is no friend like a sister,' she read. 'That's part of a poem too, isn't it, girls?'

'"There is no friend like a sister, in calm or stormy weather". "Goblin Market". Christina Rossetti,' said Jane promptly. 'Someone has been changing the scrolls. They used to be about meeting dark-haired men or secret lovers. This is much more interesting. Got another penny, Ruthie?'

'I'm going to go on the merry-go-round again,' murmured Ruth, handing over the penny. 'I don't like this mermaid any more.'

'Just let me get another fortune,' insisted Jane, and put it in her pocket without reading it. Ruth was more sensitive to the uncanny than herself, Jane knew, always threw salt over her shoulder if she spilled it. Jane could read her fortune later.

Jane looked back at the mermaid as they left and wondered what it would be like, trapped in porcelain, with no one to hear if you screamed, and shivered. This was turning out to be a fascinating day. She hoped that she might be able to see more of the mummified body. How long did it take to reduce a human body to that strange state of leather and bone? Was this deliberate embalming or the action of hot sun and desert winds?

With any luck she might be able to see a real autopsy. She followed Ruth out into the hot sunlight, agog with scientific curiosity.

Phryne was not enjoying her interrogation at the hands of a particularly sceptical policeman.

'Probably rabbit bones,' he said. 'Just to give you a bit of a scare, like.'

'I know rabbit bones, I've eaten enough of them,' returned Phryne crossly. 'And I spent all day in a ditch in Exmoor once, putting an Iron-Age skeleton together. The toe bones were the hardest to find. This is a metatarsal if ever I saw one! Have a look!'

'Lamb bones, maybe,' he said.

Constable Benson was a large, stolid constable with the beefy self confidence which arises from being able to instantly crush any opponent, if necessary by sitting on them. Phryne felt like a small, yappy terrier, trying to get the attention of an unusually obtuse Aberdeen Angus bull. Time to pull rank.

'Constable Benson, if that mummified body is not taken down and covered and conveyed rapidly to a medical officer for an autopsy, I am going to report to Jack Robinson that one of his constables needs spectacles,' she said firmly.

Constable Benson blinked, like an Aberdeen Angus bull who has been peacefully contemplating the landscape and is unexpectedly bitten in the fetlock by an exasperated bee.

'Do you know Detective Inspector Robinson, Miss?' he asked.

'Certainly. Get going! Find out where the cowboy came from. The Luna Park management must know. I haven't got all day,' said Phryne.

'Oh. Well. I'll have to make a report,' said Benson, fumbling out his notebook, searching for and locating his much-chewed pencil, licking the end and beginning to write. Phryne took a deep breath. This was going to take some time.

The Luna Park management appeared in the form of Mr Bennet, a portly, jovial man with a great display of waistcoat and watch chain. He shook Phryne's hand, obligingly ordered the dummy to be unhooked and laid on the ground, laughed heartily when told that it was a real corpse and stopped laughing heartily when the papier-mâché mask slipped and revealed a whitewashed, dreadful, hollow-eyed skull.

'Jesus!' he exclaimed in what Phryne chose to believe was an ejaculatory prayer. Several nearby nuns crossed themselves before they hurried the ice-cream dripping orphans out of view onto the River Caves ride.

Several people were examining the dummy with great interest. A pink-faced man the size of a wrestler bent over it, looking at the desiccated wrist, then snorted, stood up, collected his dark-haired friend and strode away. Several girls threatened to faint. Several bold boys approached close enough to touch and were shooed away.

The sight affected Constable Benson too. He wrote more quickly, pencil stabbing into the hapless page. 'Where did you get the . . . deceased . . . from?' asked Benson.

'Bought a whole lot of stuff from a carnival that went broke,' stammered Mr Bennet. 'From Bendigo way. Mr Dalby handled the sale. My partner. I'll check the sale note. I'm sure we got some dummies, the werewolf and the vampire from them. A travelling show, it was. You know the kind. Bloke who owned it died and his widow sold his effects. Come along with me and I'll find the note. And—Bill! Fetch a tarp and cover it up, for God's sake.'

Bill did as he was told. Phryne, Jane and Constable Benson followed Mr Bennet to the office, where he rummaged in a filing cabinet and muttered. After five minutes of dropping sheaves of paper, he found the sale note.

'Here we are,' he told them in triumph.

The sale note, Phryne saw over Constable Benson's meaty shoulder, was grimy but readable. The list of properties from Carter's Travelling Miracles and Marvels Show was given as 1. Ghost with wrappings 2. Vampire (cloak needs mending) 3. Cowboy (needs a lot of work) 4. Werewolf (bald spots on skin) 5. Misc. canvas backings and theatrical sets. Phryne noticed that the cowboy mannequin had been discounted to half price because it was so unconvincing. Mrs Carter had cleared three quid on the deal and probably thought she had done well.

'I'll use your telephone, Mr Bennet,' announced Constable Benson. 'We need to get the morgue van to collect the deceased. Then we shall see. You can go home, Miss Fisher. We know where you live and someone will come and talk to you.'

'Very well,' said Phryne. 'Who will do the autopsy?'

'Dr Treasure, I expect,' said Benson. 'He gets all the strange ones.'

'Ah,' said Phryne, and left before she could be warned not to make any enquiries on her own. The charming blond (and, regrettably, happily married) Dr Treasure was sure to welcome her interest in a fascinating cadaver.

'Miss Phryne, I wanted to see that autopsy!' objected Jane as they went down the wooden stairs to the main courtyard.

'And so you shall,' said Phryne. 'I know Dr Treasure of old. Come along, my dears, it's time to go home. We've got a new mystery,' she added with relish. 'And we may well have to solve this one all by ourselves.'

'Oh, goody!' exclaimed Ruth, a born investigator.

'Phryne,' objected Miss Eliza mildly, 'this is very unlady-like.'

The sting appeared to have gone out of Eliza. Phryne wondered if it was the spectacle of an old murder or all that ice cream which had mollified her sister.

'So it is,' agreed Phryne happily. 'But I think that body is about fifty years old. No one is going to care about him. And he was murdered.'

'How do you know?' asked Jane.

'When the papier-mâché mask slipped, I saw his face,' said Phryne. 'And I saw the bullet hole in the centre of his forehead.'

'Oh,' said Eliza, and was silent all the way home. This was a great improvement. Phryne considered that she might not have to poison Eliza after all.

Eliza remained quiet during an excellent dinner of cold lamb and salads and lemon meringue pie, and silent even after, when Lin Chung had gone home, Dot had brought out her drawn-thread work and Phryne was writing down everything she could remember about the body.

'He had cowboy clothes on,' she said. 'A checked shirt, a pair of moleskins and those leather things.'

'Chaps,' said Jane, a fervent reader of Westerns. 'And leather boots. With studs. Which weren't his,' she added.

'Because?' asked Ruth.

'They came off too easily. And he had a cowboy hat, one of those curly brimmed ones.' She wrinkled her forehead, trying to remember.

'Now how did a real corpse come to be found in the Ghost Train?' asked Phryne.

'They bought the cowboy from the carnival. Carter's Travelling Miracles and Marvels. Maybe someone decided to kill someone and hid the body by putting him amongst the dummies,' suggested Ruth.

'Yes, but this body was mummified,' objected Jane. 'That means someone who knew what they were doing eviscerated him, packed the body with sawdust, dried it in some way and that takes months. Seventy days, according to the Egyptians.'

Dot stopped listening and concentrated on her embroidery.

'Someone might have found a natural mummy,' said Phryne. 'Drag out the encyclopaedia, Jane, and see what it says about natural mummies. They are found in deserts, I believe.'

Jane hauled out the requisite volume of the *Britannica* and leafed through it. 'Mummification is a natural process where the body is desiccated by the application of heat and salt . . .' she read. Her thin finger travelled confidently down the page. 'Aha. "It is believed that the Ancient Egyptians discovered mummification by observing the bodies of humans and animals which had been buried in hot, dry, salty sand. The conditions of Egypt are peculiarly suited to this process because the sand contains a high degree of natron, which Herodotus says is used to preserve the bodies of pharaohs." Gosh. So maybe he just dies in the desert . . .'

'Is murdered in the desert,' corrected Ruth.

'And the desert dried him out.'

'How, then, did the body come into the possession of a travelling marvel show?' murmured Phryne. 'I know someone who knows all about those carnivals. I believe that he has taken a leave of absence to finish his PhD,' Phryne mused. 'It is time for me to invite my friend Mr Josiah Burton to dinner. You'll like him,' she told her sister. 'A very educated person. He is a star performer in Farrell's Circus and Wild Beast Show, of which I am part owner. I wrote to you about it.'

'Oh, yes,' said Eliza, refusing to rise to the bait.

'He's a dwarf,' added Phryne.

'How nice,' said Eliza.

'Beth, are you all right?' asked Phryne.

'I think I'll have an early night,' said Eliza, and went out of the room.

'Did anything happen to her that I didn't see?' asked Phryne, fixing her adoptive daughters with a suspicious eye. They bridled. She had told them to be good and they had been good, despite the temptations.

'Only the mermaid gave us some odd fortunes. I haven't even looked at the last one,' said Jane. 'The place made Ruth a bit jumpy so we came away. See.' Ruth fished hers out of her pocket and Jane found the others. Phryne read them.

'Very strange,' she commented. 'Why have you got two?'

'I was curious,' answered Jane. 'So I got another one. The first one was "Beware" and the second says "Ask no questions and you'll be told no lies", which is true, of course.'

'But not helpful. What did Eliza's fortune say?'

'Just a quote from Christina Rossetti. "There is no friend like a sister". I don't know why it upset her.'

'Neither do I, but something has certainly taken the edge off her temper and that's a mercy for us all. What are we doing tomorrow, Dot?'

'We're going to church,' said Dot, glad to have left the subject of mummification. 'Tomorrow is Sunday.'

'So it is. I'm going to occupy myself blamelessly with the encyclopaedia, and Jane and Ruth might like to look at Herodotus on Egypt. He's quite fascinating.'

'Not for me,' said Ruth. 'I've got to finish my romance before the books go back to the library on Monday.'

'And I've got a letter to write to my sister in Sydney,' announced Dot.

They sat companionably round the parlour table. Jane read Herodotus. 'Egypt is the gift of the Nile.' Ruth imagined a strong, hawkish face half seen in a midnight rose garden. Dot strove for unexceptionable news for her sister in Sydney, a teacher of deportment. Then she glanced at the newspaper. Someone was searching for the relatives of one Amelia Gascoigne, late of Port Melbourne, and was serious enough to pay for a quarter of a page of enquiry. Phryne read about death in the desert.

They were all very contented.

Mr Hu conducted Mr Lin to a seat at the lacquered table and poured out a cup of tea for his guest.

'What a fortunate accident,' he said suavely, 'that I happened to be passing your house and encountered you purely by chance!'

'The ancients say that there are no accidents, that every meeting is fated,' replied Lin Chung, raising the tea cup. 'It is very good to meet you at last, Mr Hu.'

Mr Hu was short, inclining to a corporation, and smooth: smooth hair, smooth skin, smooth smile. Mr Hu's Caulfield house was as plush as money could make it, and stuffed with antiquities. Long glass cases displayed Hu's remarkable collection of jade. Lin Chung's end-of-feud gift, a sleeve ornament pair of lion dogs in pure green jade, had been well received, as was the Hu gift to Lin, the Eight Immortals carved in blackwood. The T'ang craftsman had expended endless eyesight and care on tiny details: the gourd, the iron fan, the flowers around the Flower Maiden's feet. They were the size of chessmen and completely undamaged.

'My ancestor brought them here in the late nineteenth century,' observed Mr Hu. 'Shortly after the unlucky misunderstanding which deprived us of your friendship and counsel.'

'My family also regret this misunderstanding,' returned Lin. 'Which is now ended. I have the particulars.' He unrolled a scroll of paper. The handwriting at one end was so old and faded as to be almost illegible. Five or more hands had gone into its making. It was the record of every deed which the Hus had done to the detriment of the Lin family.

'And I,' said Mr Hu, unrolling a similar scroll, 'have ours. Let us compare.'

'Begin in the present and go back to the past?' asked Lin. 'Give me your advice, Mr Hu. I have never settled a feud before.'

'That is the correct procedure,' Mr Hu assured him. 'Now, I have here the sad affair of Lin Wan.'

'Is she still living?' asked Lin Chung. 'Her mother still cries for her, and she is very old now.'

'Still alive and the mother of five sons,' said Mr Hu, beaming his double-chinned beam. 'She will be delighted to see her mother again. No dowry was paid for Miss Wan, and she has proved a good mother and a good wife. Shall we say— forty pounds?'

'Thirty,' bargained Lin Chung. 'We had to pay ten pounds consolation money to the man she was betrothed to. Not to mention the shame when she ran away.'

'We will not quarrel on such an auspicious day,' agreed Mr Hu.

'What about the sale of the blackwood furniture? Grandfather Lin said that he would have made at least seven pounds a set on that deal, if Hu had not undercut his price.'

'Great Grandfather Hu told me about that,' sighed Mr Hu. 'That was an error on our part. Perhaps—thirty pounds?'

Lin grinned and emptied his cup, which Mr Hu filled again. 'Thirty pounds,' Lin agreed, making a note on his scroll. 'Now—I cannot read this line. It looks like . . . something about shipping charges? In 1891?'

'I have a note about that,' said Mr Hu. 'We both bid for a shipping contract, in the old days when both Lin and Hu operated ships between here and Canton. We outbid each other so outrageously that both sides lost the contract . . . shall we call it quits on that one?'

'Yes. And the Hu woman who ran away with the Lin man in 1880—do you have a note about that? We say that she was enticed, even kidnapped.'

'We say that he was seduced.'

'What happened to them in the end?'

'They went to Queensland. No one in our family has heard of them since.'

'Call that one quits as well, then. Now, we need blood money for the Lin man killed by Hu men in Little Bourke Street on January the twelfth, 1873.'

'Ten pounds,' said Mr Hu, consulting his own record. 'And we need blood money for a Hu child run down by a Lin wagon in the same street, earlier on the same day.'

'How horrible!' said Lin, shocked. 'Did the child survive?'

'Crippled for life,' read Mr Hu. 'But became a famous artist.'

'Shall we say ten pounds?' asked Lin, who was beginning to get the hang of settling a blood feud. It should work out in the end to a nil–nil win.

'As you suggest,' agreed Mr Hu. 'Now we come to the gold-fields and here I must beg your gracious indulgence. I find this part of the scroll very hard to read.'

'I, also,' confessed Lin. 'We have a jumped claim—no, two. And a Lin man informed on by a Hu man for selling alloyed gold to a shopkeeper.'

'What happened to him?'

'Three months jail.'

'Ah. It so happens I have a Hu man who was informed on by a Lin man for abominable practices.'

'And he went to jail for . . .?' asked Lin.

'Three months.'

'Heaven has designed this meeting to be very neat,' said Lin Chung.

'And accurate.' Mr Hu smiled his pleasant double-chinned smile. 'I count two jumped claims also. And an assault on a Hu woman.'

'What did we do to her?'

'You beat her for refusing to sleep with you. But my notes say that the Lin man was beaten by us, so badly that he was taken to hospital, so we might call that quits as well. Apart from that, we seem to be clean.' Mr Hu allowed his scroll to roll up. 'And that concludes our settlement,' he said. 'Allow me the honour of inviting you to share my most inadequate noon rice.'

Lin was surprised.

'No, Mr Hu, wait. There is one more matter. What happened to the Lin couriers, carrying four hundred ounces of gold, who were presumed ambushed and murdered by the Hu family in July 1857 at Golden Point, near Castlemaine?'

Mr Hu opened the scroll again and scanned it hastily but thoroughly, using a magnifying glass on the faded parts.

'I can find no record of such an event,' he said at last. 'Someone may have murdered the Lin couriers, Mr Lin, but it was not the Hu family.'

The smooth current of the exchange was broken. The scroll curled up from Lin Chung's weakened hand. He stared at the bland face of his erstwhile enemy. It was unthinkable that he should lie. And he had no reason to lie anyway. This was a règlement des comptes and meant to be a final settlement. Keeping something back would vitiate all agreements and continue the feud.

'Then what can have happened to them?' asked Lin at last.

'Come and have lunch with me, Mr Lin,' said Hu, taking Lin's arm. 'And this time tomorrow we shall talk to Great Great Grandmother Hu Ta. She was one of the few Chinese women on the goldfields, and like all the Hu women'—here he winced slightly—'she has a very, very good memory.'

'Thank you,' said Lin Chung. 'I will be delighted to partake of her wisdom.'

'Enlightened, perhaps,' said Mr Hu, leading the way into a sumptuous dining room and the scent of Peking duck. 'But probably not delighted.'

In the thirteenth year of the reign of the glorious Emperor Lord of the Dragon Throne Kwong Sui of the Ching Dynasty in the season of Autumn, festival of Ancestral Shrines.

To his younger sister Sung Mai the elder brother Sung Ma sends greetings. The ship is crammed with people. I find that the only place to contemplate the moon is far astern and I come here when I can. The shipmaster does not like coolies on his deck. Fortunately in the first week I cured him of a stubborn case of the itch and his boy of a fever with the bark infusion and now he allows me to walk where I will.

So I sit on the after deck with the ship's cat, watching the moon and trying to make up poems. It is very exciting to be going to another world. We have some here who have also been to the First Gold Mountain, California, where they were very badly treated and finally expelled from the city of San Francisco. They tell how some of their number were murdered by the other miners. But there was gold there and if there is gold in this Australia the Lin family mean to have it. You know how we used to joke about the Sze Yup and their coarse speech and their greed? It was all true but they are very determined. If any succeed, it will be them.

Raising my head, I look at the moon.

Lowering my head, I think of my home.

I hope you are well, little sister, and that mother's cough has cleared up. Continue with your studies and soon there may be a Gold Mountain Uncle returning with his sleeves full of nuggets to buy you a rich husband.

CHAPTER THREE

This skull was Yorick's skull.

William Shakespeare
Hamlet

Phryne went decorously to church with Eliza, Jane and Ruth. She did not often attend but it did make a soothing start to the day. Eliza, instead of sniffing at the youth of the building and the primitive nature of the worship, sank quietly to her knees in a back pew and spent the whole service engrossed in something which looked surprisingly like prayer. Phryne spared a moment to wonder what had converted her acidulated bitch of a sister into a nun and assumed that if female problems or maybe demonic possession were to blame for the bad moods, then maybe angelic possession accounted for this good one. She really didn't care. Eliza was a sad disappointment to Phryne.

'That sermon,' ventured Ruth as they left the church and came into sunshine hot enough to char-grill an ox.

'Mmm?' asked Phryne absently.

'He said that we were emerging from barbarism into civilisation.'

'Did he?' asked Phryne, settling her cloche and wishing that she had brought a broad-brimmed hat. And a camel. And was on the way to a suitable oasis, with resident sheik and a bucket of sherbert.

'You weren't listening, were you?' accused Ruth, who would have appreciated the sheik.

'No, I was wondering about the man in the Ghost Train,' confessed Phryne.

'So was I,' agreed Jane. 'It was just the usual sermon. Like that one on Brotherly Love. I've heard it so often I could recite it.'

As she showed signs of doing this, Phryne said hastily, 'We'll talk about the man in the Ghost Train this afternoon, when we go to see Dr Treasure. He has an old friend visiting, an expert on Egyptian mummies. He ought to be good value.'

'A godless occupation for a Sunday,' commented Eliza. The piety, Phryne noticed, had quite worn off.

'Yes, so you will have to occupy yourself in good works and golden opportunities while we are gone. What were you going to say about the sermon, Ruth?'

'Barbarism. He said that we have left behind the barbarism of the past. And I was thinking, Miss Crich said that the Great War killed more men than any other war—not Alexander, not the Romans or Assyrians, no one killed more people than . . . well, us. Our governments. Aren't we barbaric still?'

'Oh, yes,' said Phryne with great feeling. 'The only difference is that we are trying not to be. We at least know what barbarism is, and we reject it. That has to count for something. But not,' she added, breaking into the fast scamper of one wearing a tight-fitting skirt, 'to any great degree of success.'

Eliza, she noticed, was running beside her. And prudent Eliza, wishing to protect her milk and roses, carried a sunshade. It was frilled and delicate as befitted a lady's accessory for a warm summer's day, but it had a steel shaft and handle.

'And how do you expect the horse to get up if you keep beating it?' Phryne asked a carter, who was flailing at a fallen horse's eyes with a buggy whip.

The carter sighted Phryne's small figure and growled an obscenity. He continued to beat the horse, which was so pinned under the remains of the cart that it could not move.

Jane was interested, warm-hearted Ruth was aghast. Both of them took a step backwards to allow Phryne room to move. Eliza did not.

'See here, my man,' she began. Her aristocratic tone attracted the carter's full wrath and he came up from his stooping position roaring. Eliza was caught by the arm and uttered a ladylike shriek.

Phryne dodged around him, removed his whip with a quick twist, and called to an enthralled crowd, 'Come and heave this cart off that poor horse while I reason with this gentleman. There will be shillings if this is done very quickly,' she added as the carter dragged Eliza towards him.

Then something astonishing happened. The aristocrat, daughter of at least a hundred distinguished earls, lost her manner, her accent, and her temper. The carter found himself being dragged off balance by a fury who snarled through bared teeth, 'Shut your filthy mouth! If you call me that again, you bludger, I'll knock out your eye with this sunshade! Now take your hands off me! Who asked you to manhandle a lady, you bastard?'

Phryne, energised and warmed by the return of a small sister who had flanked her indomitably by the pig bins of the

Victoria market, poked the whip into the middle of the driver's unsavoury back. He was a big, red-faced, broken-toothed bully, greasy with breakfast sausages and stinking of beer. Phryne knew the type.

'Let my sister go,' said Phryne clearly. 'She means it, you know. And that sunshade is London made. Steel. Which eye don't you need?' The carter released Beth, who shook herself like a cat ruffled by unauthorised handling. Phryne did not allow the carter to turn around. Her gentle voice continued from behind his back, which was disconcerting. 'Now we are going to get your horse up, and you are going to behave, and the Inspectors of Cruelty will be round in the morning to make sure that you don't beat the poor beast to death because we have embarrassed you. Assuming it can still trudge, of course. How are the men going, Beth?'

'They've heaved the cart off,' said Beth. 'They've got it onto four hoofs again. It's favouring the off-fore, but nothing's broken as far as I can see.'

'Name and address?' asked Phryne, and wrote down the grudgingly given details in a small notebook. 'You may turn around now,' she told him.

When the carter realised that he had been bailed up and reproved by a woman barely over five feet tall in a cloche hat, he swelled with outrage, remembered the sunshade, and released his beery breath.

'Good, lead it carefully, now. Thank you, gentlemen,' said Phryne, distributing shillings with a liberal hand to her stalwart helpers. 'Now, Beth, I think we could do with a nice cup of tea.'

'Bugger that,' said Beth, fanning herself with her straw hat. 'We need a drink.'

Phryne and her sister walked arm in arm along Acland Street. The sun shone. The breeze blew the scent of ozone and

Turkey lolly and the vinegar scent of best black silks brought out for Sunday. Phryne was suddenly very happy.

'Good afternoon, Dr Treasure. Such a bore to bother you on a Sunday afternoon,' apologised Phryne. The room looked just as it always had. Crowded. Shelves bore books, anatomical specimens far too vividly displayed in gin-clear alcohol, a pair of crossed oars with a kangaroo skin behind them and a rather out of place teddy bear. He was a battered, humorous and much loved bear with an air of slightly cynical world weariness and someone was going to miss him fairly soon. And in all probability, they would then scream. Dr Treasure's family occupied the parts of his house without, Phryne hoped, interesting viscera in jars, and he had two small children much given to vociferation.

'You know, Miss Fisher, I've never been bored in your presence,' replied Dr Treasure, offering her a chair next to a table bearing an ominous, shrouded burden. He took her hand and kissed it.

Dr Treasure was an expert in many sciences, frequently consulted in the deepest secrecy by important persons, and very firmly married. Phryne found this refreshing. She could flirt with Dr Treasure without the risk of being invited to any impromptu game of swap-the-spouse. He was tall, with the curly blond hair, guileless blue eyes and rosy cheeks of the country boy he had been, and Phryne liked him very much.

'Well, we've laid him out—definitely a him, he's very well preserved,' observed the doctor, throwing back the covering. Phryne couldn't help noticing that it was a fine linen sheet and hoped that Mrs Treasure was not going to be told where her trousseau linen had gone. Although by now she could probably guess.

The corpse was, as the doctor had said, very well preserved. Horribly so. Even the fingernails were still on the clawed fingers. The face was still disfigured with the half-rotten papier-mâché mask. The drum-tight leathery skin stretched over the great bones of the torso, ribs and pelvis, and even the shrunken remains of male organs were evident. Phryne did not blench, because she never did, but she did not find the sight agreeable. Jane stepped forward with every appearance of delight.

'Who is this?' asked Dr Treasure, a line appearing between his brows. What he was thinking, Phryne knew, was that naked men, however long dead, are no sight for young maidens. What he said, to his eternal credit, was, 'Miss Jane, is it? Pleasure to meet you. Have you been to an autopsy before?'

'No,' replied Jane. 'But I've read several reports. You begin with a Y incision, do you not? Throat to sternum then around the navel to the pubis?'

Dr Treasure blinked.

'Ah, well, yes, though the very first action is to view the body all over, to see what can be seen. That is what the word means. "Op", to see; "auto", for oneself.' The line between Dr Treasure's brows vanished. He smiled down on Jane's enthusiastic face. 'Do I detect a future colleague in the bud, as it were?'

'I want to study morbid psychology,' said Jane. 'But first I want to be a doctor.'

'And so you shall,' agreed Dr Treasure, equipping Jane with a large apron and blousing it at the waist so that it would not drag on the floor.

Phryne had wondered how Dr Treasure would react to Jane. She looked so small, so thin, and so schoolgirlish in her good blue churchgoing suit and her round felt hat. But the admirable Dr Treasure had recognised something akin to himself in the composed young woman which had removed all his objections.

A door closed and someone came in through the house entrance.

'Ah, Ayers, there you are,' said the doctor. 'May I introduce my most learned colleague Professor Ayers, the Egyptologist?'

Phryne smiled. Ayers was from Sydney University, expert in both the pharaonic debris and the beautiful boys that littered the desert. He was a slim, elegant man about the heft and height of Lawrence of Arabia. The last Phryne had seen of him he had been headed for the sandier bits of the world with a papyrus clue to the tomb of Khufu, builder of the great pyramid. Either he was back or he had never left.

'You've caught me making final arrangements,' he told her. 'Next month I'm off.'

'I wish you every success,' said Phryne warmly. 'Allow me to introduce my daughter Jane.'

Ayers bowed slightly in Jane's general direction. Professor Ayers evidently did not like children. Phryne noticed that Jane divined this instantly and changed position around the dead man, so that she was standing close to Dr Treasure. Phryne was impressed with Jane's sensitivity and also that she did not seem to return Professor Ayers' dislike.

'Well, here's our chap,' breezed Dr Treasure, aware of an atmosphere. 'Weighs in at fifteen pounds and is fifty-nine inches in extremis—and his extremis is more extreme than usual. Beautiful condition,' he continued, knocking on the corpse's chest with his knuckles. There was a hollow clonk.

'Would that be his height in life?' asked Jane.

'No, they shrink a bit,' replied Ayers. 'The corpse is desiccated, which reduces the overall weight and the space between the joints. Give him another four or five inches for a living height. My word,' he said, drawing closer to Jane's unwelcome proximity. 'He is magnificent, Treasure. What a find, Miss Fisher!'

Phryne found the mummy more grotesque than magnificent. Dr Treasure had removed the clothes and had been engaged in cleaning the leather face with linseed oil. He offered Phryne a swab. She politely declined. The way that the dark skin had torn like paper over one cheekbone was unsettling her. 'Where be your quips, your quiddities . . .' she asked herself. 'Imperial Caesar, dead and turned to clay might stop a hole to keep the wind away . . .'

She had been unaware that she had spoken aloud until Dr Treasure completed the quote: ' "Oh that that flesh that held the world in awe, could patch a wall t' expel the winter's flaw . . . Go to my Lady, bid her paint an inch thick, to this end she must come. Make her laugh at that!" Dear me. Shakespeare always has a word for it, hasn't he?'

'Yes, it's so accommodating of him,' said Phryne rather tartly, and turned her back on the table.

Here were the chaps and the cowboy hat of his disguise. They felt new, or rather, not old enough to be original. They were filthy with dust and old spiders' webs.

'I think it's whitewash,' said Professor Ayers behind her.

'Whitewash indeed, and papier-mâché. Curiouser and curiouser. Ayers, my dear fellow, who whitewashes a mummy?'

'And why?' murmured Jane. 'It's a bit like gilding fine gold or painting the lily, you know.'

'So you read Shakespeare as well, my young colleague. Very suitable. Can you get hold of this bit from your end? I think it will peel. So. Very nice.'

'I do hope you are going to tell us, Miss Fisher,' commented Professor Ayers. 'When you have an explanation, of course. I know it is going to be fascinating. Someone makes a mummy—you know, Treasure, some consideration ought to be given to the method of mummification. I am almost prepared to swear that this body was treated in an Egyptian fashion. Give me a probe and I'll be sure.'

There was an interval in which Phryne tried not to hear sinister scraping noises, and Ayers exclaimed, 'Exactly! No nasal sinus!'

'Ah,' said Jane.

'Ah,' said Dr Treasure.

'What does that signify?' asked Phryne after a pause in which the scientific drew their own conclusions and the unscientific wondered why they had come.

Dr Treasure hurried to explain. 'Well, you see, there are various ways of preserving a body—by freezing in permafrost, by smoking, by curing, by embalming and by desiccation. I don't think he's been smoke-cured, do you, fellows?'

'No singed bits,' said Jane, who had obviously been promoted to an honorary fellow.

'No soot,' agreed Professor Ayers.

'And if he had been properly embalmed he'd have more flesh on him,' Dr Treasure continued, 'to put it crudely. Embalming works by injecting arsenic . . . well, I suppose that is not relevant.' He had observed that he was not holding his audience. 'Of course, there are also the bodies of saints and so on who have been preserved incorrupt by some means, but they are supposed to be perfect and this chap only weighs fifteen pounds. So it's probable that he was preserved by desiccation, that is, he was dried out. We don't know yet if it was natural, which he could have done himself by dying considerately in a nice hot desert, or whether someone did it on purpose with a couple of bags of butcher's salt. Professor Ayers reminded me that in Egypt the brain was extracted through the nose . . .'

'With a thing like a button hook,' added Jane helpfully.

'And has just ascertained that the nasal sinus is broken, which means . . .'

'Thank you,' said Phryne. 'I understand. Pray continue, gentlemen.'

Phryne turned back to the clothes. Jane was in her element. Phryne was not. The corpse disturbed her. She felt that this examination was somehow indecent.

The cloth of the shirt tore even under her very careful handling. There were traces of whitewash on the wide band of a cheap collarless blue and white checked flannel shirt, circa perhaps 1910. The trousers were older—moleskins, if she were any judge—and as fragile as old washleather. Phryne took up Dr Treasure's magnifying glass. Something was written or perhaps, yes, stitched into the waistband. It was so blurred and broken that she could only guess at it. Was that a T? Followed, perhaps, by a B? A washing mark, maybe. Otherwise the moleskins were cobwebby, worn, dirty and fragmentary. There was scarcely enough trouser to keep even a mummy decent.

There were no rags of undergarments, though they might have fallen entirely to dust, and no socks in the dusty boots. Poor TB, if he was TB, had not even been given a slave's loincloth before he had been dressed in these foul rags and displayed like a guy.

The boots were interesting. They looked too good to be wasted on a carnival figure, for all the walking he might do. Jane had suggested that they were not his boots because they had fallen off, but surely the total loss of flesh would explain that? If he had been about 64 inches tall he might have had a size . . . seven, perhaps, boot. Phryne borrowed some linseed swabs and cleaned one side of the left boot, noting that the soles had plenty of wear in them. Layers of dust came off and under it a splash of white and then a streak of red. Blood? No. Blood dried black. This was red clay. Under close examination she could see that both boot soles bore traces of red clay. Tenacious stuff, red clay. Phryne had once been smeared with clay during an injudicious foray into the sport called caving, and after trying to remove it from her hair had decided that it might be easier just to plaster the rest of herself with red clay and start a new fashion. Where was the nearest red earth? Not on the black soil plain. Towards Ballarat, perhaps, or Bendigo.

The boots did not have conventional cloth laces but were held together with strips of what Phryne thought might be kangaroo hide.

Then she took each boot, turned it upside down and shook it firmly. Nothing was going to make her put her hand inside. She evicted one puzzled spider, who summed up its change in circumstances with great speed for an arachnid and leapt for the bookcase. Otherwise there was nothing but more red dust. Phryne took a probe and pried at something stuck to the insole. A fragment of paper.

She drew it forth and used a delicate pair of tweezers to unroll it. Red paper, printed in black—would the mummy have been so courteous and far-sighted as to have included his name and address and possibly instructions for the future disposal of his remains?

Phryne flattened the paper at last and read 'Admit O . . . Marvels . . .' It was a ticket for the Carter show. Drat.

More information on the Carter show would be forthcoming from Mr Josiah Burton, who was coming to dinner that night. Phryne spared a moment to worry. She would not tolerate her scholarly and charming friend meeting with any affront in her own house. She must confront Eliza and make sure that if she could not cope with dwarves at dinner with the courtesy expected of an English gentlewoman then she could dine off a tray in her own apartments. A firm line was going to be necessary with Eliza, and Phryne was going to draw it as soon as she returned home.

There was absolutely nothing more to be got from the boots. No maker's tag, no markings, only a lot more red clay. Phryne had exhausted the possibilities of the clothes and therefore had to reluctantly return to the fascinated figures around the mummy.

He was bare now of paint and masking papier-mâché and he shone slightly with linseed oil. Phryne controlled her distaste as Dr Treasure began to exhibit the glories of his subject to his distinguished guest.

'Except where you broke his ankle joint, so careless of you, Phryne, he is intact. He even has all his fingers and toes. If we rehydrate him a bit we might even be able to take his finger-prints. What a piece of work is man!'

'Indeed,' said Phryne.

'He has been preserved by someone using Egyptian methods,' said Dr Treasure. 'There is no Y incision but one cut along the right side of the abdomen, here closed with stitches. This is where the viscera were removed. And the brain . . . but you already know about that.'

Professor Ayers coughed and continued: 'I presume that his abdomen was washed out with eucalyptus oil—there is still a faint scent of it about him—quite a good substitute for cypress oil. Then the body was stuffed to keep its shape.'

'What did they stuff it with?' asked Jane, agog.

'That we shall presently see,' promised Professor Ayers, almost smiling. Jane was proving an education for Professor Ayers. 'The Egyptians used rolls of linen, sawdust, any rubbish that was hanging around. The body was then laid in dry natron for seventy days.'

'As Herodotus says,' prompted Jane.

'So after the poor helpless body was gutted, stuffed and salted like a fish, what did they do with it?' asked Phryne. The scent of linseed oil and leather was giving her highly inappropriate memories of a cricketer to whom she had been very close. Extremely close. In the pavilion, if she remembered correctly. Before a county match. Thinking of sex in association with this human wreck she considered improper.

'After desiccation it was washed in wine—here I believe they used turpentine—and then anointed with resin and bandaged. Here we see no bandages or amulets but I believe my thesis is sound.'

'So do I,' said Dr Treasure.

'There's a mark on his forearm,' said Jane. 'Here.'

'You've got good eyes!' exclaimed Professor Ayers rather enviously. 'Take the glass, Miss Jane. What can you see?'

'A bruise? No, wait, it's all colours,' replied Jane excitedly. 'I don't suppose, Professor, you could just call me Jane? I'm not used to being called Miss. I'm just Jane.'

Ayers unbent. His previous experience of children of the female persuasion (loud, vain, greedy) had not prepared him for eager, intelligent, educated Jane.

'Very well. Colours? What do you make of it then . . . er, Jane?'

'It's a tattoo, isn't it?' she asked. She looked into his face for signs of agreement. Not, Phryne thought, for approval.

'I believe that it may be,' said Ayers. He took the glass and bent over the twisted forearm. 'Chinese, I think. The Chinese have always done the best tattoos. Much superior in application and artistry than the crude western ones in harsh

43

blue ink. Well, Treasure? Don't be shy. Show the ladies your illumination.'

Blushing, Dr Treasure rolled up his sleeve. There was a fish on his upper arm. Jane took the glass and examined it minutely. So did Phryne.

'Where did you get it?' she asked.

'Hong Kong. In my uproarious youth I was the doctor on a cruise ship. I don't show it to just anyone, you know. Some fellows consider tattooing to be rather low. I wouldn't have it done now, of course, but with tattoos there must be no regrets, for they're perfectly indelible. Isn't it pretty?'

'Gorgeous,' said Phryne truthfully. It was a carp, all floating fins, done in delicate etchings of orange, gold and black. She tore her lascivious mind away from wondering if the rest of Dr Treasure matched the muscular and lightly tanned arm and considered the tattoo on the mummy.

It was some sort of crest or coat of arms. The shape made this clear. Two supporters of a fish-tailed kind, then a quartered shield topped with a helmeted head. The plumes had survived intact, as had the tails of the mermen (if they were mermen), but the shield was stained, or perhaps the flesh under it had been bruised. Heraldry had never interested Phryne, but she knew her sister Eliza had made a close study of it. Eliza knew *Debrett's Peerage* almost by heart. Phryne found a pencil and tried to sketch the design exactly as she could see it.

It was blurred. Ayers finally shook his sleek head and rubbed his eyes. 'No, I can't make out any more. I have a friend who has been getting interesting results from photographing disputed manuscripts through different filters. I'll ask him to call and bring his plate camera. Now, what more have we to see?'

The autopsy now required that the body be turned over and every inch scrutinised before any cutting was done. Phryne

44

was uncharacteristically wishing that she belonged to the class who could be sent to make tea. Dr Treasure might have been reading her mind.

'Phryne, could you do me a service? Would you go into the house and ask my wife to tell Mrs Bernstein to make tea for us? Coffee for Professor Ayers and for Jane . . . what can I offer, my dear and most promising colleague?'

'Ginger ale, Miss Phryne, if you please,' said Jane decisively. Phryne went.

The house was a haven, comfortably if shabbily furnished with things which someone's relatives hadn't had room for but couldn't bear to throw away. Nothing matched but nothing jarred. The parlour contained, reading right to left, a woman playing the piano, a small girl dancing uncertainly, a baby making a spirited attempt to gum a biscuit and a large dog of the labrador persuasion. He was sitting under the highchair, salivating quietly, in the sure and certain knowledge that fairly soon, infant grasp and concentration being what they were, the biscuit would be his. All looked up at Phryne's entrance.

'No, no, please don't stop,' she said quickly. 'You make a charming picture.'

'You're Miss Fisher, aren't you? So nice to meet you again,' said Mrs Treasure. She was a plump, dark-haired woman in a stylish crepe dress. She had the air of effortless serenity usually only possessed by small dark people wearing saffron robes. 'Do meet my family,' she said, beginning to play her simple tune again. 'I am Anne Treasure, the dancer is my daughter Phoebe and the baby is my son Charles. And the dog is called Huggy Bear. As you might have gathered, I did not name him. Can I help you with anything or are you seeking refuge from the laboratory?'

'They want tea, coffee for Professor Ayers and ginger ale for my daughter Jane, and I wanted to get out of there,' confessed Phryne.

'Well, if you can take over the piano,' said Mrs Treasure, 'I shall give the order. And I think a nice gin and tonic is indicated for us. If it wasn't for the sustaining power of gin, I would never have survived child rearing. As long as you keep playing, Phoebe will keep dancing,' she added as Phryne slipped into the seat beside her.

It might have been a threat or it might have been a promise, but Phryne picked out the notes for the tune, which she recognised after a while as Ravel's *Bolero*, and Phoebe kept dancing. The baby duly dropped his biscuit on Huggy Bear, who gave an adroit twist and 'clop' of jaws. The biscuit never hit the floor. Charles missed it. Or perhaps he was taking exception to Phryne's uncertain touch on the keyboard. Just when he was reddening with intent to roar, Mrs Treasure came back.

'Mrs Bernstein will bring the tray,' she said. 'I will mix us a drink, so essential on such a warm day. I'm not going to ask about Mark's work—I never do. You may stop playing now, Miss Fisher, thank you. Phoebe, go with Miss Fraser, now, it's time for your nap.'

A large competent woman in a navy wrapper had appeared at the door. She bore the struggling baby off in mid roar. Phoebe followed, still dancing. Huggy Bear fell in behind. There might, he felt, be more biscuits.

'I like your house,' said Phryne, sipping. The crowded bookshelves held no skulls and there were no anatomical diagrams on the walls, which was an improvement on Dr Treasure's ideas of domestic design.

Mrs Treasure laughed pleasantly. She had a rich, cultured voice.

'My dear, the furniture is all castoffs. No point in having good furniture if you have children. One would be forever telling them not to bounce on the couch. Too fatiguing for me and too irritating for them. Do smoke if you wish. Mark is always trying to bring horrible things in jars into the house, and I am always telling him to take them back to the laboratory, so that's enough friction for one household. But he is a dear good fellow.'

'Yes, he is,' agreed Phryne.

It was pleasant to sit in a room which was not scented with science, but she knew she could not remain long. Someone was doubtless dying to tell her something new about their beloved mummy. Phryne enjoyed her drink and her Sobranie and waited for the tray which a severe woman brought to the door of the laboratory, where there was a table. 'And no further,' she declared. 'Not after them rats!'

'Rats?' asked Phryne when Mrs Bernstein had safely gone.

'She went in once just as Mark dropped a cage in which he had a few white rats. They rather swarm, rats, especially when they are dropped. Apparently one ran over her foot. After that she won't go near the laboratory.'

'Thank you for the drink,' said Phryne, picking up the tray and opening the door into science.

'Do come again,' said Mrs Treasure, seeming to mean it.

Phryne laid down the tray and announced, 'Tea.'

'We have made progress,' Jane proclaimed, taking her glass of ginger ale.

'We certainly have,' beamed Dr Treasure. 'We have been over the whole body and made a small incision to see what he is packed with. Most amazing, Phryne, you won't believe this. Tea? Ah, yes, tea. Thank you.'

'What won't I believe?' asked Phryne, cushioned against further shocks by a comfortable gin.

'First, we have the bullet. It was still in the skull, jammed in under the jaw. It's not a bullet, Phryne. It's a ball. Like they used in the old days. And what's more . . .' Dr Treasure paused to sip and lost his place. Professor Ayers leapt into the gap.

'We know when he was mummified.'

'We do? How? Did you find a date of preservation? Or a canning date, like they put on tinned ham? This mummy made in 1921?'

Professor Ayers did not even acknowledge her attempt at wit.

'Better. We found out what his abdomen was packed with.'

'What?' asked Phryne, feeling like the straight man in a comic crosstalk act. They were so pleased and so excited and they really needed her to be astonished and impressed.

'Newspaper,' said Jane triumphantly.

'Newspaper?' demanded Phryne, astonished as required. In fact, more astonished than was required. She really was surprised.

'And we've got some which hasn't been rendered entirely illegible by the body fluids. Here.' Ayers presented a stained and crumpled piece of newsprint.

'Part of a masthead. The something *Mail*,' read Phryne.

'And here . . .' Dr Treasure had regained the initiative as Ayers gulped his coffee. 'The pièce de résistance.'

'My God,' said Phryne very quietly. 'Gentlemen, you are amazing.'

On the strip of paper was clearly printed 'July 27th 1857. Attempted Expulsion . . .' While Phryne was still staring at it, Dr Treasure put down his cup and delivered his considered medical opinion.

'This was a healthy young European man, under twenty-five, with dark hair and probably brown eyes. He was about five foot four and well built, the muscle adhesions on the bones are marked. He was left handed and had been doing hard physical work; there are callouses on his hands. He has a tattoo on his arm which came from a Chinese source, probably a port like Shanghai or Hong Kong. If I had to make a finding of death I'd have to say that there are no gross injuries, all the other bones appear to be intact and he died of homicidal or accidental violence due to a bullet to the head. Right between the eyes. At close quarters, as there is some gunpowder tattooing. After death, soon after, he was mummified in a manner which duplicated the Ancient Egyptian. From the stitches, which are surgical silk, I assume that the mummifier was a medical gentleman with a knowledge of the classics and an experimental turn of mind. How the young man got to be where he was found, that is for the remarkable Miss Fisher to explain.'

They all beamed at Phryne. She was genuinely impressed. But while their research was ended, hers was about to begin.

'Difficult. But possible. And what would you say was the date of death, gentlemen and Jane?'

'Oh, we are in agreement about that too. Somewhere around the date of the newspaper, Miss Fisher. Look for your missing young man in about 1857,' Ayers told her.

'That's the Gold Rush,' said Jane.

'So it is,' said Phryne. 'A very good time for a murder, and a very easy place in which to disappear.'

In the thirteenth year of the reign of the glorious Emperor Lord of the Dragon Throne Kwong Sui of the Ching Dynasty, Mid Autumn festival, 15th day of eighth month.

To his younger sister Sung Mai the ku'li Sung Ma sends greetings. We seem to be travelling so fast that the clouds trail behind us, trying vainly to keep up. I can hear the sailors shouting over a fantan game below, smell the stench of the rancid pork fat our fried cakes are being cooked in and the fish which the ship's cat, whom I have named Dark Moon because of her black fur, has dragged out of the bilges and is now devouring on my bit of deck. The ropes which hold the sails are singing.

There ought to be a poem in this.

A small village, dinner is cooking, men are gambling.

The sea gods noose it and sling it across the waves.

Not one of my best. We have been thirty days at sea and they say that we will arrive before fifty days are gone.

The elder brother bids farewell, with love, to the younger sister.

CHAPTER FOUR

In her new dress, she comes from her vermilion
towers;
The light of spring floods the palace.

Liu Yuhsi, translated by Lin Yutang

Phryne and Jane returned home with the ticket and pieces of
newspaper carefully preserved between two sheets of glass. Jane
was quiet all the way home in the Hispano-Suiza. Phryne
wondered if anything was wrong. Delayed shock?

Her fears were dissipated when Jane remarked, 'Perhaps
I might rather be a pathologist, like Professor Glaister.'

'Perhaps,' said Phryne. 'Think about it when you have
finished your medical training. Dr Treasure does say that it is
one speciality where the patients don't complain.'

Jane chuckled. 'Who is coming to dinner?' she asked
eagerly. 'Did you say he was a dwarf, Miss Phryne?'

'Yes. A very educated and dignified person, and I have to
warn my sister not to insult him. I know you and Ruth too
well to think that you might stare and giggle as silly Misses

might do. Though, now I come to think of it, neither of you giggle much. And you may not ask him personal questions, Jane. I know that you would really like to and that you mean no offence, but he's a guest and guests are not to be either anatomically examined or interrogated.' Phryne paused. 'Unless they want to be, of course,' she added.

Jane bit her lip. 'You're thinking about Mrs Behan, aren't you?' she asked. 'I did apologise.'

'I know, and that the question of the real colour of her hair was only to be expected if one insists on dyeing grey-brown hair that very metallic shade of red. But it's a known middle-class fact that ladies do not dye their hair. Only actresses and prostitutes dye their hair. So your innocent question, "What dye do you use to get that lovely red colour?", was loaded with social criticism. Conversation is a minefield until you learn the conventions, Jane dear.'

'I'll never learn all the rules,' muttered Jane.

'Yes, you will,' said Phryne. 'Then you can bend them. The best advice I would give you is, "If under attack, cause a diversion".'

'A diversion?'

'Yes, trip over the dog, spill a glass of wine on your attacker, burst into song, challenge your attacker to a duel. And the angrier you get, the lower your voice should be. Never shout unless you are shouting "Fire!" Enough of this . . . I am not cut out to be a guide to youth. I think youth can get itself into enough trouble without my help, don't you, Youth?'

Jane grinned and agreed.

Lin Chung arrived at the door, dead-heating a gentleman in faultless evening costume whose top hat came up to the level of his second coat button. Lin, whose savoir-faire was legendary, bowed slightly. The top hat bent in his direction.

'Do I have the pleasure of meeting Mr Burton?' he asked.

'And you, sir, must be Mr Lin. Delighted.'

It was such a deep, cultured voice that Lin regretted that he could not see the gentleman's face. Mr Butler opened the door and admitted them, taking the gentlemen's coats and conducting them into the drawing room with his usual suavity.

Phryne had been thinking about this visit, and the fact that her entire house was built for people two feet taller than her guest. After a consultation with Mr Butler, a suitable chair had been fixed to a wooden crate, covered with blue velvet. This would allow Mr Burton to sit almost at eye level with the guests and incidentally obviate the crick in the neck which Phryne always got from conversing with her friend.

'How kind of you to come,' exclaimed Phryne, allowing Mr Burton to kiss her hand and leading him to his throne. She wanted him to be able to see and appreciate her new dress.

Phryne expected to entertain often in her sea-blue, sea-green rooms and she needed a cocktail dress which complemented the rooms. In blue or green the clothes had a regrettable tendency to meld into the general colour scheme, so guests saw an uneasy Gustav Klimt vision of their hostess's head and limbs as if emerging from the wallpaper. This clearly would not do. But red or purple were too garish and shocking in the soothing greens and one could not wear cloth of gold all the time.

She had taken the problem to Madame Fleuri, High Priestess of the Mode, who had surveyed the rooms, scribbled notes, accepted a glass of wine, scribbled more notes and then vanished into her atelier for three weeks, emerging with a dress she called 'Opalescence'. It had cost Phryne a fortune. She had not grudged a penny of it.

Josiah Burton surveyed Phryne with deep appreciation. She had always been elegant, even when—as he had first seen her—wearing a Woolworth's fuji dress with half the fringes torn off. Now she was clad in a slim sheath of steel grey silk. Over it was a cloud grey silk georgette wrap which was almost transparent, sewn with paillettes of mother of pearl down to the weighted handkerchief points of the skirt, along the scoop neck and the shoulder straps. A string of pearls swung nearly to her knees, knotted halfway. A panache of pearl shells was in her black hair. Grey silk stockings and shoes completed the ensemble. She turned to be admired, chiming a little.

'A sea-nymph,' said Mr Burton.

'A mermaid,' said Lin Chung.

'Isn't she absolutely beautiful?' asked Ruth of Jane. Jane nodded. She would never be as interested in clothes as Phryne was, but she knew an effect when she saw it. Phryne shone with a moonlight gleam against the blue and green, like the mermaid to which Mr Lin had likened her. The paillettes glinted when she moved, as though she were shedding drops of sea-water. Ruth thought that she looked even more beautiful than the heroine of her latest romance, *A Fisher Maid*.

Phryne perched on a chair to allow Mr Butler to distribute glasses of his gin cocktail, a drink which 'promotes ease and eloquence, Miss Fisher, while avoiding any sense of excess'. Phryne had asked which ingredient took away any extravagance in the drink and he had replied with a definitively straight face, 'That would be the lemon juice, Miss Fisher.' Whereupon Phryne had given up, reflecting that every religion has its mysteries.

Jane found that by carefully aligning herself with one of Phryne's many mirrors, she could gaze on Mr Burton without seeming to stare, and was lost to fashion thereafter, even forgetting to drink her orange juice.

Which didn't mean that Mr Burton hadn't noticed. He felt the avid eyes and traced their source. He said, 'Miss Jane?' and she blushed.

'What would you like to ask me?' he enquired calmly. 'Don't be concerned. I am used to being an object of interest in any gathering.'

Jane gathered her courage and looked him in his highly intelligent, dispassionate eyes.

'I beg your pardon, sir,' she said. 'And I wasn't looking at you as though you were an object. But I am curious. I want to be a doctor.'

'A useful attribute for a doctor. I have achondroplasia, which is an inherited abnormality. Characteristic of this disease are the short limbs, and therefore short stature. The skull vault and clavicle, and the facial structure, are also retarded in development, giving this dished-in appearance.' He ran a stubby, powerful finger along his tip-tilted nose. 'But I am as strong as a taller man with a much lower centre of gravity and lighter body. This gives me advantages as an acrobat: thus.'

Mr Burton, still holding his glass, executed a perfect somersault, coming down into his sitting position again without spilling a drop. Phryne and Ruth laughed and clapped. Jane said, 'Thank you! That was wonderful. And I promise not to ask any more questions. Really,' she protested, when Ruth nudged her.

'You are with the circus?' asked Lin Chung easily.

'Dwarf heaven, they call it. Where else can the Small People be at home in a world of giants?' Mr Burton smiled. 'There I met Miss Fisher.'

'Are you still with Farrell's?' asked Phryne. 'How I remember falling off Missy every day! My bruises had bruises.'

'But you did learn to do a handstand on a horse's back,' he

reminded her. 'Also, you found out who was trying to ruin the circus and you freed an innocent woman from prison. Everyone sends their love,' went on Mr Burton, allowing Mr Butler to refill his glass. 'Farrell himself, Dulcie, Wallace and Bruno, Samson, Doreen and Alan Lee, the Catalans, the Shakespeare brothers—you recall the clowns.'

Phryne did. The memory of making love in a caravan to a man with a painted face loosened her joints, but she took a sip of her drink and a deep breath.

'And it took two days to get the tar off your skin,' put in Dot, who had noticed this reaction and was distracting attention from Phryne. 'Not to mention them awful clothes. Filthy places—beg pardon, Mr Burton.'

'No offence taken,' said Mr Burton. 'They are filthy places indeed. But fascinating. I miss them. When my thesis is accepted I will go back on the road. My caravan is presently in my college's stable, as is my gallant steed Balthasar. He is appreciating the rest. One of the students takes him out for a sedate ride every day in Royal Park and the university has the best grass. But to return to what I was saying, they all hope that you will come to a performance when they get back to Melbourne in December. They want to express their gratitude for saving the circus.'

'Just a good investment,' said Phryne, waving her cigarette dismissively.

A lesser man might have said, 'Bah!' Mr Burton shot Phryne a sharp look and said in a voice loaded with more irony than an ore truck: 'Oh, indeed, Miss Fisher. An investment.'

Then he leapt to his feet as Eliza came in.

Phryne had warned her sister that if by any means—word, look, intonation, drawn breath, squint, raised eyebrow or avoidance of gaze—she conveyed any disapproval of Mr Burton she, Phryne, would give her sister, Eliza, a clip over the ear which would take a week to stop ringing, and referred to their mutual childhood for proof of her competence in ear-clipping. Eliza, who had seemed subdued during this speech, had agreed rather listlessly to be good.

Eliza wore a cocktail dress in a drab shade of brown and a bunch of silk pansies on a headband, and she carried a bound book. She had dragged her hair back into an unbecoming bun and walked as though her feet hurt, which indeed they might, due to her refusal to wear sensible shoes. She allowed Mr Burton to kiss her hand without a blink, smiled at the company, and took her seat next to the girls. She accepted a cocktail from Mr Butler, gulped it down, and accepted a refill which also vanished with disconcerting speed.

'We were talking about the circus, Miss Eliza,' said Mr Burton.

'Do you work in a circus, Mr Burton?' asked Eliza. Even her voice had lost its 'haw-haw' edge. Phryne thought her greatly improved. 'I thought that my sister said that you were a scholar.'

'One can be both, Miss Eliza. I am completing my doctorate of philosophy at present, studying the literary depictions as opposed to the real social conditions among the poor.'

'I don't quite follow,' confessed Eliza. Neither did Phryne. Lin Chung shook his head. Both young women looked blank. Mr Burton explained.

'Well, for instance, if the ladies will forgive my breach of taste, authors who write about prostitutes always follow Dickens' lead in saying that they come to bad ends, suicide and so on—you will remember Little Em'ly and her cry of "Oh, the river!" Admittedly Dickens saved Little Em'ly's life and sent her to Australia, a favourite literary device for removing inconvenient members of the cast to a place where No One Will Know.'

'Still is,' put in Eliza unexpectedly, starting Phryne on quite a novel train of thought. But Eliza had always been the good daughter, she told herself. Stayed in the manor and did the flowers. Went to the hunt balls. Poured tea for the county. Had memorised Debrett.

'Indeed,' agreed Mr Burton. 'Whereas most prostitutes stop being prostitutes when they have, for instance, paid off their debts, saved enough to open a business, accepted a proposal of marriage, got diseased, educated their children, divorced their husband, inherited money or decided to move to another city and get a straight job. Prostitutes do not kill themselves at a greater rate than the general population. But what is even more curious is, from Dickens onwards, the authors know that they are not depicting the truth. If they have done any research at all, actually talked to any of these women, they know that they are just people, and have all the varied motives which people have.'

'Then why doesn't someone write a realistic book?' asked Phryne.

'Because no publisher would publish it,' said Mr Burton.

'You are right,' said Eliza, gulping down her third cocktail. Phryne glanced at Mr Butler, who made an almost imperceptible movement which might have been a nod. The next cocktail for Eliza would be plain orange and bitters. 'Look at Beatrice and Sydney Webb. They wrote the truth about the conditions of the working poor in London and they had to establish their own publishing house to get it released. None of the nice people who owned and rented out those dreadful buildings, running with rats, wanted to know what state they were in.'

'And that's regrettable but not unexpected,' said Phryne.

Eliza leaned forward in her chair and said earnestly, 'I've

seen them, Phryne! Terrible. Pigs wouldn't live in them. Rats and . . . er . . . bugs. So filthy that no scrubbing could ever clean them.'

'And you have seen them?' asked Phryne, with a delicate hint of disbelief. She wanted this new Eliza to keep talking. Eliza flushed a little.

'I have! I went with Ally, Alice, I mean Lady Alice Harborough, we . . . I mean, she was starting a housing mission in the East End. Those houses were a disgrace. Even the ones owned by the church, Phryne!'

'What's a housing mission, Miss Eliza?' asked Ruth. She knew all about houses which could not be made clean by scrubbing. She had spent her childhood scrubbing them.

'One buys a house,' said Miss Eliza. 'One of the awful ones, to start with, because they're cheap. Then one hires otherwise unemployed men to clean, replaster, sewer, plumb, wire for electricity, then paint and tile and so on. There are a thousand details and they have to be right. The people are people, not animals. They like nice things. Everyone likes nice things, don't they?' Everyone nodded. They liked nice things, that was agreed.

Eliza had entirely shed her affected accent and in her voice one could hear a faint echo of Collingwood and Richmond. Phryne found this consoling. Perhaps Beth had not gone forever.

Eliza continued: 'Then one rents the rooms to people. They pay less than a commercial rent but they agree to keep the place clean and in repair—and they do, they really do.'

'Of course they do,' said Ruth. 'If they went from one of those bone-dirty houses to a nice clean house, then they'd keep it clean. It's not hard to keep new houses clean. But not old ones, eh, Jane?'

'No.' Jane looked down at her hands as if momentarily surprised to find them clean and soft, with neat short nails, instead of the grimy claws they had been. 'Not even possible, I think. No matter how much you scrub.'

Mr Burton seemed enlightened and was about to comment when Phryne signalled him to remain silent.

'So one repairs one house,' commented Phryne. 'There is a lot of the East End, Eliza, and all of it frightful.'

'One has to start somewhere,' retorted Eliza. 'With the rents from the first house one buys a second, and so on. Ally— Lady Harborough has seven houses now, a whole street. It was the only street which didn't get typhoid last year.'

'And you work with this charitable lady?' said Mr Burton. 'That is good of you.'

'No!' Eliza jumped as if she had sat on an unexpected hairbrush. 'No, I just heard . . . I just heard about it. In passing. May I have another cocktail, Mr Butler?' she asked in her county voice. 'They are most agreeable, are they not?'

Mr Burton, a little surprised, agreed that Mr Butler's cocktails were marvels of their type and the conversation became general. Phryne cursed under her breath. Beth had almost emerged through Eliza then, and just as she was getting interesting Eliza had popped back like the Demon King in a pantomime. Damning and blasting all sisters, Phryne led the way into her dining room, clinking a little as she walked and trailing her undersea clouds of glory.

Dinner was one of Mrs Butler's best efforts. After a very hard working life with a jovial gentleman, Mr and Mrs Butler had only agreed to oblige Miss Fisher if she did not entertain a great deal, so Phryne had given most of her dinner parties at the Windsor, a very superior hotel. She might have a few people for drinks, perhaps, or those little lunches at which Mrs Butler excelled, but Phryne did not like large parties cluttering up her small house and usually only invited close friends to share the Butler cuisine. This suited the Butlers.

Tonight, with the added spur of Miss Eliza's freely expressed views on Australia not being a patch on Europe, and St Kilda not even being a patch on Melbourne itself, Mrs Butler felt that she needed to make a point about the advantages of fresh vegetables, admirable dairy products, eggs which had only been snatched from the hen an hour before and the sort of meat which even the famed farmers of the whole continent of Europe could not equal. Much less surpass.

Therefore, laid out on the buffet was the Cold Collation of the Gods. Small cups of perfectly seasoned vichyssoise were gathered at one end of the white-draped buffet. Plump pink prawns studded the seafood aspic as thickly as daisies in a springtime meadow. A whole baron of beef squatted glistening in a bed of dark green bitter lettuce, rare, paper-thin slices rolling from its side. An entire salmon, sliced and decorated with radish flowers, lay shining in a silver dish. A nearby salver held oysters, freshly opened, with lemon juice in a jug beside. Little squares of rye-bread toast, sliced onions and hard boiled eggs accompanied the black pearls of the Beluga caviar, a gift from the Russian ambassador, which were piled with a lavish hand into their silver dish bedded in crushed ice: the manner in which Phryne always served caviar. An aspic gallimaufry of poultry (the recipe a closely guarded secret which Mrs Butler had promised to her favourite niece, to be communicated on Mrs Butler's departure to the Grande Cuisine du Ciel) reposed on a broad salver, a golden jelly which trembled slightly. In it one could discern dark meat and white—duck, perhaps, chicken, maybe pigeon, perhaps quail?

With the beasts of the field and the fish of the sea and the fowls of the air went the fruits of the earth. A forest of crisp greenery decorated the salads: the potato salad creamy with mayonnaise which had no acquaintance whatsoever with condensed milk and mustard powder. The salade Russe which added an agreeable note of deep pink. The Caesar salad on which the egg had just set. Bunches of tiny carrots, crisp celery, the first tomatoes, asparagus in hollandaise sauce shiny with cream, sliced cucumbers bursting with vitamins and lettuce of several types completed the table. There were four sorts of chutney, three types of mustard, and mayonnaise with lemon for the fish and without for the salads, and also a perfect vinaigrette.

With the French windows open onto Phryne's small, enchanting garden where the wisteria and jasmine were just coming into bloom, it seemed to Mr Burton a vision of a gourmet's heaven.

'Did you always garden, Miss Fisher?' asked Mr Burton, trying not to salivate. The college kitchens were known for specialising in Edible Stodge, at which they excelled. He lusted after fresh fish. Oysters. Caviar! But the admirable Miss Fisher, provider of this feast, was speaking. He dragged his attention away from the table.

'No, it isn't my doing at all. Lin's wife, Camellia, a most accomplished young woman, planned it and supervised the planting. It's very pretty, isn't it? The Chinese do the best gardens in small spaces. Do have some caviar, Mr Burton.'

Overcome, Mr Burton pressed her unoccupied hand. The right was engaged in scooping caviar onto his plate.

'Miss Fisher, could I ask you to call me Josiah?'

'Certainly, and please call me Phryne.' Phryne was touched. Mr Burton was a complex, dignified man and it was a pleasure to be considered one of his friends. 'And more caviar, perhaps?'

'One can never have too much caviar, Phryne,' agreed Mr Burton. 'And some of that seafood aspic. Some salmon. A couple of oysters, perhaps.'

'Phryne, this is an amazing feast,' said Lin Chung. 'Please excuse me if I do not indulge in it too freely. I have already eaten one banquet today.'

'At Mr Hu's? Of course. You have solved your feud. How did it go?'

'Basically a no-score win,' said Lin. 'Perhaps just a few grains of caviar. And one slice of that roast beef.'

The guests sat down with loaded plates. Dot, Phryne noticed, favoured fresh vegetables with a big dollop of mayonnaise and roasted meat. Jane had discovered the gallimaufry and was dissecting it carefully, identifying each delicious sliver before she ate it. Ruth, who was a steady, patient eater with years of semi-starvation to avenge, had started with a spoonful of everything and was working her way through. So far all of it pleased her.

'Phryne, this is a banquet!' exclaimed Eliza. 'You could feed a hundred . . . no, of course, it is very nice. Very nice indeed. I believe I will have some salade Russe. And some salmon. I didn't know you got salmon here, except in tins.'

'Do try the gallimaufry,' said Phryne, intrigued. 'Mrs Butler is very proud of it.'

Mr Butler poured the wine, a straw-coloured hock from South Australia, where the vines had been tended in German, which made them pay attention and get on with growing and producing Rhine quality wine, alsbalt! It was refreshing and slightly lemony, with a good bite of tannin. No one said anything much for the next ten minutes, leaving Lin Chung to carry on a light conversation over the clatter of cutlery.

'The most surprising thing about settling the feud was how matter-of-fact it was,' he told Phryne, who was capturing the last Beluga pearls with a handy spoon. 'Mr Hu had his list and we had ours and we just went through them one by one. The missing woman, Lin Wan, and her children are coming to visit her mother tonight, so I'm rather glad to be out of the house—it will be full of noise. Also, Grandmother is displeased with my entirely accidental meeting with Mr Hu. She smells disobedience.'

'And the gold? Will they be bringing it around on a handcart?' asked Phryne, sipping her wine.

'No, it seems that it wasn't them. It wasn't the Hu family who killed those couriers. We were wrong. Now I must try and find out what happened in 1857, and that is not going to be easy. It might not even be possible. But I will begin by talking to Mr Hu's venerable great great grandmother, and my own even more venerable great great uncle, and see what they say. Assuming they can remember anything at all, of course.'

'Fascinating,' said Mr Burton, who had eaten as much caviar as was decent, and then a little more, and was starting on his oysters. 'The feud is settled, then, as though it was an ordinary business transaction?'

'Yes. We have a list of grievances and so have they and we make what Paris calls a "règlement des comptes".'

'And unlike Paris you do not settle it with machine guns,' commented Phryne. 'Mr Butler, do tell Mrs Butler that this is one of the most superb dinners of the year.'

'Of my life,' agreed Mr Burton. 'My college would get an Anti-Michelin Award, their speciality being "Unidentifiable Beast in Cold Lumpy Gravy".'

Mr Butler bowed gravely. He was delighted to see that Mr Burton had not only a healthy appetite for his size, but a healthy appetite for a six foot wharfie after a three day fast.

Mr Butler approved of gluttony. It was, he thought, a nice, comfortable vice. Never caused any noise or trouble and the sufferer just expired of an apoplexy, regretted by all those who had attended his excellent dinner parties. At his direction, Mr Butler placed a spoonful of each salad on Mr Burton's plate, on a bedding of lettuce and mayonnaise.

Phryne sent her plate back for more roast beef and said to Mr Burton, 'Josiah, if you would be so kind as to cast your mind back to your early days at the circus, I want to hear all about Carter's Travelling Miracles and Marvels Show,' said Phryne.

'Carter's?' Mr Burton swallowed his last oyster. Perfect. Very fresh, creamy, with just the right touch of lemon juice. 'They followed Farrell's for a while, many years ago. Before my time, really. But I did hear rather a lot about them, and some of their properties were knocking around for sale for years. Why do you want to know about Carter's? It was a very low, sensational carnie show, full of feejee mermaids and Jenny Hanivers.'

'Mr Burton, what is a Jenny Haniver?' asked Jane.

'It's a sort of shark, which can be configured (when dead and dried) to resemble any sort of monster. What I meant was, the show was as fake as it could possibly be, and not too scrupulous in its methods either. One of the reasons why it went broke. But before we get onto that, why on earth are you interested in that piddling little raree show?'

'I think we will tell you that after dinner,' said Phryne. Lin, Jane, Ruth and Eliza murmured an agreement. Mr Burton decided to trust them, picked up an asparagus spear and used it to emphasise his points.

'Old Mr Carter started the show, late in the nineteenth century. He came from over Ballarat way, or perhaps it was Bendigo. Someone told me his father had been a gold-miner.

He had a tent show, with boxers, you know, and later added a freak show.'

'Mr Burton,' said Jane reprovingly.

'Who is better entitled to talk about freaks?' asked Mr Burton, smiling at Jane. 'It is a glorious title. His freaks included, if my memory serves, a thin man, a Chinese who spoke in tongues (though perhaps he was just speaking in Chinese), a dwarf called General Thomas and a fat lady. Also some of those dried-up remnants of God knows what—Jenny Hanivers. Horrible things. I never look at them. Carter's show moved along the same circuit as all of the travelling shows, crisscrossing or following a circus depending on whom he had quarrelled with lately. He was a bad-tempered, cross-grained old man but basically honest. For a carnie. His son was a miser.'

Temptation overcame Mr Burton and he ate his pointer before the hollandaise dripped onto the tablecloth. Phryne supplied him with another one.

'A miser? How very unpleasant,' said Ruth. She associated misers with the old woman who had almost worked her to death.

'So my father said. He joined the show after General Thomas, his father, left it to retire. Father lasted about two weeks with Carter. He told me that the show was doomed. Only a madman would starve his horses. And his performers. "How can he maintain a fat lady if the poor woman hasn't had a square meal in weeks?" he said. Grandfather had made a tidy sum and told my father to come home to Eltham and work in the orchard for a few months while he looked around for another position. As it happened, Father stayed. He had a natural talent for apple trees and we didn't have another son in the business until I found out that I couldn't prune trees but I could climb them—right up to the top.'

'Then Mr Carter died.'

'Starved himself to death,' said Mr Burton, eating his asparagus with relish. 'Then his wife tried to keep on going but the whole concern was so run-down by then that she sold it all and went into a convent. True,' he assured Ruth, who was staring at him with wide eyes. The convent was a Fate Worse Than Death in her romances. 'The Good Shepherd, in Eltham. She is a poor, thin, devout, trodden down and much tried woman and the nuns are very kind to her. Farrell calls in when we are passing to bring her some Turkey lolly. Only thing she lacks, she says.'

'Very good choice,' said Dot. She could not imagine that poor Mrs Carter would want to try marriage again after Mr Carter. And at least the nuns would feed her regularly. Speaking of which, could Dot manage another bit of lettuce and a slice more of beef? Probably. And some asparagus before Mr Burton ate it all.

Dot had never met a dwarf before. Once one got used to his stature, it was just like talking to a well-spoken, intelligent and courtly man, and Dot was quite comfortable in his company, which was not what she had been expecting at all.

The pace of eating slowed to a stop. People put their elbows on the table and nibbled favourite foods. Mr Butler wheeled in a silver trolley on which reposed dessert. It consisted of a large and complex fruit salad sorbet: lemon ice studded with pineapple, mango, plum, peach, apricot, strawberry and passionfruit. Coffee was already made and the diners tasted tiny, delicious mouthfuls of sorbet and sipped their coffee, and when Mr Burton said, very deliberately, 'You know, I am not sure that I deserve a dinner like that,' there was general agreement.

. . .

67

Phryne led her guests into the parlour, where there were soft chairs for those who wished to repose and more coffee and liqueurs for those who wished to stay awake. Mr Burton listened closely as Phryne explained her Ghost Train discovery and Jane explained the findings of the autopsy.

'But how very curious!' exclaimed the dwarf, looking at their exhibits. 'Yes, that's a Carter's ticket all right. That newspaper does look old enough to be 1857. Attempted expulsion at . . . could be anywhere. That was a rather turbulent year.'

'I know where it was,' said Lin Chung quietly.

'Where?' asked Phryne.

'I told you about it, Phryne. That's close to the date. The twenty-first of July 1857. That's when Constable Thomas Cooke stopped a riot against the Chinese. At Golden Point, near Castlemaine.'

'Yes, you told me. And that's when your gold went missing too. How very odd! But we haven't got the place, Lin dear. It could be a coincidence.'

'Of course it could,' said Lin.

'And can you make anything of this sketch, Eliza?' asked Phryne. Eliza, who had done herself well at the table and was feeling sleepy, roused herself to look.

'It's very vague, Phryne. Can't really see the quarterings. But there aren't many supporters with tails and fins—that definitely looks like a fin. A merman, a mermaid, or maybe a heraldic dolphin. We could look it up.'

'So we could.' Phryne smiled at her sister for the first time since she had seen her get off the boat at Station Pier. Eliza almost returned the smile. Then she got up, murmured that she was very tired and the company should excuse her, and went out.

Phryne swore softly and went back to the puzzle.

'And it would be nice to find the rest of the newspaper,' said Lin. 'At home we have the report on that riot. And if not we can always enquire about the name of the local newspaper.'

'We will do that tomorrow,' said Phryne. 'After we have all been interviewed by the police again.'

'Mr Burton, do your family still grow apples?' asked Dot, deciding that it was time for a change of subject. Mr Burton evidently agreed.

'I am feeling far too complacent to talk about social conditions or about old murders, Phryne. Let's have a little music and some light conversation, eh, to aid digestion?'

Phryne went to the gramophone. She selected 'Danse Macabre'. She felt it was appropriate.

In the thirteenth year of the reign of the glorious Emperor Lord of the Dragon Throne Kwong Sui of the Ching Dynasty in the season of Frosts Descend.

The elder brother Sung Ma sends greetings to the younger sister Sung Mai.

It is a strange place, a ship. After a week it is the most uncomfortable place in the world, so small, like a prison. After that it becomes familiar and comprises the whole world. Every morning we rise and wash and eat, the men play games or gamble or sing, the crew tend the ship, the cooks cook the meals, the doctor—that is me, most unworthy, but I am the only one—looks after the sick and we are all, from Dark Moon hunting rats to the shipmaster directing the course, perfectly fitted into our places. Sometimes we have storms, only small ones, sometimes we go fast or slow, sometimes we see dolphins or other ships, and yesterday we saw a whale. It was a vast mass of flesh, the largest animal I have ever seen. It surfaced and rolled, slapping the sea with a tail as big as the ship, then dived again and we were all afraid it would surface under the ship and sink us. But it did not. The Goddess of the Sea called it away, perhaps, to save our lives. I am going to play chess with the captain. Good night, little sister. I hope all is well with you.

CHAPTER FIVE

The year is drawing to an end
The leaves are turning golden
I want to go home
I want to go home
I have loitered around this mud flat far too long.

Su Tungpo, translated by Lin Yutang

Phryne slept very well, assisted in her slumbers by an absence of Lin Chung, who was too indecently overfed to consider amorous dalliance, and the presence of Ember the black cat. Though a little more portly than the statue of Basht which decorated Phryne's mantelpiece—like his mistress, Ember was devoted to the pleasures of the table—he knew exactly where to sleep to provide himself with the most restful night. Ember's notion of restful did not include being either rolled on or ejected because he was sleeping in the exact centre of the bed, as thoughtless felines did. He occupied a position to the left of Phryne's head, in the hollow between her chin and her shoulder, or, on hotter nights like this night, removed himself a little way to the side where the curve and fall of her hip made a nice dent in the bedclothes and he could catch a refreshing breeze from her open window.

Phryne rose betimes. For Phryne, betimes was between nine and ten o'clock. Ember had risen earlier, exiting through his own door, at the rattle of milk cans which did not even cause his mistress to roll over. Unless Phryne had visitors, she preferred to breakfast in bed. But the morning was so warm and delightful that she descended to the breakfast parlour to partake of café au lait and a croissant from the French bakery in Acland Street. She was feeling rather lazy and French and disinclined to do anything more effortful than a short swim or a stroll. She again blessed the happy chance which had taken her to St Kilda, this slightly tatty city by the bay, where a walk along the plage was only a wish away, rather than a hot, gritty, expensive taxi ride away, arguing with a grumpy driver over centimes. Perhaps she did not feel so French today after all.

It was Monday. Jane and Ruth had gone to school. Dot, whose betimes was much earlier than Phryne's, was sewing something. She came to the table for another cup of tea and Phryne asked her what it was.

'A pillowcase. For my glory box. My last one. I've got all my bed-linen now,' announced Dot proudly.

'Congratulations,' said Phryne. 'Now you can get married.'

A pang struck her that Dot was going to leave.

'No, I can't,' said Dot, 'I have to make ten teacloths, three tablecloths, six damask napkins, twelve cotton napkins and the wedding dress. And the petticoats. And the underthings. And the nightie. And the negligee. Could take years.' She grinned. 'At least I've got the man. Hugh's in no hurry. He has to be promoted to Detective Sergeant before he can support a wife. And I'm in no hurry. I like it here. Miss, is there something wrong with your sister?'

'Yes,' said Phryne, comforted. 'And I'm wondering what on earth it can be. She came here in a fine flaring rage, determined to hate and despise everything, so it doesn't sound like she wanted to leave home. You know, Dot, I believe that Father has adopted the fine old family tradition of getting rid of inconvenient relatives by sending them to Australia. It worked with him.'

'She almost said as much,' agreed Dot.

'But she was always the good girl,' protested Phryne, allowing Mr Butler to pour her another cup of café au lait. 'She always did exactly as she was told. She stayed at school, whereas I ran away to France. She went from boarding school to a finishing school and then she went home like a good girl. She was presented at court, she went to all the dances, she had a season, or a modified post-war season . . .'

'And she didn't catch a husband,' said Dot. 'That's what the season is for, isn't it?'

'Yes. That's why I wouldn't do it. I stayed in France and, until they relented, I never replied to any of the telegrams or letters. Finally they gave up and said I needn't. The season is a stud, a saddling paddock, where all the young gels parade and all the mothers scheme to snare my Lord Brutal, Duke of Huntin' Shootin' and Fishin' or His Dryness the Earl of Tedium. But Beth—Eliza—seemed to like it. She told me all about it whenever I saw her. About her dances and her young men and her masquerades.' Phryne drank some coffee thoughtfully.

'Do you think it's a man? An unsuitable man, I mean?' asked Dot.

'Almost sure to be, wouldn't you say? And it must be serious. The aristocracy never really mind their daughters taking unsuitable casual lovers—I mean, that's what stable boys are for—but mésalliances, non. She must have threatened marriage and she must have stuck to it, otherwise Father would not have rusticated her. I didn't know she was so proof against being shouted at. My father gets his way most of the time because he is convinced that people only do as they are told when you shout at them. I remember him in Paris, the one time he came, shouting at those ignorant Frenchies for refusing to understand English.'

'What if they don't do as they are told?' asked Dot, who was familiar with the method.

'He shouts at them louder and for longer. Until they either run away or crack, generally. It works, for him. But Father is an unmitigated bully. Always has been. Beth used to be putty in his hands. Couldn't stand loud noises.'

'I wonder who he is?' asked Dot.

'Well, the mail is here,' said Phryne. 'Perhaps he's written.'

Mr Butler entered with the letters on a silver tray. He was ambushed at the breakfast parlour door by Eliza, who grabbed the letters, sorted swiftly through them, scattering some on the floor. She grabbed one, pressed it to her breast and ran away, all without a word. Phryne heard her footsteps on the stairs. Mr Butler looked staggered.

'My dear Mr Butler!' said Phryne. 'I do apologise for my mannerless family. Let me just pick up the letters, there, and you can give them to me and then I suggest that you go and have a sit-down and a little pick-me-up. You have had a shock. Well, Dot,' she observed, as Mr Butler tottered off to his pantry for a small glass of port, 'that would seem to be proof.'

'She certainly wanted that letter before you saw it,' agreed Dot.

'But did she really think I was going to forbid her to correspond? I am not the stuff of a Victorian father, Dot dear.'

'Perhaps she isn't thinking too clearly,' soothed Dot.

Phryne sorted through the letters. One pile was business. One pile was trivia—invitations, thank-you letters, cards for gallery viewings and at homes. The smallest pile was always personal letters. Phryne fanned them in one hand.

'One from Father, by the look of it. One from Mother. My, we are attracting attention! And one I do not recognise. Neat handwriting, posted in Melbourne.'

Phryne ran her letter opener under the flap and there was a bright flash. She had dropped the knife and retreated to the other side of the table before the bang; Phryne could move very fast when roused. The letter caught fire and Dot swatted it with a handy plate. Nothing could make Dot burn good linen.

'You all right, Dot?' Phryne stood up.

'Yes, you?' gasped Dot, fanning herself with the plate.

'Yes. That was flash powder. Magicians use it to cover up the substitution of the pretty lady with the donkey. Someone has a quirky sense of humour, Dot dear, and when I catch them I shall insert flash powder into various crevices on their person and light it. Anything written on that enclosure?'

'It's a bit singed,' said Dot. 'I think it says "STAY AWAY FROM THE CORPSE OR BECOME ONE" but the edge has burned off.'

Mr Butler, Mrs Butler, Molly the dog and the butcher's boy all appeared from the kitchen, expostulating.

'Pithy,' said Phryne. 'No, no need to worry, Mr Butler—you are having a morning, aren't you? Someone sent me a joke which backfired rather literally. They will, in due course, be sorry. In future, Mr B, take the mail into the garden, in case we get any more little surprises. That will be all,' said Phryne, and the Butlers went back to their tea. Phryne lit a meditative Sobranie. Dot said nothing, grieved by the black soot on the breakfast cloth.

'Never mind about the cloth,' said Phryne, blowing a smoke ring. 'The Chinese laundry will get it out. Dot, this is a very interesting development.'

'It is?' Dot was cross. 'That could have blown your hand off! Not to mention the damage to the furnishings.'

'No, there wasn't enough powder to do any real harm. It's just a warning. But don't you see, Dot, if someone is trying to stop us, it means that the body in the Ghost Train is relevant to someone alive today. I thought it was just an old mystery.'

'Well, it isn't a new mystery,' objected Dot, still ruffled. Magician's tricks in a lady's parlour! The idea! 'That nice Dr Treasure says the man has been dead since about 1857.'

'Yes, and that long dead, who would care about him? But someone does.'

'Why on earth would they worry about a man who's been dead for seventy years?'

'There is the rub, I agree.' Phryne blew another smoke ring. 'Why indeed?'

When the doorbell rang Dot went herself. The Butlers were upset and if anyone had come to follow their trick with a real threat they would have Dot to deal with.

'Yes?' she said militantly.

'Detective Constable Laurence,' said the mountain of blue serge in front of her eyes. 'To see Miss Fisher.'

'Come in,' said Dot. As he passed her the policeman sniffed. 'Gunpowder?' he asked mildly.

'Flash powder,' replied Phryne from the door. 'Come in, Detective Constable. We have a tale to unfold.'

While Phryne was talking, Dot was examining the policeman. Dot did not like cops per se, although she was engaged to marry one and she really liked Detective Inspector Jack Robinson. This was a large household supply policeman, mild of eye and benign of glance, without the impenetrable stupidity which had been so noticeable in the police constable at Luna Park. He was listening, he was making notes, and he wasn't interrupting Miss Phryne to ask her if she was sure. This was always irritating, because Phryne was always sure.

'Then someone sent me a letter which exploded,' she finished. 'I noticed that it was posted at the GPO, then it went bang. The letter just says "Stay away from the corpse or become one".'

'So someone is still interested in this old murder,' said Laurence. 'This does change things, Miss Fisher. I came here to tell you that as the coroner agrees with the police expert that the body is over fifty years old, that no further action would be taken. But it means more searching. If he was killed in 1857, I don't even know that we'd have records. I know the police force was different then. There was a special unit of goldfields police with their own commander. History is a bit of a hobby of mine,' he confessed quietly, as though admitting to a shameful vice.

'And 1857 is the Gold Rush, and if my friend Lin is right, this man died in Castlemaine or thereabouts, which must have been one frightful mess of men and mud and murder. I shall have to go there and see what I can see.'

'Miss?' asked the policeman and Dot, at exactly the same moment. Dot waved the policeman to go first.

'But, Miss Fisher, if someone is threatening you . . .'

'Pfui,' spat Phryne. 'What would you have me do, my dear police officer? Sit at home all day and take up tatting? That wouldn't stop anyone from killing me if they really wished to do so. And they don't, or they would have. That letter could have borne a fulminate charge strong enough to blow me up— but it didn't. So they don't really want to kill me. They just want to warn me off.'

'Yes,' said Dot. 'And the sensible thing is to be warned off. Who cares about a seventy year old dead body anyway?'

'The very question I was asking of myself, Dot dear. What a clear thinker you are! What importance could he have to anyone alive? Was he someone's grandfather, perhaps? He was a bit young to even be a father, though that is a biological skill which most boys pick up quite young. Mr Burton says that Carter's show was broken down and full of unidentifiable vaguely organic things which he didn't look at, being a man of delicacy. I wonder when they acquired the mummy, and from whom? Well, that takes care of today, Dot dear. We are going to Eltham, to interview Mrs Carter.'

'But she's a nun!' gasped Dot.

'And?'

'You can't just walk up to a convent and demand to see a nun. They're cloistered. You have to write to Reverend Mother and make an appointment.'

'What about emergencies?'

'Miss, the man is dead seventy years, one more day won't matter,' argued Dot, who felt strongly about the sanctity of convents.

'I suppose so. What enquiries will you be making, Detective Constable?'

'Er . . . well, Miss Fisher, we shall have to investigate . . . well, actually, I don't know.'

'Yes, it is difficult, isn't it? No scene of the crime, no suspects, no name. But we do have a clue. The newspaper. You can call the constable in Castlemaine and ask him to search for a local newspaper with the title . . . *Mail*. And then turn to the paper for the period around the 27th of July 1857 and find out the rest of the heading. Attempted expulsion at . . . somewhere. That would be very useful. That would prove the origin of the newspaper. But it isn't significant for our man,' she added. 'He should look for any accounts of a murdered man. You have the description. Someone killed him and someone else must have missed him—because they are still missing him.'

'Yes, Miss Fisher,' said Laurence, scribbling in his notebook.

Lin Chung was sitting in the garden under an arbour of white star jasmine, watching a very old man make tea for an incredibly old man. This took time and the process could not be rushed.

Lin was nervous. Defying—even in a mild and roundabout way—the grandmother whom he had obeyed all his life was less pleasant than he had anticipated. He was very fond of that alarming old lady and did not want to hurt her feelings. But Lin Wan and her children had been welcomed so delightedly by her old mother that he felt justified in solving the feud. Feuds! In the twentieth century! People would think that all Chinese were barbarians, nailed to their past.

Therefore watching the slow movement of old Uncle as he fanned the brazier and dropped the tea leaves into the pot was soothing. Great Great Uncle Lin Gan was sitting at his ease in a padded chair, sucking his teeth. Age had shrivelled him, burning off all fat and muscle and taking his hair with it. He still had a long beard of which he was inordinately proud and was otherwise a light armful of bones and bad temper. He reminded Lin uncomfortably of the mummy from the Ghost Train.

Lin, trained from childhood to be courteous to his elders, usually avoided Lin Gan because his only conversation consisted of (1) The Good Old Days coupled with (2) The Bad New Days when boys were not polite to their elders, food had no taste and the weather was cold enough to freeze his bones.

And now he didn't talk much, but sat in the sun when there was any, by the fire when there wasn't, and gazed into the past, where he had been young and strong and bold.

The tea was poured. Lin Gan tasted, spat, tasted again, and nodded to old Uncle Wang that he could go. When the uncle had gone, Lin produced a flask of Scotch whisky, which he knew the old man loved, and unscrewed the lid. The tortoise head came up and the black eyes bored into Lin's.

'Young men should not drink whisky,' he snapped.

'I know, Great Great Uncle. I brought it for you.'

Great Great Uncle gulped his tea and Lin filled his cup.

'That's good,' said Lin Gan when he could breathe again. 'More.'

'Tell me,' said Lin, tipping a spoonful of spirit into the cup, 'about the goldfields.'

The old man eyed him suspiciously.

'Why? You never wanted to hear those tales when you were a boy. Still are a boy, of course.'

'I wish to profit by your wisdom,' said Lin, withholding the flask. 'With a little age we get a little wisdom,' he added.

'Maybe. I went there when I was six. You never saw such a sight, boy, as those goldfields. As though thousands of moles the size of horses had been digging for their lives. Humps and hummocks and holes everywhere, and mud you could drown in. And they hated us, boy. Don't you mistake that. Even the children used to run alongside us chanting "Ching Chong Chinaman, go home, go home!" and they'd throw stones. That place was a pit of scorpions, a vision of the Nether Hell.'

He held out his cup. Lin added some whisky.

'Most of them wanted to go home,' said Lin Gan. 'Most of them were going home as soon as they could. Most of them wanted to swagger into their own village with a pocketful of nuggets and be a Gold Mountain Uncle with the pick of the girls. They used to sing a song . . . how did it go . . .?'

In a thin trembling voice such as a spider might have had, he began to sing.

'Don't marry your daughter to a baker, he never comes home. Don't marry your daughter to a scholar, she'll sleep each night alone. Marry her to a Gold Mountain Uncle, with sleeves that clink and shine . . . I think that was how it went. We sang a lot of songs while we were working.'

Lin felt that the subject was established and he could attempt to guide the ancient man's recollection.

'Venerable One, do you remember the murdered couriers?'

'The Hu murdered them,' snarled the old man. 'I hear you have settled the feud. And that your grandmother is very angry with you.'

'They didn't do it,' said Lin, suppressing a private wince.

'Eh?' demanded old Lin Gan. 'Didn't do it, you say? Of course they did.'

'It was someone else,' said Lin. 'Mr Hu would not lie about that. Tell me about them. Did you know them? What else could have happened to them?'

'There were four,' said the old man slowly, holding out his cup again. 'I don't remember all their names. Servants, not Lin family. Sung Ma was the leader. I remember that he was sick, someone said he was sick, but he went anyway. They carried the gold in baskets, baked inside loaves of bread. Needs four men to carry that much gold. It's heavy. Your great grandfather, my brother, he was in Melbourne, buying the land for this house. He had started building, I think. We moved up here from where we landed, down in Spencer Street—that was foul land and marshy, and we got sick. This is drier. When the others saw what my brother had done, they came here too, and we are still here. Give me another drink, to take the taste away!'

Lin obliged. The old man smacked his lips.

'The couriers, yes, they jogged off—they laughed at our gait, you know, the yellow-haired ghosts—and then they were gone. I always thought the Hu killed them. We tried to find them. Hu said they had not seen them, the Loong family saw them go past their camp and onto the main road, a woman called Ah said they bought tea from her, after that—nothing. They had vanished completely, baskets, bodies, gold and all. But that goldfield was a very dangerous place. The miners were always brawling. And drinking and brawling some more. Heaven had abandoned that place.

'We searched but we could not find the couriers. If they had gone on the road the Hu must have seen them so we assumed it was them. Then there was the riot and we no longer felt safe, even though the Protector of Chinese came and said it will be all right. Lin Chiang moved the family onto the mullock heaps, land that the miners had abandoned, where no man could complain of us, and then we found that there was good land by the river, already dug by the miners, so we started a garden. Good deep rich soil. We grew greens and onions and potatoes for the miners and we found quite a lot of gold in the tailings, so we stayed.'

'We had a market garden?' Lin had not known this. The old man grinned, showing three remaining teeth.

'It was the only supply of fresh vegetables to the diggings for a long while. Those fools used to dump their horse dung, used it to fill old mine shafts. None of them could farm. We collected night soil and dung—the people paid us to take it away!—and our garden bloomed. We used to go into Castlemaine once it had a market, when it grew to a town. Even then they spat at us, even refused to deal with us. Until they got scurvy,' Lin Gan chuckled. 'Then they bought our cabbages again. Fools.'

'Venerable One, what happened in the riot?'

'We heard the camp roaring,' he said, looking back into the past. 'Always noisy, the goldfields, always a babble of languages, but this was different. It was like a tiger roaring, a roar that says "I am strong". A roar that says "I am hunting and you are my prey". I was scared even before we heard them coming up the hill, hundreds of feet, and that mob noise ahead of them as they came on like wild boar, breaking trees, snapping branches. We wanted to run, but we were against the foot of a rise; behind that was a marsh. There was nowhere to go. I remember cousin Chung saying that when he heard the noise he ran through a whole speech he was intending to deliver to the Black Judge of the Netherworld. I was too scared to do anything. I just stood there and wet my pants.'

His hands were trembling and Lin had to hold the cup to tip the whisky into his mouth. He recovered enough to continue.

'There were hundreds of them, all roaring, led by five men, two lascars as black as demons, three of the straw-headed ones. And then, just as I knew we were all going to die, out stepped Constable Cooke, the one we called 'Gem-eye'. He had bright eyes, like gems. He was a big man and he stood there, not moving, as the mob yelled and poured up the hill, and then they stopped, because he didn't move. And they yelled at him to move and he didn't move, and I don't know what he said because I never learned English, but then he raised his rifle and pointed it at the five leaders, one after another, and then all of a sudden, like a dam breaking, they backed down. I never saw such a thing before. He never moved. They backed away and then they ran and they were all gone and it was quiet again. Then

Gem-eye, he walked over to us and said that we'd be safe that night and he'd call the Protector, and he said that the mob would have to go over him before he'd let them hurt us, and then he sat down under a tree with his rifle in his hands and he stayed there all night.'

'That was a brave man!' exclaimed Lin Chung, who had never heard this account before.

'And not even Chinese,' said Lin Gan, still amazed after seventy years.

'What happened then?'

'He went back to his police station when the Protector came to us. I heard that the mob had broken all of his windows. He was in trouble because of that. Glass was very scarce and expensive. We used to give him vegetables as soon as we had a garden. I heard—yes, I am sure—that he was dismissed from the police force and he went to the quartz mine. We didn't see him again. He was a good man. They don't make men like that these days. I can still see him, standing like a sea-wall, quite still, while the waves broke on him.'

Lin Gan stared back into the past for some minutes. It was not kind to tire the old man. Lin stood up.

'Thank you for your wisdom, Venerable One,' said Lin Chung, handing over the flask. The old man caught his arm.

'Sit a while, Great Great Nephew.'

Lin sat down again.

'You did well to settle the feud,' said the old man. Lin suppressed a stare of astonishment.

'Thank you,' he managed.

'And your grandmother will forgive you her demotion in time,' continued the old man, sipping a little whisky.

'I hope so,' said Lin.

'I like your wife Camellia,' observed Lin Gan. 'She is clever with gardens. I saw her planting, I saw the garden she designed for your concubine and I watched her tie up this very jasmine. She will be a good wife to you.'

'I hope so,' said Lin.

'But you must leave us all for a time,' said Lin Gan, his old eyes as bright as bradawls in his walnut face.

'I must?' asked Lin, overwhelmed by unaccustomed compliments.

'Of course,' said Lin Gan, presenting him with the empty flask. 'You must go to Castlemaine, and find out what happened to our four hundred ounces of gold.'

In the thirteenth year of the reign of the glorious Emperor Lord of the Dragon Throne Kwong Sui of the Ching Dynasty, Sung Ma in what ought to be the Beginning of Winter the ku'li greets his sister Mai.

Soon we are going to land. We have seen new birds—land birds. They are also very strange. One was blown aboard, screeching like a soul in the Ninth Hell. It was as big as a chicken, as white as paper, with a crest like crocus. It snapped with its black beak and screamed for a while and then flew off, making a terrible cry, and after it flew seventeen others. The sailors are still lighting incense. They are sure that they are spirits. I feel that if they are spirits they have come back from the dead in a very odd shape and a very bad temper, so probably they are birds. I burned some incense to Kwan Yin in case they aren't.

The elder brother sends his love to the younger sister.

CHAPTER SIX

*With an elevation of over 900 feet above sea level,
an invigorating climate without extremes, and
generally healthy conditions, Castlemaine is an
attractive place for a holiday.*

Victorian Government
Tourist Bureau guide book

'A fine kettle of fish!' exclaimed Dot. She kicked at an inoffensive passing stone. She was returning from the telegraph
office, having worded a suitable message fit for a Reverend
Mother's eye, which Phryne's might not have been. Just once,
Dot thought, I would like a whole month to go past with
nothing much happening. A few parties, a few dinners, a little
art appreciation, swimming now that the weather was
agreeable, reading and sewing in the evening in that nice garden
which Miss Camellia had so magically made.

The garden comforted Dot. Previously Phryne had had
a yard with dustbins and hens. Now she had a bower with a
bamboo hedge, a fence to hide the chooks and the dustbins
behind, a fernery with white azaleas called 'Phryne' and a
planting of sweet smelling trailers—jasmine and wisteria. Lin

had provided bamboo furniture and it was just the place to sit in on a hot night with a shandy and a mosquito candle on the table. When the plants grew higher it would be entirely private.

And it would be pleasant to go to Eltham in the big car. Dot was almost reconciled to driving, though not driving with Phryne. Phryne drove like a demon.

Perhaps we could take a picnic . . .

Dot woke from her reverie just in time to see a totally unbelievable but definitely real khaki-coloured motorcycle roaring towards her down the footpath. The rider was helmeted and masked in a muffler. The machine was almost on her before she threw herself over a low fence and into someone's privet hedge. And when she struggled out of the hedge, it was just a drone on the horizon.

'Bloody disgraceful! Are you bloody all right, love? Someone bloody call a bloody copper!' bellowed a woman in a baby's bottom pink art silk dress so short it showed her garters. Dot, very shaken, leaned a little into the strong arm, imprinting her cheek with fifteen jingly gold bracelets. A reek of patchouli washed over Dot. Her rescuer was clearly one of St Kilda's working girls. Which didn't mean that it wasn't a timely rescue or that Dot wasn't grateful. Wasn't her own sister employed to teach deportment to Tilly Devine's girls in Sydney? Dot took a deep breath and stood up, leaning on the whore's arm.

'He just come out of bloody nowhere,' exclaimed the woman. 'Down the bloody pavement and bloody almost hit you!'

'Thank you,' murmured Dot. 'Can you see my handbag?'

'Here you are, now sit down here until you get your bloody breath. I never bloody saw such a thing! Bloody gutter crawlers are bad enough . . .'

Dot sat down on the fence and considered herself. A little

scratched, a little shocked, nothing worse. One stocking ruined, as always. Adventure and stockings did not go together. Someone else approached.

'Here you bloody are!' exclaimed the woman. 'Never a bloody copper around when you bloody need one! You want to bloody do something about this! Some fucking bastard just ran this lady down.'

'Name?' asked an official voice.

'Dot Williams,' said Dot. Her vision was blurry. All she could see was blue serge and buttons. The space above the buttons gave a gasp.

'Miss Williams? You're Hugh Collins' intended, aren't you? There's going to be hell to pay over this. Mabel, did you see it?'

'I bloody did,' declared Mabel. 'He come off the road there, just at the corner, and came bloody roaring down here as though there was no next bloody Wednesday. And I'll tell you another thing for free. He was bloody aiming at her.'

'You sure?' The policeman sounded sceptical. The arm around Dot stiffened.

'Of course I'm bloody sure. I got his number, if that helps the constabulary in their bloody enquiries.'

'You got his number, Mabel? Good girl. What was it?'

'MW 471. Saw it clear as bloody day. Now if you're quite bloody finished, I gotta get this lady home before she bloody expires on the pavement. If you don't bloody mind.'

'Can you walk, Miss Williams?' Dot could see the policeman now. He was a young man with a concerned, grave face. 'I can call for a car but it'll take a while.'

'I'm nearly home,' said Dot. 'If Miss Mabel would come with me, I can walk that far.'

'I can bloody do that,' said Mabel. 'Come on, love. One foot in front of the other.'

Mr Butler received his third shock of the day when Dot limped up to the front door, leaning on the arm of a lady of the night and accompanied by a policeman. Phryne and Eliza jumped up when they came in. Dot was as white as her dowry bed-linen and Phryne was horrified.

'Sit down, Dot dear, ask for anything you want. Tea for Dot, Mr Butler, and stiff drinks all round. Do sit down, Constable. Hello, I'm Phryne Fisher, nice to meet you.'

Mabel, already uneasy in this elegant parlour, took Phryne's hand gingerly.

'Well, I'll be off, love,' she said to Dot.

'No, do stay. Have a drink and tell us what happened. What's your fancy?' asked Phryne. She grinned at Mabel and Mabel suddenly felt better.

'Gin and orange, dear, if you're having one. Well, it was bloody awful,' began Mabel. 'I come from the Town Hall where Carmel the Comm, I mean, Miss Shute, gimme a lecture on how the workers' revolution would triumph, two bob and a food voucher. Then . . .'

Phryne listened carefully. The constable made notes. By the time she had absorbed two stiff gins, Mabel had lost her fear. While Phryne turned her attention to Dot, Mabel found herself talking about her life to Eliza, the other lady, who seemed sympathetic and was so good a listener that Mabel forgot she was in a lady's parlour and talked as she would to her girlfriends.

Phryne gave Dot a swift physical once-over, took off her stocking and bathed her skinned knee and sat down beside her.

'Try to drink all that tea, Dot dear, you've had a shock,' she urged.

'I can see it when I close my eyes,' said Dot, proud that

her voice did not tremble. 'The bike getting closer and closer, the wind of it as it passed.'

'Yes, the thing to do is let it run, like a ciné film. After a while it will slow down and then it will stop and go away forever. But if you resist and order your mind to forget it, the sight will lodge in the back of your head and give you nightmares. Believe me, I know what I'm talking about. Now drink up,' urged Phryne.

'There's brandy in this tea,' protested Dot.

'There certainly is, and as soon as you finish it you are going to bathe and lie down until you feel better. And when I lay hands on the bastard who did this, I am going to make him really wish that he hadn't.'

Dot drank the tea. The immediate effect of brandy in the middle of the day was to make her sleepy. The motorcycle came and went in front of her eyes. Phryne escorted her upstairs, inserted her into a soothing bath into which she poured a large handful of Egyptian Asses Milk Bath As Used By Cleopatra and left her to soak while she found a long, silky, autumn leaf patterned gown which Lin Chung had given Dot for her birthday. Phryne was seething with cold fury. It was one thing to threaten Phryne herself. But to attempt murder on Dot was another. When she found that motorcyclist she would chain him to the back of his own bike and take him for a nice long drag.

Dried and dressed, Dot wanted to come downstairs again. To lie in her bed and watch that motorbike approach would be too uncomfortable. Phryne installed her in the garden under the bamboo bower with a glass of sherry cobbler, the newspaper—someone was still seeking Amelia Gascoigne's relatives—and her sewing and rejoined the group in the parlour.

To her amazement, Mabel and Eliza were getting along swimmingly. This was clearly not the first time that Eliza had spoken to a whore. The obscenities with which Mabel punctuated her speech did not faze Eliza at all. Clearly Eliza had spent a fair amount of time with Lady Alice What'shername in the East End. Phryne stuffed a banknote into Mabel's hand as she was leaving.

'I don't bloody need this for just doing what I bloody did,' she protested, shaking her bottle blonde head.

'Take it because it would make me feel better,' said Phryne. The shrewd eyes surveyed Miss Fisher appraisingly.

'Your sister says you're a detective. You gonna find that bloody bastard?'

'Yes,' said Phryne gently.

'You gonna nail his balls to a tree?'

'Both of them,' said Phryne. 'With two separate nails.'

Mabel grinned. 'Should happen to more of 'em,' she declared. 'Ta-ra, then!' and she went down the steps.

The constable was taking his leave. 'I'll let Hugh Collins know,' he said. 'He'll likely be around as soon as he hears. This is an attempted murder, Miss Fisher. I'll report to Detective Inspector Robinson.'

'How reliable is Mabel?' asked Phryne. The grave policeman considered the question. He seemed too young to know as much as he evidently knew about the street trades of St Kilda. His eyes were grey and weary and his voice low.

'Drinks a bit—they all do. Doesn't drug, though. Been around for years, Mabel has. I reckon if she says that's how it happened, then that's how it happened. I'll let the beat officers know she's helping us and they can give her a bit of leeway. That'll keep her sweet. Been on the game for more than ten years, poor old girl. Well, I'll be off. Got to trace that number.'

Mr Butler showed the constable out. Then he returned to Phryne.

'Miss Fisher, I really . . .'

'I know, I know,' said Phryne. 'This is quite above and beyond the call of duty. But think about it, Mr Butler, and please don't give your notice. I can't go through all that again.'

'I was about to say, Miss Fisher,' said the butler, drawing himself up to his full height, 'that if Mrs Butler and I can be of any assistance in apprehending the villain who attacked Miss Williams, you have only to ask.'

'Thank you, Mr Butler, that is very kind of you,' replied Phryne. 'If the occasion arises I shall let you know. I've left Dot in the bower, perhaps Mrs B wouldn't mind keeping an eye on her through the kitchen window? Dot hates being fussed over. And another drink for my sister and me. What's your pleasure, Eliza?'

'Just tea,' said Eliza. 'Isn't this interesting! Mabel tells me that one does not starve in Australia.'

'No,' said Phryne, accepting a gin and tonic. 'Not starve to death, not usually. Provided you're first at the pig bin you can get the best vegetables and there's usually a bit of work to be picked up here and there, but times are hard and getting harder. Food's not as dear as in England and the climate is kinder. You don't freeze to death here if you have only one blanket. You got on well with Mabel, Eliza. I was most impressed.'

Eliza blushed and ruffled her hair, a gesture Phryne remembered from childhood.

'Oh, well, it's the same as the East End but not so dirt poor. It's all people.'

'Eliza, why did you get sent to Australia? I've got letters from both Father and Mother today but I haven't read them yet, and I won't if you don't want me to, but can't you tell me what is going on?'

'I'd like to, Phryne, but I can't. I really can't.' Eliza's voice was strained, near to breaking point.

'Why can't you?'

'I just can't. Read the letters. Perhaps Father has told you.'

'I won't if you don't want me to,' Phryne said again.

'No,' said Eliza, and burst into tears. 'No, please don't.'

'All right,' said Phryne. 'And when you trust me again, as you used to, you shall tell me yourself. But tell me this—is it a medical problem? Would you like to see a very discreet lady doctor who is a close friend of mine?'

'No!' exclaimed Eliza. Muffling her face in her handkerchief, she upset her tea cup as she sprang to her feet and rushed out of the room.

'Sisters,' said Phryne to Mr Butler when she went into the kitchen for a dishcloth.

'I have had the same problem myself, Miss Fisher. Do allow me,' said Mr Butler as he preceded Miss Fisher to the parlour. 'In my sister's case it was religion. One of those ranting ones. Most unpleasant while it lasted.'

'What cured her?' asked Phryne, watching him remove tea from the small table with precise, economical movements, never spilling a drop on the carpet.

'She fell in love, Miss Fisher. With a most eligible young man in the ship's chandler's line.'

'We can hope, then,' said Phryne.

'We can always hope, Miss Fisher,' Mr Butler told her as the doorbell rang.

It was Hugh Collins in a fine state of disarray. Phryne grabbed his arm.

'Dot's all right,' she said sharply. 'But if you rush in looking like that you'll startle her and she's had enough shocks for one day. Straighten your collar, comb your hair, take a deep breath. Dot values her self control. You don't want to puncture it.'

Obedient to the voice of female authority, Hugh Collins did as he was bid. When he was the picture of a tidy young gentleman again, Mr Butler took him out to the garden and Phryne sagged back in her chair.

Mysteries all around, and now an attempted murder. Who cared that much about a man seventy years dead?

Later in the day Phryne answered the door to reveal a huge bouquet of white peonies and Lin Chung.

'Camellia sent these,' he said, handing them over. 'And I have news to relate.'

'That is very kind of Camellia. They're beautiful. I trust she is well?'

Phryne accepted the blooms and gave them to Mr Butler to arrange. She approved of Lin Chung's new wife, a Chinese widow with green fingers and perfect English. Before she married Camellia had agreed to Phryne's concubinage, and they had become friends.

'I have news to relate too,' she said. 'Sit down and let's swap.'

The conversation lasted through three cups of Chinese tea (Phryne) and a glass of lemon squash (Lin).

'How curious! You see what this attack on Miss Williams means, Phryne,' said Lin, putting a hand on Phryne's knee. She covered it with her own.

'I see that a nasty and possibly final revenge is about to be wreaked on the motorcyclist as soon as I lay hands on him,' said Phryne. 'What are you trying to say?'

'Someone must have seen us find that body. How else would they have known that Miss Williams was part of it?

Someone at Luna Park saw us talking to that stupid policeman.'

'Y-e-s,' drawled Phryne. 'It would not have been hard to find out who I was. That bone-headed cop might have told anyone who asked. And I left my card with Messrs Bennet and Dalby. What do you suggest? An employee? A visitor?'

'The only people I am sure weren't in it were the nuns and the orphans,' replied Lin, 'and that's only because they were roped together.'

'That might explain the strange messages from the mermaid. They were all in the "beware" category, as far as memory serves. I'll ask the girls when they get home . . . Lord, what about the girls? Are they in danger?'

'They will be, if Miss Williams is in danger,' said Lin.

Phryne corrected him sharply. 'Will you stop calling her "Miss Williams"? You usually call her Dot.'

'Sorry, I've spent the afternoon being excessively polite to my oldest ancestor. My great great grandfather's brother, Lin Gan. It's odd, Phryne, but I always ran away from him when I was a child because he was so censorious. Now he seems almost heroic, though all he did in the riot was to stand and stare.'

'You're not a child any more,' said Phryne. 'And perhaps he approves of you, just a little.'

'Yes,' said Lin, 'he does. Which is why I have to go to Castlemaine.'

'When?'

'Wednesday, I expect. First I must speak to the old Hu lady, then I will take the car. That will get me out of Grandmother's way, at least.'

'And out of the firing line, with any luck,' said Phryne.

'If that is the case, then I shall not go,' said Lin. 'I can at least be as brave as my ancestor.'

'Lin, dear,' said Phryne.

She leaned forward, soliciting a kiss, and his smooth lips had just touched hers when Phryne heard a shocked gasp and opened her eyes.

Eliza was standing in the doorway. She said, 'Oh, sorry!' and fled. Phryne leaned forward more emphatically and kissed Lin Chung hard. His inner lip was like silk; he tasted of lemon squash. Heat bloomed in Phryne's spine, grounding with a thud at the base. If the delicious Lin was going to Castlemaine, Phryne thought, it might be an idea if she followed him.

'But I have a suggestion,' he said, once he had freed his mouth and got his breath back.

'And that is?' asked Phryne.

'I will leave my own bodyguard with you. You like Li Pen. Your household knows him. No one gets past a Shaolin monk.'

'He is supposed to be looking after you, beautiful man,' Phryne pointed out.

'Yes, but this is my decision. You and I, Silver Lady, we take our own risks. But I cannot undertake any journey which might leave your family in danger. My own family is well guarded. Anyone getting into the Lin compound will have only a few moments for prayer before the dogs eat him. But until Molly gets a little bigger or we train Ember to claw on command, this household needs a guard.'

'And Ember has always been of the view that training is something which happens to inferior animals, haven't you, my precious?'

Ember paused in his saunter through the parlour to blink, twice, and move on.

'Well? Shall I send Li Pen?'

'Yes,' said Phryne. 'I agree with you. And I may be joining you. Where will you stay?'

'Apparently we still have a market garden at Golden Point,' said Lin. 'I haven't been instructed in all the ramifications of the Lin family business. I was trained as a silk buyer. I don't know much about the rest of it, though I now must learn. There are still Chinese people in Castlemaine. The person I am looking for is a lady called Mrs Ah, who saw the couriers last.'

'She must be pretty antique by now,' commented Phryne.

'I am an expert on antiques,' said Lin. 'If you come to Castlemaine, where shall I find you?'

'Let's look at the book.' Phryne rose and extracted a touring guide from the small walnut bookshelf. She flipped through the pages. 'Ah, yes. The Cumberland looks like the best hotel. Thirty-nine rooms. Nothing with a private bath, though. Oh well. One must suffer for one's revenge. My wharfie friend Bert told me that the secret of successful travelling is never to stay at a hotel called Railway or Commercial. There's the Imperial as well—I shall have to see when I get there. Now kiss me again before the girls get home and think of the pleasures of a good, large, impersonal hotel. I'm beginning to feel a touch constrained in my present home.'

Lin obliged enthusiastically. Just in time to hear another shocked gasp from Eliza, who had come back again, and who fled again in the same way.

Phryne pushed Lin away and sat up.

'A nice, big, uncaring, uninteresting hotel,' she told Lin. 'I look forward to it. How am I to find you in Castlemaine, then?'

'I shall telegraph,' said Lin. 'And now I must take my leave. I will send Li Pen soon.'

'I shall lay in a store of Vegemite,' said Phryne. Li Pen was one of the few Shaolin monks to admit to a taste for bread and Vegemite. 'And get Mrs Butler on to vegetarian cooking. I'm sure that Mrs Beeton has a chapter on it.'

'He would be just as happy with rice and steamed greens,' said Lin.

'But Mrs Butler wouldn't be,' said Phryne. 'She likes a challenge.'

Lin smiled, kissed Phryne's hand, and departed, leaving her restless. She wished for a moment that she had never acquired all these followers and family and could just ravish her beautiful lover on the floor of the parlour. But living in the world meant living with people and it was time to get up, see how Dot was, greet the returning daughters and perhaps—for the day seemed to be getting warmer—go for a swim.

No. Until Li Pen arrived they were rather confined to the house, which made Camellia's garden more attractive than ever. At least it was outside. And if anyone came over the wall, Phryne could belt him with a rake. This made her feel slightly cheered as she walked through the house.

Mr Butler joined her after a few minutes with the afternoon post. He looked a little apprehensive. Dot took her sewing away to a safe distance.

'Put it down here, Mr B, and we shall sort,' said Phryne bracingly, suiting the action to the word. 'Bills, bills, a postcard, a letter from Peter, a card for Lady Mary's At Home, nothing explosive. You may come back, Dot dear. I'm thinking of a little trip.'

'A trip, Miss Phryne?'

'Yes, just to Castlemaine. I feel that the solution to our mystery lies there, or somewhere near. Someone had Castlemaine newspapers to hand when they needed to stuff a mummy, and I feel that makes him local. First, of course, we must talk to Reverend Mother about Mrs Carter, and then we must make sure that you are all safe. So Lin has lent me Li Pen.'

'Oh,' Dot was a little cast down. 'So we aren't coming with you.'

'No,' said Phryne as gently as she could. 'It also means that I am leaving you with Eliza, which is a filthy rotten trick. I apologise for that, Dot dear. But she seems to have mostly lost her anger, so she might be easier to live with now. If you can find out what on earth is the matter with her, Dot, it would be a mercy. But I am not going to read my letters from my parents until she says I can, and that leaves me a bit gravelled for lack of matter. Try to find out who the man is, there's a dear. She indignantly refused a delicate hint that she might like to see Doctor MacMillan, so events haven't proceeded too far. And if she should confide in you, Dot, do try and convey to her that I do not in the least mind if she marries a Welsh coalminer, even if he sings, or a wharfie with a three day beard. I will cover up for her and I will keep Father away. I just want her to trust me. I just want my little sister back, Dot.'

Dot drew a thread through her drawn thread work and said, 'I understand,' very solemnly. 'And it will be nice to have that Mr Li here while you are away,' she added.

'Yes, Li Pen is an asset,' agreed Phryne.

They sat for almost an hour in the shade of the bamboo house. Phryne listened to the hens clucking behind the screen. It was very quiet. The tall bamboo fence which Camellia had ordered cut out a lot of traffic noise. There didn't seem to be anything you couldn't do with bamboo.

She must have said this out loud because someone answered quietly, 'You can make scaffolding out of it. You can cook rice in it. You can build houses from it. Beaten flat, you can make a cape of it that will keep out the rain. And it makes a fine, unbreakable weapon.'

'Hello, Li Pen,' said Phryne. 'You move like a shadow.'

'My master sent me to guard your household,' he said reasonably. 'One cannot do that by stumping up and down like an elephant.'

'True. What do you mean, bamboo makes a weapon? It's only wood.'

'I will show you,' said Li Pen. He walked along the bamboo screen, selected and removed one piece, and danced with it. It was the only word to describe it. In the centre of the spinning, whirling staff, there was Li Pen, easy, relaxed, and any attacker would have been whipped and stabbed and tripped and flattened and utterly at his mercy in around five seconds. In the middle of the whirlwind of deadly blows and kicks he danced, his face quite calm, and Phryne was suddenly much more comfortable about leaving her family. Li Pen was quite possibly the best defence anyone could have, not excepting a Hotchkiss gun.

In the thirteenth year of the reign of the glorious Emperor Lord of the Dragon Throne Kwong Sui of the Ching Dynasty, Sung Ma the elder brother greets Sung Mai the younger sister.

We have landed at Melbourne. The solar calendar month is April and the year is 1855. The city is a poor, bare, busy place with few mountains and only one river, which is brown. I bade farewell to Dark Moon and the shipmaster and went with the Lin family to their compound in the city. There we were fed and rested the night. I had the honour of an introduction to Lin Hua, the head of the clan. He stays in the city and engages in trade. His brother Lin Chiang is on the goldfields. We will begin to walk there tomorrow. Mr Lin was kind enough to replenish my medicine box and lend me a copy of a novel, Gold Plum Vase, *to beguile my leisure. I am* not sure that I shall have any but it was kind of him. I left my copy of Su Tungpo's poems with him for safekeeping. I can recite all the poems in it and Mr Lin was very pleased to see it. His family have been in this city for several years and they mean to stay. His great house is already being built. It is very beautiful but will be surrounded by a great wall, like a castle.

Barbarian people hiss at us in the street. They don't want us here. Just let me get some gold, and I will gratify their wish and leave immediately.

I will send this letter back with the ship. May the goddess have you in her hands, little sister, and your mother and sister. Ask Uncle if you are in any difficulty.

CHAPTER SEVEN

Every woman knows that the most strongminded
woman in a house can set up a domestic tyranny
which is sometimes a reign of terror.

George Bernard Shaw
An Intelligent Woman's Guide
to Socialism and Capitalism

Tuesday began badly. Phryne heard the phone ring, leapt out of bed, and stepped full on Ember's tail. He yowled with pain, gave her a disgusted look, and stalked out of the room, forcing Phryne to chase him to apologise. That meant the sacrifice of her breakfast bacon to soothe Ember's hurt feelings. The girls had been reproachful when Phryne told them that they had to stay in the house unless they took Li Pen as an escort, so they had declined to go swimming and were playing a noisy and irritating game of snakes and ladders in the parlour. Dot was still pale and experiencing motorcycle films before her eyes. Mr and Mrs Butler were trying to be staunch and this was always trying. And Eliza had retired to her bed and refused to get up, saying that she had a migraine and adamantly refusing the services of a doctor.

Phryne dressed suitably, dealt with all the immediate problems, and was about to order Dot back to bed also when a telegram arrived from Reverend Mother Immaculata of the Good Shepherd informing her that Mrs Carter, now Sister Elizabeth, was coming into Melbourne to be seen by a specialist and might be properly interviewed at the Motherhouse of the Convent in Victoria Street, Fitzroy. Phryne made her dispositions instantly.

'Good. Dot, go back to bed and allow yourself to be looked after. Mrs Butler, look after Dot. If my sister asks for a doctor, call Doctor MacMillan. Mr Butler, I leave my house in your hands. No one is to leave the house without Li Pen. Molly, be good. You may go and lick Dot better if you wish. Now, I'm off,' she declared, and went out to the Hispano-Suiza. The inmates of the house heard a roar and the car was gone.

'Well, I might be better for a bit of a rest,' confessed Dot. She allowed herself to be helped up the stairs by Mrs Butler, followed by Mr Butler bearing a refreshing orange crush and two aspirins. They were followed by Molly, with Li Pen bringing up the rear.

When Dot had been clad in her nightdress and tucked into her bed with a couple of aspirins and a glass of orange crush inside her, an interesting new detective story to hand and an affectionate black dog lying at her feet, she sighed with relief. She really was that tired. And Molly was a nice dog.

Mr and Mrs Butler descended the stairs and listened at Miss Eliza's second-floor door. They heard some sad little noises which might have been sobbing. On enquiry through the door, Miss Eliza said that she wanted quiet and told them to go away.

There seemed nothing left to do but to descend further to the kitchen, where Li Pen shelled peas, Mrs Butler cut up a chicken carcass for a nice stock to make chicken soup for Dot, and Mr Butler read them snippets from the paper. In the parlour, the snakes and ladders noise had died down now that Phryne was not there to be impressed by the magnitude of their disappointment. The house settled into peace. Molly fell asleep. After a chapter of her new Agatha Christie, the book slid quietly to the floor and Dot dozed off, the motorcycle, with decreasing frequency, buzzing through her dreams.

The really noticeable thing about convents, thought Phryne as she drove the car into the convent's stable yard, the thing which you could not miss about convents, was the wall. Make it high, the religious had ordered, make it thick, top it with broken glass, make it absolutely plain to any passer-by that this is a wall meant to keep all oversexed youth, maniacs and heretics out and all devout women in. This was an unusually solid wall, even for a convent, and it was matched by the sort of door which was usually known, in Gothic fiction, as a dread portal. It was four inches thick, had iron hinges and was studded with square head nails, in case the said attackers actually got over the said wall. They would have been foiled by this door even if they had brought their very own battering ram.

Phryne got out of the car and climbed the steps. She pulled a bell which rang somewhere deep and echoing inside. A little hatch opened in the middle of the door.

'I'm Phryne Fisher,' she said to the square inch of face she could see. 'Here to see Sister Elizabeth.'

'Reverend Mother telephoned,' said the Portress, who sounded very young. 'Come in, Miss Fisher, if I can only get this darned door open.' There was a sound of crunching and scraping. 'There we are.'

Phryne entered into the wash of scent which always accompanied all-female establishments of a virtuous kind: yellow soap, furniture polish, candlewax, incense and roses. There was a faint under-scent which Phryne recognised as femaleness; musk, perhaps, and blood.

Sister Portress, who appeared to be about sixteen from her fresh complexion, bustled Phryne along a corridor shining with cleanliness, skidding a little on the freshly waxed floor. She showed Phryne into a parlour remarkable for its lack of comfort, which had to be deliberate. A horsehair sofa of uncompromising firmness sat next to two straight-backed, hard-seated chairs. A table bore a devotional work of paralysing dullness and the whitewashed walls bore a Sacred Heart. This image always made the more-or-less Protestant Phryne uneasy; it seemed primitive, even cruel, the visible heart wrapped around with its thorny crown. The blond Christ appeared unaffected by it, Phryne noticed. He was smiling.

Phryne smiled back.

Two nuns entered. One was old and comfortable, and had brought her knitting. The other was a thin woman, heavily lined, with eyes so tired of the world that Phryne regretted her own irruption into this peaceful place.

'I am Sister Mary Magdalen,' said the older nun, sitting down and angling her needles. She had an Irish accent. 'You may stay ten minutes. You may not touch Sister Elizabeth. At any time she can decide to end the interview and then you must go.'

'Can I shake hands?' asked Phryne.

The nun shook her head. 'Not unless you're a relative.'

Phryne ordered her questions so as not to waste time.

'Very well, then, hello, Sister Elizabeth, my name is Phryne Fisher and I've got involved in a very odd mystery to which I think you may be the key. Mr Burton suggested I talk to you. He sends you his best regards.'

'Then I'll talk to you,' said Sister Elizabeth. 'Mr Burton was very good to me when . . . when my husband was alive.' Her voice creaked, as though it was not often used.

'You were Mrs Carter, were you not, of Carter's Travelling Miracles and Marvels Show?'

'Yes,' said Sister Elizabeth faintly.

'The show had several dummies which you sold to Luna Park,' said Phryne. 'Can you remember them?'

'Yes,' said Sister Elizabeth. 'A vampire, they were just coming into fashion with Varney the Vampire and Count Dracula, you know, and a werewolf, and . . . a couple of others.'

'One was a cowboy,' said Phryne, watching all she could see of Sister Elizabeth very carefully. The white wimple outlined her face in a starched frame. The faded blue eyes blinked once or twice and then she shook her head with a whisper of veil.

'No, no cowboy. There was the Wild Colonial Boy, of course.'

'The Wild Colonial Boy? Tell me about him,' urged Phryne. Mrs Carter took up her rosary and the beads ran through fingers which trembled.

'Hold up, Sister,' said Sister Mary Magdalen bracingly. 'Take a sniff of the salts, now.' She gave Phryne a hard stare. 'She doesn't like to talk about her former life,' she told Phryne. 'It upsets her.'

'I'm not surprised,' said Phryne. 'And I wouldn't have bothered her but I need to know about the Wild Colonial Boy. I really need to know,' she emphasised. 'It's me or the cops,' she whispered.

Sister Mary Magdalen responded, 'We can't be having with that, at all. Have another sniff, Sister.'

Sister Elizabeth sniffed and gasped.

The older nun gave her a brisk pat. 'There you are, Sister,

now let's get this over with and you can go back to the garden.'

'You work in the garden?'

'Finest roses in the whole convent,' boasted Sister Mary Magdalen. 'That's why she took the name Elizabeth, after Saint Elizabeth of Hungary.'

'The miracle of the roses,' said Phryne. Dot had told her that roses were the only scent allowed in convents in honour of this saint, who had lied to her husband with divine permission and reward. Phryne was wearing Floris Tea Rose for that reason.

'I always wanted a garden but we never stopped travelling,' said Sister Elizabeth, a little recovered. 'You wanted to know about the Wild Colonial Boy. My husband's father bought him somewhere; on the Bendigo road, I think. From a man. A deceased estate, I think. But the Wild Colonial Boy wasn't a dummy. He was a real man, God rest his soul in Heaven.'

'Amen,' said Sister Mary Magdalen and Phryne in chorus.

'I told my husband it was indecent,' protested the nun. 'I said it would be only proper to give him a Christian burial. But Joe wouldn't listen. People did come to see him,' she added. 'He was a bushranger. Someone had embalmed him. A doctor or someone. Then they sold the body to old Mr Carter. There was . . .' Her brow wrinkled under the wimple. 'No, I can't recall. Something funny about the sale. They told us to keep him hidden and not to show him in . . . some place. I don't remember . . .'

'No matter. Thank you very much, Sister Elizabeth.' Phryne was very tempted to prompt and didn't. Sister Elizabeth was probably very suggestible and she did not want to contaminate her testimony, should it be needed.

'Wait,' said Sister Elizabeth. 'I've been here three years now and I was going to ask Reverend Mother to throw away the worldly things I brought with me into the convent. But there's something there which might help you. If you can wait, Sister Portress will bring it to you. Tell Mr Burton hello from me.'

'Farrell's will be back in December,' said Phryne. 'They'll call when they are in town.'

'Yes,' said Sister Elizabeth. She stood, smoothed down her habit, and went out. Sister Mary Magdalen rose also.

Just at the door, Sister Elizabeth turned back. Her face was anguished.

'You'll bury him?' she asked. 'A proper burial, in sacred ground?'

'Yes,' said Phryne. 'I promise.'

Sister Elizabeth burst into tears and went out. Sister Mary Magdalen gathered up her knitting and gave Phryne an approving nod. 'That will do her the world of good,' she said. 'That dead man's been on her conscience a good while, I'd guess. You stay here and I'll send Sister Portress with the things. God bless you,' she said briskly, and followed Sister Elizabeth.

Phryne read the devotional work, 'An Admonishment to Young Women', for ten minutes. Sister Portress rescued her before she committed the sin of throwing the book at the wall, shoved a cloth bag into her hands, and hurried her out, as though the worldliness of this scented, terribly fashionable lady might be contagious.

Outside, Phryne got into her car as the dread portal slammed behind her. She examined the bag. It was a grubby cash bag, probably postal in origin, with 'pennies' stencilled on the front. Inside were a variety of objects. Red tickets, identical to the one found in the mummy's shoe. A roll of flyers for Carter's Travelling Miracles and Marvels Show. A description of the exhibits, which included the 'Wild Colonial Boy, Last of the Bushrangers, preserved by a secret art'. Under the rest, a postcard.

There he lay, the spit and image of the mummy as cleaned by Dr Treasure. He was dressed in better clothes but the boots looked the same with their kangaroo hide laces. And that was the face. She stared at it for a while, wondering how she was going to be able to give him a Christian burial as she had promised. Who knew if he had been a Christian? But at last she knew where he had come from.

As she cranked and started the Hispano-Suiza and drove off down Brunswick Street, waving at outraged traffic cops, she was singing it.

'There was a Wild Colonial Boy, Jack Doolan was his name . . .'

Lin Chung was escorted into a small hot parlour where two old ladies were seated, one either side of a small, bright fire. He began to sweat instantly. It must have been a hundred degrees inside. The scent of sandalwood incense was almost a stench. Old Lady Hu was evidently a Buddhist. A gemstone statue of Kwan Yin stood on the mantelpiece. An ancient piece and probably beyond price.

'Let the young man sit down,' said a very old lady. 'Bring tea,' she ordered.

The attentive Hu maid vanished so fast there was a sort of 'flick' as she went.

'Close the door, there is a draught. A draught at our age can be fatal. I am Hu Ta. Well, you are the young man of the Lin family, who have at last admitted that we did not steal their gold, is that correct?'

'It is correct,' said Lin. 'We were misinformed.'

'By the Hakka, the tartar barbarians. Can't even speak a decent language. Or possibly by the Sam Yap. We are Sze Yap, of course, as are the Lin family, I believe. Those Hakka degenerates,' said the old lady. 'They always hated us. I have always thought that they stole the gold themselves. And now over seventy years later you are going to find it? A noble quest,' she said caustically. 'Not one which will be attended by any success, of course.'

'Probably not,' sighed Lin. 'But I must try, Venerable Lady.'

'Hmm. What do you wish to know?'

'Do you know anything about the fate of the couriers, Lady Hu?'

The title pleased the old woman. She had less beard and more hair than Great Great Uncle Lin Gan, but not a lot more of anything else. Her tiny bound feet in minute red slippers were resting on a footstool. Lily feet. How did it feel, Lin wondered, to have your insteps broken in order to please some man? A childhood of torture did not seem to have broken her spirit, however. Her eyes were as bright as new pins and she had clearly not overlooked anything in her whole life. She decided to talk to him.

'You have to understand about those goldfields. They were like—like a vision of eternal damnation. There were few women on the fields. I and my sister—she is dead now, poor thing—were born there. My father, Ah Sen, did not expose us or punish our mother for our birth, because with so few Chinese girls in Australia he had hopes of a great marriage for us. There were four of us. I am the only one with the lotus feet. Two were married to Australian Chinese and they did not need us to decorate a boudoir. They needed us to work and walk and bear sons. One of us, my sister Ky, married an Irish ghost, Liely. But he was a good ghost. He had a farm where he bred horses and his household was all Chinese—the cook, the gardeners. When he asked my father for my sister when she grew up, Father was pleased. Provided she was to be lady of the

110

house, not a concubine. They do not understand concubinage here and treat the women badly, as though they were whores. Hu women have never been whores. Except for Hu Lah, and that was different,' she said defiantly.

Lin sat in a trance of heat, feeling his life force drain away. He was not going to be able to ask questions. It was unthinkable to interrupt an elder and she would dismiss him instantly from her presence if he did. He just had to try not to melt and wait to see if she directed her discourse towards something he needed to know. He felt convinced that she knew this and was playing with him as a cat plays with something inoffensive and squeaky before it eats it.

'My other two sisters went to ordinary Chinese but I was destined for Mr Hu, a rich man, so they prepared my feet and me to be a rich man's wife. I left my sisters behind and went into the Hu household, a very well run household. I had no mother-in-law to torment me! My husband came out here alone and it was only later that he sent for his old mother, and she was very old by then.' A malicious gleam in the old eyes told Lin that the old mother hadn't been given any scope to torment young, confident Hu Ta. It had probably, he thought, been the other way round. And what she had done to her daughters-in-law didn't bear thinking about. 'We left the goldfields with an adequate fortune and my husband built a house in Caulfield, a western house, unlike some who cling to Chinese ways,' she said, a stab at the Lin family's very Chinese architecture. 'Unlike, as it might be, the Lin family, who stayed on and became peasant farmers, which was, of course, their heritage,' she added, making her opinion patent.

'I was very busy, ordering my household. I have five sons,' she said proudly, 'eleven grandsons, fifteen great grandsons.'

'You are to be congratulated,' said Lin conventionally.

Insults to his family passed him by. She was trying to bait him, but instead he was feeling sorry for her, a fact which he knew would colour his dialogue and annoy Old Lady Hu Ta very much. Such a small thin woman, to bear so many children! And she hadn't even mentioned daughters, which was to be expected. There must have been daughters. But she had paused to be praised and he inserted a thin conversational wedge.

'Your honoured father, Lady Hu, what was his honourable profession?'

'He was a miner,' she said. 'They all were.'

'A Gold Mountain uncle,' said Lin, and sang a particle of Great Great Uncle Lin Gan's song. 'Don't marry your daughter to a scholar, she'll sleep all night alone . . .'

The old lady chuckled and chanted the rest of the couplet.

'"Marry her to a Gold Mountain uncle, with sleeves of golden shine, don't marry him to your daughter, marry him to mine!" I remember them singing that. The songs used to change every week but that one stuck. Who sang you that song, young man?'

'My Great Great Uncle Lin Gan,' said Lin Chung, expecting scorn.

'Is he still living?' asked Lady Hu. 'He was a handsome man! My sister was in love with him. It was not possible to keep us in proper seclusion on the goldfields. We were supposed to stay in the house but we had to do all the work—to fetch water, to tend animals—so sometimes we had to go outside and there we would see young men because the goldfields were full of young men. Then we would run inside, of course, a modest woman should not be seen. My sister saw Lin Gan and cried over him, because she could not have him even if he asked for her, because we were at feud with the Lins. Such a pity. Still, probably for the best. She would not have been happy in a family that could believe that we would steal from them,' concluded Old Lady Hu Ta.

Lin said nothing in reply. There was a pause.

'But I am pleased that this misunderstanding has been cleared up,' said Old Lady Hu, softening her manner a little, in the same way a cat sedulously avoids alarming its mouse too much until its tail is clear of the hole. 'I am glad that Hu Wan could go back and see her aged mother. Age is to be served, young Mr Lin.'

'Indeed,' murmured Lin, almost slain by heat.

There was no fun left in him any more. Old Lady Hu allowed the reappearing maid to serve him tea then let him take the requisite three sips dictated by courtesy before she said abruptly, 'I am tired. Go away. Look for the couriers somewhere near the third blazed tree on the Moonlight road. That is where we saw them last,' and she waved a hand and Lin Chung escaped.

He leaned for a moment on the wall outside the oven-hot room. Mr Hu joined him.

'I did warn you,' said Mr Hu sympathetically. 'I hope your information was worth an hour in one of the hotter hells. If you will come this way, honoured and exhausted guest, I will provide you with some cold if inferior beer. You did well,' said Mr Hu suavely as he led the way into a small garden. The air blew coolly over Lin's hot face. He mopped his brow with a silk handkerchief.

The gravel was raked into patterns. An interesting boulder allowed water to trickle over its face down into a pond containing goldfish. So much for not clinging to Chinese ways. If there was a garden more Chinese than this, Lin had never seen it. He sagged down onto a rustic seat.

A maid brought a large jug of beer and two glasses and

stood by, hands folded over her tray. Lin drained the glass, refilled it, drained it again and the maid went back to the kitchen for another jug. This was obviously a ritual with persons who had been interviewed by Great Great Grandmother Hu Ta.

'I only just survived, Mr Hu,' he answered.

'With that old dragon lady, surviving is as much as any man can boast,' said Mr Hu, taking a sip of his beer. 'She has, all by herself, terrified three generations of the Hu family. We used to have to dose my mother with laudanum as soon as she was sent for, and all by herself and without a weapon Hu Ta is definitely responsible for three heart attacks, a sudden fit of insanity and a miscarriage. She was sorry about the miscarriage, I admit. But she excused it by saying that so weak a pregnancy must have been a girl. No one has ever made her change her mind and in accepting your offer to settle the feud I acted without her instructions.'

'You're a brave man, Mr Hu.'

'You too, Mr Lin.'

They toasted each other in beer. Lin was beginning to feel that he might not burst into spontaneous flame after all.

'She said she was pleased that the feud was settled,' he said. Mr Hu gave a deep sigh of relief.

'She really said that?'

'Yes,' said Lin. 'Before telling me that my family were peasant farmers.'

'So was her father,' said Mr Hu, mopping his brow in turn. 'Her father worked at a farm as a gardener. He never was anything else but a gardener. You have done me a great service, Mr Lin! I would never have dared to ask her what she thought of the settlement. Tell me, is that one of your trade silk handkerchiefs?'

Lin handed it over.

'We can't get silk like this,' said Mr Hu regretfully. 'So fine, such a good colour.'

'You can if you buy it from me,' replied Lin. 'But going to get it nearly cost me my life. I won't be sending anyone to replenish our stock, so now is the time to buy. Not a lot of silk is going to come out of China for the next few years. All the news we have heard is bad.'

'Yes,' said Mr Hu. He seemed to have gained weight. His smooth face was smoother and lines had ironed out around his eyes. Great Great Grandmother must be a severe responsibility, Lin thought. 'Hu lands have been stolen by warlords, Hu women ravished, Hu houses burned by bandits. Better to be here. They may not like us,' said Mr Hu, 'but they aren't actively trying to kill us.'

'Indeed,' said Lin, and drank more beer. 'I have an idea,' he said, after another chill mouthful.

'What is the honourable idea of my honourable guest?' asked Mr Hu, deliberately overstressing the courtesy. It was his third glass of beer.

'Let's bring Great Great Uncle Lin Gan to visit Great Great Grandmother Hu Ta,' said Lin. 'Her sister fancied him in the past. She might marry again and you can get her off your hands.'

Mr Hu stared at him and burst out laughing.

'You are a very, very bold man,' he chuckled, 'for wanting to bring Old Lady Hu into the same house as Old Lady Lin.'

Both men looked solemnly into their beer glasses. That was, indeed, a sobering thought.

In the thirteenth year of the reign of the glorious Emperor Lord of the Dragon Throne Kwong Sui of the Ching Dynasty, the elder

brother Sung Ma greets his younger sister Sung Mai. 21st March 1855 in the solar calendar, probably the season of Grain in Ear.

Today we started walking. Although I have stout sandals and nothing to carry I am finding this difficult. The others trot along, ta'am over shoulder or across the neck, carrying 100 catties— almost one hundred and thirty pounds in western measures—and only stop for tea and even then they do not seem tired. After a morning's walking I am exhausted. Mr Lin sent me to ride in the cart. He said it was because he wants me to learn English so as to interpret for him, but really he is being kind to my blisters. I am studying my text and writing this as we bounce along and behind I can see a long tail of blue coats, black trousers and straw hats. Three hundred Chinese going to the goldfields. May the gods be kind to us!

CHAPTER EIGHT

I see the traveller's unwaking sorrow
The vagabond spring's come in a clatter.
Too profusely rich are the flowers,
Too garrulous the parrot's chatter.

Tu Fu, translated by Lin Yutang

'Of poor but honest parents he was born in Castlemaine . . .' sang Phryne on her way home. All places were tending to Castlemaine—what did she know about Castlemaine? Until recently, home of the Castlemaine XXXX beer, which both Bert and Cec, her wharfie friends, liked. Home of the toothsome Castlemaine rock, a carefully made sweet of which Ruth was very fond. Somehow connected with a big wheel, which was probably not the one engineers sang of, and a woollen mill, something to do with ham and bacon; all this and only some seventy-five miles by road and seventy-eight by rail from Melbourne. The guidebooks said that there were several excellent hotels. Phryne was looking for one in which she could entertain a Chinese lover without comment, which ruled out the Midland (a coffee palace, anyway—Phryne did not approve of the temperance movement) and the Cumberland (arguably too big and too public). That seemed to leave a Railway, a Commercial, and the Imperial Hotel, opposite the Town Hall— not too many rooms and probably, if Phryne knew hotels, a reasonable scatter of backstairs. It lodged visiting politicians, she was told, and that argued that the management had a relaxed view of what Dot would call 'goings-on'. Otherwise it would not lodge politicians. More than once, anyway.

The Imperial might, she thought, be just the ticket. She had a feeling that openly accommodating a Chinese would cause the sort of scandal that even wealth and connections and rank might not be able to ride out . . . And Phryne was determined to get Lin Chung to herself for a while. Her intentions were purely carnal, and it had been far too long since they had been properly indulged.

Now to see what had happened at her own house while she had been away interviewing nuns and making rash promises.

The house was blessedly tranquil. Mr Butler met Phryne at the door with an 'all quiet' report.

'Miss Dot is lying down, the young ladies are at school, Miss Eliza is still in her room and perhaps, Miss Fisher, you might care to enquire as to her health? Mrs Butler felt sure that she heard her crying.'

'I'll do that,' said Phryne. 'Can you obtain the number of the Imperial Hotel in Castlemaine? I want a private room, with bath if possible, and as far away from the street as they can manage. If they're full, get me a room at the Cumberland. For tomorrow night and possibly longer. The game, Mr Butler, is afoot.'

'Yes, Miss Fisher,' said Mr Butler. 'Lunch is at one, Miss Fisher.'

Phryne climbed the stairs. It was time that she had a talk with Eliza. She would be no use to the household in an emergency if she was still having the vapours. What dreadful choice had she made that Father should send her all the way to Australia to forget? Eliza had never shown any interest in fortune hunters. Or rather, they had shown no interest in her. Of course, she had no money of her own, but when she turned twenty-five she would have a respectable settlement from Grandmother's trust, not to mention a fair whack when Father finally failed to bully Death into waiting on the stairs for one more moment.

Phryne tapped. No answer. She tapped again. A bleary voice half screamed, 'Go away!'

Phryne retreated to gather some supplies. When she returned, she was carrying a key, a flask of cognac and two glasses, a bucket of water, a bottle of Dr Proud's Anti Hysteria Nervine (containing rare Indian herbs, and which Mrs Butler kept to hand for moments when souffles fell flat), a novel, an ashtray and a chair. She put her bucket and tray on the floor, sat down on the chair, and said to the door, 'I'm going to sit here, Beth, until you let me in. Sooner or later you are going to come out, and then I am going to come in. No hurry, I've got all day.'

She poured herself a drink, opened the novel, lit a cigarette and began to read.

An hour passed. Phryne had heard the footsteps approach and knew herself perused through the keyhole. She read on. This Dorothy Sayers was a superb writer. To dare to have a detective who had come back from the Great War shell-shocked, a frail, breakable human being instead of the usual Sexton Blake superman—wonderful. She was rereading *Who's Body?* and was just getting to the most audacious Lord Peter's song about insisting on a body in the bath when the door creaked open and a defeated voice confessed, 'I have to go to the lavatory.'

'Off you go,' said Phryne, shifting her chair a little to one side and rising. 'But I'm coming with you.'

She escorted Eliza to the guests' lavatory, waited for a decent interval and escorted her back to her room, where she displaced all her impedimenta into the room.

'The cognac and the Nervine are for you. The bucket is also for you if you decide to have hysterics,' she informed her sister. 'Though I hope you won't because Mr Butler will give me hell about water on his polished floor.'

Eliza sat down on her bed and began to weep.

Phryne picked up the bottle and flask, poured her a slug of Dr Proud's concoction and then a slug of cognac to take away the taste of valerian and mistletoe, and said, 'Come along, old thing, you can tell me. You'll be making yourself ill if you keep this up. Really, my dear, it cannot be that bad, whatever you've done. What is it? Stable boys? Horses? A scandal about racing drivers? Did you get exasperated with a lover and plug him with a .45? Duelling? Drug addiction? Necrophilia? Methodism? I've really heard it all, what with one thing and another. Cough it up,' she advised, inelegantly.

'I'm a socialist!' blurted Eliza through her clenched hands.

'Yes,' prompted Phryne. That appeared to be it. There was a silence. Eliza peeped out between her spread fingers.

'I said, I'm a Fabian socialist,' she restated. Phryne utterly failed to reel in horror.

'That's nice,' she said.

'I believe in the greatest good for the greatest number! I'm against inherited wealth! I believe that all means of production should be in the hands of the workers!' Eliza's voice was gaining strength, either from the Nervine, the cognac or the lack of reaction from her sister.

'Good,' said Phryne. 'Now, what is worrying you?'

'Father said I was a traitor to my class!' Eliza began to sob again. 'He dragged me out of the waltz at the Hunt Ball and denounced me to the county! He said I was no daughter of his and told me it was all Mother's fault! He forbade me his house! He threw me out! He told me to go and live in London with Alice and never darken his door again!'

'He always was a fool,' said Phryne. 'Never mind, Eliza. Do you want to darken his door—why darken, anyway? I'm sure I never darkened a door. Not just by standing there. Dry your eyes,' she suggested. 'So you're a Fabian. How interesting. I thought you might have been, you know. Getting on so well with Mabel, not the first lady of the night that you've met, I'll wager. Instinctively almost telling me that my dinner could feed a hundred paupers. Quoting Beatrice and Sydney Webb. And reading *The Intelligent Woman's Guide to Socialism and Capitalism*. My copy just came out from England. Shaw has such a clear way of putting things, hasn't he? It was the first time I felt I understood how capitalism worked.'

'But, Phryne,' Eliza began, anxious to make sure that her sister knew the worst. 'You don't understand. We have rejected revolutionary Marxism. We stand for evolutionary socialism, for gradualism. And in the meanwhile, I want to work with Alice and live in the East End and help the poor until they can find justice. Until the system evolves to support them.'

'I know a couple of wharfies who'll love to meet you,' said Phryne.

'You don't mind?' Eliza whispered. Phryne patted her shoulder.

'Of course I don't mind. Just don't try to redistribute my capital.'

'It's all right for you,' muttered Eliza. 'You've got your settlement from Granny and your French pension and all that money from all those pictures you bought in Paris. I've got a year to go before I'm twenty-five and Father won't give me a penny. He sprang for the trip to Australia provided I didn't come back until I "got over these preposterous notions" and was ready to marry the nice man he's picked out for me.'

'Oh? And which nice man did Father find for you? Leaving aside my serious doubts as to Father's taste in men, the last time I looked the English aristocracy was entirely composed of married men, those unlikely to marry at all, the effete and the brutes—not a wide choice. All the good ones were snaffled early and the remains—well. They are remains. Or possibly dregs is a more exact description.'

'Oh, Phryne, it's terrible,' Eliza wept afresh. 'I only got two offers in my second season, which Father said was the last, he wasn't going to pay for another. There was Roderick Cholmondeley, the sole heir of the Duke of Dunstable, a mere boy—he's eighteen, younger than me. And he's only interested in football. Or cricket. Or hunting, or polo, or hockey or fishing. And he's stupid. They couldn't get him into university, even though he was a good chance for a Blue in about three sports. He can hardly read and write.'

'So, one is an oaf,' said Phryne. 'And the other?'

'He's elderly,' wailed Eliza.

'But an old friend of Father's?' hazarded Phryne. She could see how this was going. Disappointed in his eldest daughter, who had turned out to be Phryne and could not be married off, even under chloroform, Milord had decided that the much more pliable Eliza could be sold to the highest bidder. And the highest bidder had been . . .?

'Oh, Phryne, he's awful. It's the Marquess of Shropshire.'

'Ugh,' said Phryne. She remembered Theodoric, Marquess of Shropshire, which otherwise was a rather nice county and deserved better. A thin, acidulous widower (twice) with pinpoint pupils and a sidelong approach which had always reminded Phryne of a spider. He did not drink or smoke and his sole amusement appeared to be making money and outliving his wives. The young Phryne had instinctively recoiled from him when she was fourteen. The twenty-eight year old Phryne was fairly sure that his other recreations involved opium smoking and probably the sacrifice of young virgins to Mammon in some underground temple lined with banknotes. Wasn't there some scandal about a parlour maid? And another about vast war supplies fraud? Was it not, in fact, the Marquess of Shropshire who had supplied to the War Office, at huge expense, rainproof coats which proved to be as absorbent as tissue paper? The Blotting Paper Marquess, the semi-frozen soldiery had called him (amongst other things). That was the man. And there was some Australian connection, was there not, some ancestor who had come back with a fortune? Or was that someone else? Eliza would know, and she appeared to be talking to Phryne again. And, come to think of it, waiting for a response.

'Outrageous,' said Phryne. 'You shall not marry him, or the oaf, or anyone else, if you don't want to. Father must have taken leave of his senses, not that he ever had many. Is he still getting through a bottle of port a day?'

'More, sometimes,' said Eliza. 'Just before I left he had a bottle of claret and a bottle of port at lunch, double that at dinner. Mother was worried, but . . .'

'Mother always is,' concluded Phryne.

'And it never makes the faintest difference,' agreed Eliza.

She was sitting up, mopping her face, ordering her curls. Apart from the scoured complexion of the fair, who look like skinned rabbits if they are so unwise as to cry, she was looking better. Her voice, too, was firmer.

'So apart from being an exile and a class traitor, is there anything else you would like to tell me?' asked Phryne. This got a watery smile.

'Oh, yes,' said Eliza. 'But I can't tell you that, yet.'

'All right, you can keep your other secrets for now, you socialist you,' said Phryne. 'And what gave you such a shock at Luna Park?'

'Why, I saw two people that I knew. It's always a surprise, seeing people in another place when you expect them to be home in England.'

'Who did you see?'

'About the first one I'm probably wrong, but I thought I saw Alice, in a flowered hat, but when I looked again she was gone. She would come and see me if she was in Australia, don't you think? We parted in friendship. It's probably because I so want to see her. You do that sometimes, eh, Phryne, mistake a stranger for someone you miss?'

'Certainly,' agreed Phryne.

'But the other I am sure about. It was that halfwit Roderick. His father must have sent him out here to try and make me change my mind. And Father probably encouraged it. He likes him—what did you call him?—the oaf.'

'Like calls to like,' said Phryne.

'But, Phryne, it's serious,' urged Eliza, grabbing Phryne's cognac hand and almost spilling her drink. 'Before Father sent me away Roderick was threatening all sorts of things—to kidnap me, to make me stay with him, to . . .'

'Rape you?' prompted her sister.

Eliza blushed purple and nodded.

'Have no fear,' said Phryne. 'Come downstairs and I will introduce you to Li Pen. He is Chinese, you must make up your mind to that. But if he is told to guard your body, nothing short of an army will get to you and I would put good money on Li Pen against even a biggish army. He's a Shaolin monk, devoted to chastity, vegetarianism and martial arts. And, incidentally, Vegemite. He's staying here with you and the household while I go to Castlemaine and get to the bottom of this business about the mummy. And Lin Chung needs to find four hundred ounces of gold which went missing on that goldfield in 1857, so I shall probably meet him there.'

Eliza had formed an opinion on Lin Chung, who had always been very polite to her. For one trained on Madame Lin, Eliza was a mere passing annoyance.

'He's very nice, isn't he? So elegant. Like a big cat—a panther, say. And his clothes are divine.'

'Come along,' said Phryne, making a note to ask Ruth to share her romantic novels with Eliza, who clearly had similar tastes. 'You need to meet Li Pen and then you will feel a lot more secure. If Roddy gets past Li Pen I shall personally join a monastery, and think of the shock for the poor monks.'

'Father is quite wrong about you,' said Eliza as they descended the stairs.

'Why, what does the old buffalo say?'

'He says you don't care,' said Eliza. 'But you do, or you wouldn't have been so patient with me.'

'Shh,' said Phryne. 'Don't tell anyone, or I shall lose my air of fashionable languor. Li Pen? This is my sister Eliza.'

Li Pen got to his feet from his sitting position without moving through any intervening space, a trick which never failed to enchant Phryne. He bowed politely to Eliza, who took in his shaved head, his neat blue garments and his beautiful, remarkably bright eyes. She smiled tentatively. Li Pen looked very, very foreign, like an extra from a Sax Rohmer novel.

'She is being pursued by an unwanted suitor who has

threatened assault, kidnapping and worse,' Phryne went on while Eliza blushed again. 'If you see him, twist his head off.'

'As the Silver Lady says,' responded Li Pen. 'The lady her sister need have no fear.'

'But Roddy's awfully strong,' protested Eliza, surveying the light, lithe monk.

'Shall I have to do penance for boasting?' asked Li Pen of Phryne.

'No, this is a demonstration for the purpose of making Eliza feel safe. Go ahead. And make it impressive.'

Li Pen took the poker from the fire irons and stroked it between his hands, which suddenly made a complicated motion. He held the poker out, knotted in a decorative bow.

Eliza hefted the artifact. The poker was made of good solid iron and she had only seen a little flurry of movement, not the heave-ho of a fairground strongman. She stared.

Li Pen took the poker back, twisted it the opposite way, and straightened it out again.

'I'm convinced,' said Eliza. 'Thank you for looking after me, Mr Pen.'

'Mr Li,' corrected Phryne. 'Now, come for a walk along the seashore and let us talk of many things, including whose coats of arms have mermen as supporters and why that detestable young man is in Australia.'

'And other things,' agreed Eliza.

There was still a shadow over her, Phryne thought; we aren't through this by a long chalk, but a beginning has been made. A Fabian socialist in the family, she added to herself. Father must have had whole litters of kittens. How I wish I'd seen it. She chuckled quietly, collected her hat, Li Pen and Eliza, and went out for a walk by the sea.

. . .

The Lin family holdings were much greater and more diverse than Lin had ever imagined. On the reluctant instructions of his grandmother, Lin was being conducted through the business by his eldest uncle, who had survived the reign of Grandmama by being jovial and cheerful, enjoying his wife, playing with his children, relishing his excellent dinners and consuming his many cups of wine, and never taking any criticism personally. It was well known that Uncle had the hide of a hippopotamus, but he was a jolly chap and it was a pleasure to be instructed by him.

'Your grandfather was anxious to diversify,' he told Lin. 'Pass me another cup of wine, will you, nephew? He foresaw that trade with China might be interrupted and he wanted to make sure that we had a good stake in this country. After all, we are staying. We are Australians now. That's why he bought the paper-making business here, and the vineyard in South Australia. He thought that it would be unwise to sell only luxuries, so we still have market gardens and a pig farm, not to mention the restaurants. Cousin Lin Po is running a poultry farm to supply them and we also get delicacies and flowers from Lin Tao in Castlemaine, only two hours by train. We use most of our own produce in the restaurants, which means that not only are we better, we are also cheaper, and we can grow our own sort of vegetables, straw mushrooms and Chinese greens, water chestnuts and marrows. Lin Tao has high hopes of lychees soon. We also sell lotus flowers to the flower market. They grow on the fish ponds. Which we also sell. Trout, as it happens, and fancy goldfish. If the fancy goldfish don't sell we let them grow into carp and eat them.'

'What about a drought?' asked Lin Chung, fascinated. 'That would wipe out the crops. What do we sell then?'

'Unlikely,' said Uncle Lin. 'All of our gardens are on large rivers. If the Maribyrnong dries up our trouble will be as nothing to the trouble of the rest of Melbourne. The pigs and the poultry are all close to the market gardens—'

'For the manure,' said Lin, who was getting the idea.

'And to share transport to market. If we lose our agricultural production through some disaster—it would have to be the State deciding to take them away, something major like that—we still have wine and paper, we still have silk, we still have restaurants and we still have fan-tan and the lottery.'

'Which are illegal,' said Lin, to get a rise out of Uncle.

'Not at present.'

'Only because there are no Chinese policemen.'

'And may the Gracious Lady Kwan Yin protect us from there ever being any. While the games are played with beans and only cashed later, no one can prove that fan-tan is an illegal gambling game. And we get ten per cent. The more terrible the times, the more people gamble. Gambling gives them hope.'

'Even so . . .' Lin did not know how he felt about being a gambler. His uncle laughed and poured another cup of wine for both of them.

'You like this? South Australian and in a few years it will be almost drinkable. Look at it this way, scrupulous one. Men will gamble. We do not cheat them. If they win they can collect their winnings and there will not be a couple of people outside to relieve them of their so-heavy wallets and beat them to a pulp if they protest. We run an honest game. If we are not there—if young Lin Chung decides he is too moral to be concerned in such trade—then who will run it? Criminals,' said Uncle, banging down the empty cup. 'There are no people with one long fingernail and strange tattoos concerned in gambling in our establishments. But if the space is empty, it will be filled. Heaven does not allow empty spaces.'

'Very well, Uncle,' said Lin. 'I bow to your wisdom.'

'Good thing too. What is the use of wisdom if it is not bowed to?' Lin Chung filled the cup again. He wondered why Uncle did not just get a large glass, or a pint pot.

'So, from the beginning, our wise ancestors decided that we should do many different things. We have to avoid being noticed: it is not good to dominate any market, or there will be envy. Heaven also does not look favourably on any man growing too great. You will be expected to advise of new opportunities and other markets which your inherited business sense will undoubtedly lead you towards.'

'I have always thought that there is a lot to be done in the making of garments,' said Lin Chung. 'It is always better to have a dress that one could sell at fifty guineas rather than a length of silk to be bought for ten.'

'Very risky, women's clothes.'

'I was thinking of undergarments,' said Lin reminiscently. 'Chemises, knickers. Pyjamas. They are not very susceptible to fashionable changes.'

'Ah,' sighed Uncle, clearly thinking of the same thing. He shook himself. 'Yes, possibly, but they would have to be at the very top end of the price range to be worth making, and those women prefer to have their clothes made by hand and to measure.'

'So they do,' agreed Lin, recalling how stockings rolled down Phryne's admirable legs, to be followed by a slither of knickers, and underneath . . .

Uncle rapped him smartly over the knuckles with an empty wine cup.

'Pay attention, nephew. To continue. There are no great holdings in shares in other companies. Most of our capital is in business or in land. We own several office buildings in the city, which are leased through an agent. The holdings are all here and you may take away the list and study it. Have some more wine. You are going to Castlemaine?'

'Yes, tomorrow.'

'Have a care. You can forget, in the city, especially in Little Bourke Street, how few Chinese there are in the outer world. There are very few in Castlemaine, though once there were thousands of us. You will be a curiosity in the town unless you have a suitable disguise.'

'A disguise, Uncle?' Lin Chung was taken aback.

'You want to make enquiries, you want to ask questions of people who believe that touching a Chinaman will give them jaundice,' said Uncle Lin placidly. 'There is only one proper disguise which will make you acceptable. I have arranged for it to be found—once I wore it myself—and here is our cousin with the garments. They are badly made but we have time to tailor them properly.'

Lin was worried. His uncle was not smiling.

'Do I really need a disguise, Uncle? You are not joking?'

'I never joke. And when I do, you will know, because you will laugh,' said Uncle Lin. 'Here you are. Try it on. Good. Your cousin will make the alterations. In that garment they will not like you, but they will not harm you and they might even talk to you. Are you taking your Shaolin with you?'

'No, he is keeping Miss Fisher's house safe. Something very odd is happening there.'

'If it happens when Li Pen is on watch it will be sorry,' chuckled Uncle. 'Probably better. He would certainly object to accompanying you, dressed like that.'

Li Pen turned in front of the mirror as his cousin applied pins. The collar was tight and uncomfortable and he wasn't at all sure that he could carry this off. What, after all, did Lin Chung know about being an Anglican clergyman?

He drank another cup of wine to take the taste out of his mouth and tried to remember where he had left his school copy of *Hymns Ancient and Modern*.

In the thirteenth year of the reign of the glorious Emperor Lord of the Dragon Throne Kwong Sui of the Ching Dynasty, 20th of April in the solar year 1855.

The elder brother Sung Ma sends greetings to his little sister Sung Mai. In this strange place the seasons are upside down. When I left home it was nearly spring, here it is nearly autumn to judge by the way the poplar trees are shedding their leaves. I must assume that this season is Stopping of Heat. We reached the goldfields after four days. The landscape has been ruined by all the holes dug by miners and the water and fire lines are completely disturbed. No wonder the place feels so disharmonious. The earth dragons must be very angry. The weather begins to be cold but the air tastes crisp, like a bite of Hami watermelon. Here with this letter I send my first gold to be given to you, little Mai, and your sister Lan, as a dowry. You must keep it safe. Tell Uncle that his unworthy nephew has provided it for you both and that he should find you good husbands. I am sending it by a trustworthy man, Chang Li, who lives near us and whom I have known since we were children. He has made his fortune and is going home. May I soon do likewise!

It is twenty ounces of alluvial gold and I dug it up while I was clearing a place for my tent. Mr Lin allowed me to keep it when I told him that it was your dowry. I have been caring for those who have developed water-on-the-chest, which I believe is caused by lack of fresh fruit or greens in the diet. I have prescribed us all as much fruit as we can buy in Bendigo and Mr Lin has sent the cart.

This is a rich place but there is much misery and filth and when the cold comes it will be worse. But soon we will be gone, I hope, if the fates are merciful to us.

The loving elder brother bids his little sister farewell and good fortune.

CHAPTER NINE

Late at twilight I passed the verdant hills
And the mountain moon followed me home.

Li Po, translated by Lin Yutang

It was morning. Breakfasted, Phryne was packing. In actual
fact, she had thrown a load of clothes onto her bed and was
considering what she might need when Dot came in, wearing
a beige dress patterned with terracotta nasturtiums, and a
worried expression.

'Miss? Let me do that. How long are you going to be away?'

'I don't know. Say a week.' Phryne sighed with relief and
sat down to watch Dot sort, fold and pack the clothes. Anything Phryne folded instantly developed extra creases. Anything
Dot touched flung itself into a perfect package and threw itself
into the suitcase. 'Not the good underwear, it may have to be
washed locally and local laundries are hell on silk. Two light
suits, I think, and one evening dress, cocktail length. The
Mayor may invite me to dinner. Or not, of course, but it is a

good idea to be prepared. Paste or theatrical jewellery, I do not want to worry about it. Plus the male disguise and some cosmetics. And my gun. They play a little rough in the country, Dot, all those big strong men with shotguns and rustic ideas of humour. I don't know what this may entail.'

'I wish you were taking me! Or at least Mr Bert and Mr Cec, or Li Pen!' wailed Dot. She didn't like guns. Phryne's neat little pearl-handled Beretta was both strangely fascinating and horribly repulsive, like a gaily patterned coral snake.

'Bert and Cec are busy with their taxi, and in any case they seem very urban. Though I might be doing them a disservice. I will consult them, Dot, if you like. It never hurts to have a reserve, as the Duke of Wellington would say. And Li Pen is here to protect you and the girls and the Butlers and Eliza. If anyone tries anything with Li Pen around they will be puréed faster than you can say knife, otherwise I would not be leaving you. I don't want any more incidents and Mr Butler is to open all mail in the garden, is that clear? And don't tell anyone where I have gone.'

'Of course not, Miss Phryne,' said Dot, shocked.

'Miss Eliza may be better company than we thought, Dot dear. She has told me one of her dreadful secrets. She is a Fabian socialist.'

'Ah?' asked Dot, sorting stockings. 'Like Mr Bert and Mr Cec?'

'Precisely my response. My father seems to have split a gusset and flung her from the house, pausing only to watch her bounce and stating that until she recovered her senses and came back willing to marry either a brute of a boy or a very nasty old man, she was no longer his daughter.'

'It sounds like the plot of one of Miss Ruth's romances,' observed Dot, flicking a nightdress and dropping it back into perfect folds. She laid a sheet of newspaper over it which bore a plea for the relatives of Amelia Gascoigne to contact the paper, where they would learn something to their advantage. It seemed to be everywhere, thought Dot.

'I know. Father has always been the complete Victorian Paterfamilias and now he has the scope to conduct the whole blood-tub melodrama. Why do you think I moved to Australia? As far as one can get in the civilised world from Berkeley Square, W1 where the old grump resides when in London. And I was tossing up about a move to Easter Island.'

'You wouldn't have liked it there,' said Dot placidly.

'I know. But it does have a lot of granite heads and I was thinking of dropping one on Father. The brute of a man, he's had poor Beth cowed since she was a child, and he must have got such a shock when she wouldn't agree to marry either of his chosen ones. Which brings me to the point of all this gossip. Roderick, only heir to the Duke of Dunstable, is here. Eliza saw him at Luna Park and got the shock of her life. He's been threatening abduction and rape and she's frightened of him.'

'He being the brute of a boy?' asked Dot.

'Illiterate but nonetheless nasty,' agreed Phryne.

'He'll be sorry if he tries conclusions with Mr Li,' said Dot.

'Exactly my view. But just in case, I thought I'd warn you. Eliza can tell you what the little bounder looks like. Bash him with a skillet if he causes any trouble and bury the body under the hydrangeas.'

'We haven't got any hydrangeas,' objected Dot.

'Ask Camellia for some. I'm going to ring Bert. Back soon,' said Phryne, and breezed off. She looked in again. 'Put in a hundred cigs and fill my flask with the Armagnac, will you?' she added.

Dot kept folding. Just a little peace and quiet, she thought, and with Mr Li to stand guard and no Phryne, Dot might just get on with her trousseau nightdress.

Having contacted Bert, found out that he and Cec had been shearers in their time and arranged for a reserve in case of emergencies, Phryne decided not to annoy Dot while she was packing and to sit quietly in the garden with Li Pen and discuss philosophy. The Shaolin proved amenable.

'The Chinese have a different relationship with their gods than any of the one-god religions,' he remarked. 'Chinese gods do not require adoration. They would not know what to do with it. They do not forgive sins.'

'Then what are they for?' asked Phryne, lighting a cigarette.

'They take care of the things which they are required to take care of,' he replied. 'For instance, the goddess Nu Kua is responsible for walls. She rebuilt the walls of heaven once when there was a spill from the Great River of Stars. You may ask for her attention in any matter involving walls. But not anything else. Walls are her . . . her . . .'

'Speciality?' suggested Phryne.

'Area of responsibility,' said Li Pen. 'An especially brave soldier, like Ch'uan Chung-li, might find himself turned into a god and then his care is soldiers. But there is also a god for soldiers, Kwan Gong. The goddess Songshi Niang Niang looks after childbirth and it is only childbirth that she is allowed to care about.'

'I see,' said Phryne. 'A feudal heaven to match a feudal earth.'

Li Pen bowed his shaven head.

'The Silver Lady is very acute. Some gods are common to all who have not been enlightened by the Divine One. The

Emperor of Heaven is always the August Personage of Jade. Tou Mou is always the Mother of Stars. Wen Chang cares for scholars. But there are local gods as well.'

'Lares et penates,' said Phryne. 'Spirits of springs and woods.'

'Yes,' said Li Pen. 'These can also be brave or wise people who have become gods. And there are also the ancestors, who take a keen interest in the doings of their grandchildren. All of them are beseeched, but not in the way followers of the one-god religions do. Chinese gods do not require adoration. They require the matter to be brought to their divine attention, and then they will act, or not, and one cannot make them.'

'Harsh,' said Phryne.

'Do you think so? Is it better to think that your prayers have not been answered because you are a bad person, or because the goddess happens to be busy that day? I remember when there was a great drought in Guandong province, when I was a child. We did not beat our breasts thinking that we had been sinful, though we probably had been, it being the nature of men. We brought out the statue of the Land God, that we called Grandpa, and drenched him with water and had water fights and laughed, so that he might think that we had plenty of water and send more.'

'Shows a nasty vindictive streak in the gods, though,' commented Phryne.

'But it rained,' said Li Pen, smiling.

'Can't argue with that.'

'And there are also gods for people who are outcasts,' he said quietly. 'There are the Taoist Eight Immortals: they protect soldiers, the sick, whores, old people, entertainers, barbers, musicians and actors. Shall I tell you a story?'

'Tell me,' said Phryne.

'Once Li T'ieh Kuai the immortal was a fair young man, tall as a tree. He came down from heaven and left his body in a field while he danced with the butterflies. When the butterflies flew away, he came back and found that farmers had discovered his body, thought he was dead, and burned it. What was he to do? He had to find another body in order to re-enter heaven. He flew about weeping, but everyone who had a body wanted to keep it. Finally he found a dead beggar in a field, an old man with a crippled leg. He took that body and regained heaven, but forever after he was Li of the Iron Crutch, and he cares for the sick.'

'Nice,' said Phryne.

'It serves. The Gracious Lady Kwan Yin, who is an aspect of the Lord Buddha, is also in those shrines. The Chinese will reject gods who do not give good service and collect new ones as they require them, and I suppose that they always needed a goddess of mercy.'

'Trust me, Li Pen, everyone needs a goddess of mercy. I'd better be going. You will take care of them while I am gone?'

'I will. And you, Silver Lady, you will take care of my master?'

'To the best of my ability.'

They did not shake hands, as monks are not supposed to touch women. Li Pen paused, seeing her hand fall to her side.

'Another, very short story, Silver Lady?'

'Certainly.'

'Two monks at the side of a river see a woman with a child, too frail to brave the water. The first monk says, "We are required to help the poor but we are also not allowed to touch women. What shall we do?" The second monk picks the woman up, carries her and the child across the river and the two monks continue on their way. After a few li the first monk says, "But we are not supposed to touch women!" And the second monk says, "Are you still carrying that woman?"'

'Shake hands,' said Phryne, and took his firm, slim hand in farewell. Li Pen smiled at her, which he did very seldom, and went back to watching bees in the wisteria. Phryne went back to her room.

Her clothes were packed, her car loaded, and she swung away into the street with her household crying farewell and a song on her lips—which at least was not 'The Wild Colonial Boy'. That was something to be thankful for. She was thinking about sex and gods and she was singing:

'If you don't like my peaches, why do you shake my tree?
'If you don't like my peaches, why do you shake my tree?
'Get out of my orchard and let my peach tree be!'

Phryne, against all appearances, had the St Louis Blues. It was far too long since she had been free to act as she liked, what with daughters and households and sisters. This Castlemaine trip might be just the thing for some of her wilder impulses.

She drove gently out of the city onto the Bendigo road, still singing. The Hispano-Suiza was behaving perfectly, the day was sunny but not blinding, and most of the morning traffic had got where it was going. She might even take the big car up to a very high speed—say, sixty miles an hour—if she found a straight stretch of road without lurking country cops, who always had speeding fines in mind when they saw a big red car.

Lin Chung, reluctantly but accurately attired in his cassock and collar, entered the Lin family Bentley and tried not to catch anyone's eye. His enthusiastic uncle had gone over the main points of his story—a Canton mission, not too big, driven out by passing warlords, come to Australia to minister to the remnant communities in various towns. It made a nice story and provided he was not examined too closely on matters of doctrine, he might pass. He was not at all sure that this was a good idea, but Uncle would be hurt if he abandoned it too quickly. No one seemed to have noticed and he sat back behind the curtain, watching the city fleet past. He had a load of presents for Uncle Lin Tao of the market garden, and of them he had made several smaller bundles, full of treats for any indigent Chinese person he might meet. Thus he would at least acquire merit, and might even get some answers to his questions.

Lin Chung's recent and dangerous sojourn in China had been educational in many ways. He had heard about the starving children of the past, but never had he seen any until the potbellied infants of Canton came, hands outstretched, to the big car and thence every night in his dreams. He had expended all that he dared in charity but knew that those children had very little chance of surviving. He had heard about famine but the smell and taste of famine was another thing altogether. And during his short captivity by pirates he had learned useful, though painful, lessons about power, about dominance, and about cruelty. He had plans for the Chinese people of Castlemaine, if they were indeed poor and uncared-for. That silk trip had netted the Lin family several fortunes in silk and antiquities. One of the three Shang incense burners which he had bought for ten copper cash, a load of rice and three sheep from some starving farmers had sold in London for three thousand guineas. Though the money did not belong to Lin himself but to his family, he felt that since it was he, Lin Chung, who had risked his life for it, he had a reasonable say in its expenditure. The Lin family would be able to send all of its children to the nth generation to Melbourne Grammar and Presbyterian Ladies College just on the interest.

The thought made him smile. He opened his *Book of Common Prayer* and began to read.

'When the wicked man turneth away from his wickedness that he hath committed, and doeth that which is lawful and right, he shall save his soul alive.'

Phryne was at Diggers Rest before she risked letting the car go. The engine roared. Massive pistons slid. The road rolled away, the trees flashed past, and she did not slow down until she was coming into Gisborne, where there was bound to be an interested member of the constabulary with a notebook and a strong sense of his duty to the local shire's revenues. She rolled to a stop next to the Gisborne pub and decided that, since she had travelled so far, so fast, lunch and a glass of pub squash would hit the spot. After turning down several pressing offers from young men eager to further their acquaintance—with her car— she sat down in the Ladies' Lounge and was served the usual country meal, viz, steak, eggs, and vegetables out of which all nourishment, impudence and even colour had been boiled. The decor was Travelling Salesman, the prevailing colour a nice shade of mud, and the skipping girl was the only person in the pub who seemed at all pleased to see Phryne, and she was a poster advertising vinegar.

A little depressed but adequately nourished, she was soon back on the road to Kyneton, which she hoped (with police presence) to reach in two hours or (without police presence) one hour, when she could have sworn that the black Bentley which followed her at a decorous pace was the Lin family car. But it was carrying a clergyman. As far as she knew, there were no ecclesiastical Lins.

She shook her head, jammed her cloche down firmly over her forehead, and leaned on the accelerator. The great car leapt under her hands. It was almost as good as flying.

Apart from a brief shower of rain while passing through the

forest, which necessitated stopping and wrestling with the hood, always a task which ruined the fingernails and pinched the knuckles, the journey was uneventful and most of her blues were blown away as she went at a proper twenty miles an hour through the agreeable hamlet of Chewton and into the town of Castlemaine.

'Nice place,' said Phryne to herself. Unlike some of the places she had passed through, Castlemaine had an almost cocky sense of self assurance. The straight, well-planned streets and the solid stone buildings, town hall, State Bank, market and post office, told the visitor that this hadn't just once been the richest goldfield in Australia but presently had the best beer as well, and did anyone want to make anything of it? This was a well-found, well-served gem of a little place that knew exactly what it was, which was the best place in the world, and have you tried our clotted cream and our superlative jam on our very excellent scones at Penney's tea-rooms?

Phryne liked it immediately. She parked the Hispano-Suiza near the market next to a dilapidated grocer's van and strolled into Mostyn Street. A passing gentleman, politely removing his hat, directed her to walk along Hargraves Street to Lyttleton, where she would find the Imperial Hotel opposite the town hall. It was three o'clock in the afternoon on a cloudless day and the air was fresh and scented with baking. Divine. Phryne fell into her Parisian saunter and enjoyed the walk.

This was an old place. Everywhere the buildings were stone, and those which had crumbled over the years had been repaired and prinked-up with kalsomine. She saw several young women wheeling perambulators, which was a good sign. Once a town began to decay, the young people moved out and with them went the future. She passed a doctor's surgery, a chemist's shop and the Supreme Court Hotel before she turned the corner into

Lyttleton Street and the Imperial Hotel burst upon her in all its slightly off-key glory.

Well, well. Someone had decided that a hotel, to be a hotel within the meaning of the act, had to have dormers and a lot of windows; so far so good. They had then added a French mansard roof, made of tin, and more wrought iron than seemed entirely decent. It was charming, commodious, and unlikely.

Phryne loved it. She hoped she was staying there.

She walked into the pub, was gestured at by a barman, and went in the second door, where a blonde girl was sucking a sweet and reading a film magazine in front of a bank of pigeon-holes.

'Hello, I'm Phryne Fisher,' she said, and the girl almost choked on her lolly.

'The Hon. Miss Fisher? What your butler rang up yesterday about? Yes, Miss, er, my lady, we have your room, it's a nice one, with a balcony, and you have a private bath, just like he said. Bill! Come and get the lady's things!'

'I parked my car over by the market,' said Phryne. 'I shall go and fetch it later. Where can I park it?'

'In the stables, my lady, Bill Gaskin will show you. Bill!' Her voice rose to a screech.

Someone grumbled in the background, 'All right, hold yer horses,' and Bill Gaskin came into sight. He was a younger man than she had expected from the voice and seemed to have been doing something relating to coal. Or possibly soot. He had barely distinguishable features and those she could see looked sullen.

'I'll just go and get the car,' said Phryne. 'Then shall I come round to the side?'

'Yes, Miss, them big green doors,' he agreed, without enthusiasm.

'Bert and Cec send their fraternal greetings, comrade,' whispered Phryne to Bill as she went out. A gnarled hand detained her.

'How's the dock strike?'

'Worse than ever,' she replied. 'I don't know what Mr Justice Beeby was thinking of, really I don't.'

The hand released her and the blackamoor grinned, showing white teeth. Phryne had found a comrade.

'I'll wait by the gate,' he promised, sounding like something out of Tennyson.

Phryne had parked the Hispano-Suiza in the stable yard of the Imperial Hotel and her bags had been carried up by the indefatigable Bill Gaskin. He had stopped for a few moments to gossip about the wharf strike and recommend her to tip his son, the waiter, before a bell had summoned him to the kitchen to clean silver.

Nice place, thought Phryne, sitting down on her bed. She had a chair, a table, a light, a private bathroom with a claw-footed enamel bath in which one could actually sit, an abundant supply of hot water and wardrobe space, and a good reliable mirror. The decor ran to red plush and heavy carpets and the picture on the wall was the usual hotel moorland with sheep, or possibly buffalo—it was always hard to tell. But someone had filled a little glass vase with loose, old-fashioned roses, the towels were fluffy and the bed-linen crisp and lavendered.

Phryne bounced a little. Good. The strings were new and did not twang unduly. She found a bedspring symphony musical accompaniment to amorous pursuits distracting. She kicked off her shoes, lay down on her bed, and closed her eyes, making a mental list of Things To Do In Castlemaine.

1. Find an eccentric doctor or undertaker who decided in the 1850s to make a mummy by the Herodotus method.
2. Find out who sold the body to the Carter travelling show as the Wild Colonial Boy.
3. Reason backwards and find out where the doctor or whoever got the body he used as a basis for his experiment.
4. Find out who, in fact, the mummy was when he had breath. And then
5. Find out who killed him, and why, and the corollary of that was
6. Find out who, in the present, was warning Phryne off.

All of which sounded like a lot of bother, she reflected, and fell asleep.

She rose in time for dinner. The dining room at the Imperial was heavy on the red plush, but also heavy on real silver cutlery and white napkins, much washed but originally good. Phryne elected for a summer salad and cold roast beef, a dish of which she was inordinately fond, and ordered a bottle of Tahlbilk red, an original shiraz which had escaped the phylloxera epidemic because the vineyard was so isolated that the nasty little creature would have had to plod miles to get there—and never did. Someone found a corkscrew and opened the bottle and rather tentatively offered it to Phryne to taste. The Imperial was not used to ladies who drank red wine, but covered its surprise admirably.

There were several other guests. A plump lady in blue and a plump lady in pink, dining together, nodded politely to Phryne. They resembled each other so closely that they had to be sisters. Only close family bonds would endure matching hats of blue and pink roses. A party of sporting gentlemen, exchanging improbable fishing stories to judge by their wide, expansive gestures, stared at her and looked away again. Two young men in dinner suits had their backs to her; they were laughing and drinking a lot of beer. Well, it was the vin du pays.

Phryne allowed a young waiter who wasn't too sure about the procedure to refill her glass and began her enquiries by asking him, 'Who would remember the goldfields, do you think, in this fine town of yours?'

'You a journalist, Miss?' asked the waiter. He knew about the New Woman and her Professional Engagements. His aunt had done her best with his cowlick but his straw-coloured hair stood up at the crown like a cocky's crest and he radiated, like the Elephant's Child, insatiable curiosity.

'No,' said Phryne. 'I'm thinking of writing a book.'

'Ah,' said the waiter, wisely. 'Then I reckon you ought to go and have a word with Mr Harrison. He'll be along shortly for his tea. Been here ever since the year dot and his dad before him. But he can talk the hind leg off a donkey, Miss, I have to warn you.'

'Then all I shall have to do is listen,' responded Phryne. 'Let me know when he comes in, will you?'

She slipped a shilling into the boy's ready hand and he raced off to stand guard by the door and nab Mr Harrison as soon as he came in. Phryne sipped on, beguiling her dinner with a glance at the guidebook produced by the Castlemaine Chamber of Commerce. Visitors were enjoined to see the market building, which had Ceres on the top, walk in the botanical gardens, which had been designed by Baron Von Mueller, visit the memorial to the South African War, and perhaps even pan for a little gold in the Campbells Creek (gold pan hire from Williams General Merchant, Hargraves Street). The Theatre Royal was offering novelty acts and showed a film every night (sixpence, a bargain if you counted the extra newsreels). Phryne had already seen Garbo and Gilbert in *Flesh, and the Devil*.

And one could drink in a different hotel every night and it would be weeks before you needed to repeat yourself. By then, Phryne reflected, you wouldn't be able to remember the first one anyway. One coffee palace, the Midland. She would appreciate temperance movements more if they were not so shrill, declamatory and arrogant.

Still, it seemed a nice little town, and just as Phryne's Peach Melba arrived, so did Mr Harrison, and she ordered him a beer.

To the most munificent and much missed elder brother Sung Ma from the unworthy younger sister Sung Mai much love and greetings. Season of Great Snow, 11th day.

It seems so long since you went away, elder brother, and there is so much to tell you. Now that you have been sending gold, Uncle is pleasant to Mother and he has arranged very suitable matches for me and our little sister Sung Lan. I am to marry the son of the magistrate, Li Chu. I am told that he is a very studious young man and he wanted a wife who could read and write and join him in his poetic pursuits. He has passed his second literary examination and we are going to the capital Canton to take up his post as assistant secretary. Little Sister is to marry Butcher Lo's son, who is the one who goes hunting a lot and has a merry laugh. Little Sister is such a good housekeeper that I am sure she will be happy. Uncle says that Mother may stay in his house as long as she lives as there is now enough money to support her. She is pleased. I shall miss Mother when I marry but I miss you even more. Come home, Elder Brother! You have found enough gold. Heaven frowns on excess and you have now been away for a year. We had the New Year celebrations without you and my heart was heavy.

The younger sister sends a handful of withered petals to the elder brother, and also her heart.

CHAPTER TEN

To search for gold is to look for the moon at the bottom of the sea.

Taam Sze Pui (Tom See Poy),
Palmer River, 1877–82

Mr Harrison was an old man and once he had been a giant. Shoulders fully two axe-handles across still strained his good shirt. Phryne knew it was his good shirt because someone, probably a sister, had darned it so meticulously. His corporation was beautifully solid, a good belly which he had obviously been cultivating for many years. His hair had lost the battle to stay on his head and had slipped to the back. His eyes were a muddy blue and his complexion that of a ruined redhead. His gleaming teeth were masterpieces of the dentist's art. In his youth, Phryne suspected, Mr Harrison might have been a bit of a knut—possibly, even, a masher. He sat down at her table and engulfed her hand in a large, gnarled paw.

'Young Billy Gaskin said you wanted to talk to me,' he said in an unexpectedly low voice.

'I do indeed,' Phryne replied. 'I am interested in the history of this charming little town. Young Billy thought that you might be so kind as to share your memories with me.'

'Delighted,' said Mr Harrison. 'You might like to look at this while they bring me my tea. I never talk while I'm eating. My old mum taught me that.'

Phryne accepted a slim volume bound in blue cardboard. She averted her eyes from Mr Harrison getting bodily into his steak—his teeth were justifying their maker—and read *Reminiscences of the Gold Fields* by his father Jim 'the Blacksmith' Harrison.

The volume was locally printed and bound and because this was, after all, Castlemaine, someone had made a good workmanlike job of it. It had been proofread by, Phryne guessed, an elderly schoolteacher and thus contained no mistakes. And Jim had an interesting story to tell, though his prose style was overelaborate and in need of a nice cup of senna tea and a good lie-down.

'You can't imagine what those times were like,' the text began. Phryne read on as Mr Harrison demolished his tea. He had sent back his plate for another steak and more vegetables as the first one had barely touched the sides.

They were the roaring days. They were the days when men were men. My dad walked off his job in a wholesale hay and feed store in Port Melbourne with his pick and shovel on his shoulder and took only two days to get to Castlemaine in 1851, when the field was fresh and there was still an abundance of 'the riches of the earth'. The government was down on miners and made every man pay thirty shillings for a miner's licence, whether he was going to dig or not. This made the shopkeepers and grog sellers wild.

It also meant that women could dig with impunity and some of the more abandoned and degraded females did, like the celebrated Five Women claim which some miners decided to knock over one night. Two men were shot but the constable did nothing about it and the Five Women left the field with their ill-gotten gains, never a licence between them and they were so proud of themselves. Black Douglas the Bushranger swore to teach them their place but never a sight did he get of them once they left the field, heading for Ballarat one morning in May 1855. My dad said three were young, good-looking women too, the others being half-castes, and there were plenty of miners who would have taken the white women to wife and provided a respectable state for them but these independent Misses did not care for the holy state of matrimony. Dad said they were Irish. He told me never to cross an Irish woman and he never did himself, Mum being from County Tipperary and she had a terrible temper when roused, God rest her soul.

There were remarkable finds in those days. Everyone in the world was going to the diggings to try their luck. Ships were becalmed because their crews had all jumped ashore at Melbourne. One Captain Aubrey decided to do something about this. He left four men on board his ship, the *Golden Fleece*, and took seventeen crew to Castlemaine, agreed to share and share alike. They marched here and began to dig and struck it rich in a week. Then they marched back to sell their gold in Melbourne, where they got three pounds seven shillings an ounce, then they marched onto the ship and away. They didn't even stop for a celebration until Hong Kong. They say that there are inns called The Golden Fleece up and down the North

Road in England, all financed by that one captain's discipline and ingenuity. He also got top rates for his cargo because everyone else had lost their crews.

My dad and his mate made friends with some of the miners. They came from all over the British Empire and some from outside. There were Californians who were very dirty on the Chinese and some lascars as black as your hat and of course the Celestials, the Chinese, who used up too much water, hogged the best sites and made Sundays hideous with their caterwauling music and opium smoking. There were various attempts to rid the goldfields of this plague and curse but none succeeded because the government was protecting them, and all we could do was drive them to the fringes, where they lived on the tailings, grew vegetables, and stayed out of a decent man's sight.

Dad's best mate was George Duncan, and next to George was an English new chum called Thomas—always Thomas, not Tommy—Beaconsfield, who was the son of a Marquis, or so he said. His mate was a pink-faced bloke called Chumley. Together they worked hard but never made a big strike, only enough 'colour' to act as encouragement to keep trying. But you can't keep the British lad down. Thomas and Chumley left one night without a farewell, leaving their claim to Dad and George and then they did strike it pretty good, cleaned up and left the field. George went home to Hobart but Dad stayed here and established a blacksmith's. Dad told me lots of stories about the goldfields . . .

Phryne lifted her head and examined this rankly prejudiced old hound more carefully as he patted his lips daintily and picked up a spoon to engulf the Imperial's very good apple pie and cream. He looked back. Phryne simpered. Old mashers were susceptible to simpering and she wanted to test her theory. She had perfected the simper in front of a mirror. It had taken weeks.

'Just let me get this pie inside me and I'm all yours,' gasped the old masher, confirming her hypothesis. Phryne thought about applying the simper again, but decided that Mr Harrison might self-combust if overheated, and rewarded him with a slight smile.

Phryne sipped at her glass of wine, Mr Harrison gulped down his first pot of beer, and the Imperial dining room began to empty. One of the two sisters gave Phryne a sympathetic smile as she gathered coat and handbag and left a tip for Young Billy. The sporting gentlemen went out, still shouting boasts about the croc they shot in the Palmer River—a likely story, thirty feet long, indeed, thought Phryne. They had probably shot a boat. The beer-drinking young men called for another round. An old waiter went across, presumably to suggest to them that they might remove into the bar, where the beer was fresher, being closer to the source.

'Now, Miss, what would you like to know?' asked Mr Harrison.

'Your father was on the goldfields, it says in this very well written little book. I am interested in finding a relative. He was a doctor, at least, he trained as a doctor. He might have been an undertaker, perhaps, or a herbalist, even a showman of some sort. He was a rather eccentric gentleman with a fascination for the classics. The trouble is, I don't know his name,' said Phryne, deciding to unleash her simper again. 'He was actually called Fisher, but we know that he was on the fields under an assumed name. Perhaps you can help me?'

Mr Harrison's face fell.

'I'd be real pleased to help you, Miss, but I'm not sure I can. There was some real strange people on the goldfields. Professors and bushrangers and gentlemen and thieves.'

'And sometimes you could tell the difference,' murmured Phryne.

He gave her a puzzled look and she mentally slapped her own wrist. That cynical murmur did not match the simper.

'But doctors—my dad didn't hold with doctors. He always said with a bottle of Dr Collis-Browne's Chlorodyne, a turpentine poultice and a good belt of rum you could beat any disease.'

This was, Phryne thought, very likely true. If the chlorodyne and turpentine didn't kill the germs, the rum would at least ensure that you died happy. In any case, people were tougher in the old days, the reason being, the weak children died as babies. Phryne thought of her own grandmother, who had boasted of raising nine of her sixteen children, and shuddered slightly.

'But men were men in the roaring days,' said Mr Harrison reverently.

'Tell me of these men,' breathed Phryne, seeing that by asking a direct question she had upset the old ruffian's whole memory structure and hoping that she might be able to sieve some particles of 'colour' out of the Harrison bonce if she shut up and let him talk. In furtherance of this plan she suggested a remove to the lounge, ordered another bottle of wine and refills of beer for Mr Harrison, and allowed Young Billy, cocky's crest erect with interest, to lead her to the only part of the Imperial prepared for the reception of ladies.

It was furnished in the usual plush, with the usual pictures and one gold-framed picture of an old man entitled 'I Allus Has One at Eleven' but the brass was polished and someone was in charge of fresh flowers, which lent the beery air a scent of refinement. Phryne stopped to sniff at one arrangement of gum tips and freesias, a fascinating combination of scents.

'The flowers are from the nursery, and Smithy there trained at Buda, so he's real good at roses and bulbs and all them old-fashioned flowers,' Mr Harrison told Phryne. 'Pity that we can't show you around Buda, Miss Fisher. Beautiful house. But the old sisters, they don't like visitors. Mind you, they do let the children play in the gardens on Sunday afternoons, though.'

'Perhaps we can borrow a suitable child,' said Phryne artlessly. 'Now, do sit down in this nice well-stuffed chair and tell me all about the men of old.'

Mr Harrison was entirely hers. He waited gallantly until she sat down and Young Billy refilled her glass, took a swig of his own and began what was evidently a long recitation: 'Men was men in them days . . .'

Phryne suppressed a sigh, drank her wine, and listened.

Mr Butler, opening a parcel in the garden, was relieved to find that it contained photographic reproductions of what seemed to be a blurred crest of some sort rather than the explosive device he had expected. The note accompanying these said 'What fun, Phryne! Best we can do through the filters, but they are a lot clearer and my friend has tinted them to near an exact match of the colours we have. Keep me posted? Chin, chin', and it was signed Mark Treasure. Dr Treasure was a gentleman of levity unbecoming to his profession, thought Mr Butler severely. He tucked the note in with the photographs and delivered them to Dot.

'They're ever so much better than that sketch,' said Dot, examining them closely. Mrs Butler asked her to remove them immediately from her nice clean kitchen table which had just been scrubbed and let the cook get on with serving dinner. Li Pen was peeling potatoes. He gave Dot a shy look and returned to his peeling. He was going to do penance for the remarkable vegetarian dishes which Mrs Butler was concocting for him, but he was prepared to do that in a good cause. Soupe julienne had not previously come to his attention.

Dot gathered the insulted photographs to her bosom. 'This is one thing which Miss Eliza could really help with,' she said to Mr Butler. 'If only I could get her to talk to me.'

'Well, see what you can do,' advised the butler. 'She's in the blue parlour. Dinner in a tick, and it's those little rissoles. And everyone loves Mrs B's shepherd's pie. And I've opened a bottle of the good riesling. That ought to mellow Miss Eliza a bit.'

Dot sighed. The trouble with alcohol and Miss Eliza was that it seemed to make her shriller. Still, one could but try. Dot knocked at the blue parlour door.

'Dinner, Miss Eliza,' said Dot. Phryne's sister put down her improving tome—what a book, thought Dot, it must have cost a fortune in excess baggage—and got up.

She was greatly improved, Dot considered. She had been crying but was now in a state Dot called 'mopped-up' and her smile was unforced. Her hair was loosely gathered at the nape of her neck rather than being wound into that tight, unbecoming bun. Her accent, when she spoke, had lost all of its Home Counties abrasiveness.

'Good! I am quite hungry. What is Mrs Butler giving us?'

'Leftovers, Miss Eliza, but they'll be tasty,' promised Dot. 'Shepherd's pie made with the cold roast and a lot of little vegetables and salad. Miss Phryne tells me that you're a socialist,' she added. Eliza stiffened.

'Yes,' she said bravely.

'Lots of socialists in Australia,' said Dot easily. She wanted this over with so Miss Eliza wouldn't flinch every time someone mentioned socialism. 'Perfectly respectable here. Miss Phryne has a lot of socialist friends. And there are Mr Bert and Mr Cec, they're IWW—Industrial Workers of the World, you know. They're nice, even if they are red raggers. You'll fit right in, here.'

'You know, Dorothy, I'm beginning to think that I might,' confessed Miss Eliza.

Dinner was not so much leftovers as the more refined form of réchauffé known only in French cookbooks. The rissoles and shepherd's pie were masterpieces of their type and the mixture of finely cut vegetables was heavenly. The girls tucked in heartily and Miss Eliza followed their example, knowing that there was apple and pear sorbet to follow.

Given a hint by Dot, Ruth and Miss Eliza discussed romance novels and found that they had a number of favourite authors in common. This left Jane to consider the mystery of Fermat's Last Theorem, about which she had ideas, and Dot to wonder what Phryne was doing. Getting into hot water, in all probability, hell-raising being something of a Phryne specialty. Dot ate less and less until Jane, returning from a mathematical trance, nudged her.

'It will be all right, Miss Phryne is a very capable person,' she urged.

'How did you know I was worrying about her?' asked Dot. The girls were really coming out of their rescued-and-grateful shells; Jane would not have made this comment six months ago.

'You get a little line between your brows, just there,' said Jane, touching with the tip of a forefinger. 'I don't think we need to worry about her tonight, anyway,' she added. 'She just got to Castlemaine. She hasn't had time to get into any trouble.'

'That's true,' agreed Dot, resuming her dinner and analysing her mouthful. Mrs Butler made the most beautiful shepherd's pie. The potato was creamy and crisp on top. Was there, perhaps, a morsel of cheese in the crust? These were mysteries.

Miss Eliza allowed Mr Butler to pour her a second glass of the South Australian riesling and said soberly, 'Ladies, I have to tell you about a man who is . . . well, not to put too fine a point on it, he's . . .' As Eliza seemed to have stalled and the household needed the information, Dot provided a translation.

'Chasing you,' said Dot. 'Threatening you. And if we see him, we tell Li Pen, and that will be the end of the problem.'

'Is Mr Li that good?' asked Miss Eliza, hopefully.

Three plaits bobbed as three females nodded.

'He is,' said Dot. 'You can trust him, Miss Eliza. Now, what is this man's name, and what does he look like?'

'His name is Roderick Cholmondeley, and he is . . . oh Lord, I am no good at this. He's made like a bruiser, Father says, like a prize fighter. He's about six feet tall and he has blue eyes and fair hair which is cut very short. He is . . . dangerous. He made . . . threats. My father wants me to marry him and I never shall.'

Ruth's eyes were as round as marbles.

'Gosh!' she said. 'Just like in *Lady Joan's Secret*! I didn't know there were fathers like that any more!'

'Well, there are,' said Miss Eliza. 'Phryne was right when she told him to . . .' There was a significant pause while Miss Eliza sought for another way to put this other than the coarse and biological phrase which Phryne had actually used. 'She told him to keep his matrimonial plans to himself, because she would find her own mate. Furthermore, she was going to Australia, and he was at liberty to . . . er . . . make his own plans as long as they didn't include her. She was always bold! I was so shocked at the time, you know, that she could do that—just tell Father no to his face and off and leave her family.'

'And leave you,' said Dot gently.

'She asked me to come too,' said Eliza, defending her sister for the first time since she had come to Australia. 'I was too scared. She bought me a ticket and told me to meet her at the docks and I couldn't, I just couldn't run away without a word and I . . . let the boat go with the tide. I have regretted it ever since,' she added. 'Then I met Alice and we began our work in the East End and I was happy again until Father ordered me to marry either this brute, Roderick, or a horrible old man who is the Marquis of Shropshire and I really couldn't so I told him . . .'

'You told him?' prompted Ruth very softly. 'You stood up to him?'

'No,' said Miss Eliza bitterly. 'He caught me out in a lie about the East End and made enquiries as to what I had been doing and then he bellowed at me that unless I left everything I held dear, recanted socialism, abandoned Alice and married one of his candidates, he would send me to Australia to my worthless sister—that's what he called Phryne—and we could both . . . well, we could both get on with it.'

'You're better off here,' commented Dot. 'I've heard about Miss Phryne's father. He's not a nice man and you don't want to be anywhere near him.'

'No, but I haven't any money,' said Miss Eliza. 'Not until I am twenty-five.'

'Stay here until then,' advised Dot. 'Li Pen will set this Roderick to the right abouts, even if he is a bruiser. It's not the size of the dog in the fight, my father used to say, but the size of the fight in the dog. Can you describe this Roderick Cholmondeley any better than big and blue eyes, Miss Eliza?'

'I've got a picture of him,' said Eliza. 'He gave it to me. I'll show you after dinner.'

'Now, we've got our orders, girls,' said Dot solemnly. 'First sight, call Li Pen, raise the alarm. We don't want to take any chances with this one. We may not have to go so far as Miss Phryne suggested and bury him under the hydrangeas—'

'We haven't got any hydrangeas,' objected Jane, who botanised freely.

'Miss Phryne ordered some from Mrs Lin,' said Dot.

Miss Eliza was momentarily surprised, then joined in the laughter, and Dot had hopes of her recovery.

Miss Eliza went to her room and brought down a picture of a scowling, heavily muscled youth in very expensive clothes, and several books on heraldry.

'Do you understand how precedence works?' asked Miss Eliza. The girls looked blank.

'The ranks go like this,' explained Miss Eliza. 'The highest is the King, of course, and then the princes and the royal dukes. Then ordinary dukes. Then we have marquess and marchioness, earl and countess, viscount and viscountess, baron and baroness, all of whom are addressed as my lord and my lady, then baronets and knights, called Sir, whose ladies are just called Lady. That is why my friend is called Lady Alice and Phryne and I are just Hons. Clear?'

Jane shook her head. 'No, but do go on.'

The girls laid Phryne's sketch and the photographic prints on the table and examined them under the strong magnifying glass.

'Definitely a shield,' said Ruth. 'This is exciting! And do you think those things are mermen, Miss Eliza?'

'Possibly, or mermaids. Or they may be dolphins—heraldic dolphins do not look like real ones. Now, here is a sample coat of arms. It consists of the shield, the helmet, the mantling, the crest and the supporters. The main body of the coat of arms is the shield—I am sure that this is a shield. Such a pity that the colours are so pale. The photographer has done his best with the tint but he can't have been sure either. It was quartered, that's for sure. And I'd say that quarter was red, that is gules, and that one was blue, that's azure. This I believe was sable with, perhaps, a bend on it?'

'Sable being black? Yes, two of the quarters are black, and both have this funny sort of bendy stripe on them,' observed Ruth.

'How keen your eyes are! Yes, I see what you mean. A chevron, argent, I do believe.'

'Argent must be silver,' said Jane. 'And this is a star.'

'A mullet of how many points?'

'Six,' said Ruth, who had the clearest sight. 'So, we have two quarters with the chevron on them, and one with a gold star on a red field.'

'A field gules with a mullet of six points, or,' corrected Miss Eliza.

'And this blue quarter seems to have a snake,' said Dot. 'Or a coil of rope, perhaps. That doesn't sound very aristocratic.'

'Can you see the snake, girls?' asked Miss Eliza faintly.

'Yes. The only other thing it could be is a spring, and that's even less aristocratic,' said Jane.

Eliza made a choking noise and groped for her bag. Dot was concerned.

'Why, Miss Eliza, you look ill. Jane, pour her some more wine.'

'I'll just get my salts . . .' Miss Eliza found her smelling salts and took such a deep sniff that the ammonia knocked her head back. 'What colour do you think the helmet is?'

At a loss for a safe answer, the girls inspected the pictures again.

'I think it's meant to be white,' said Jane. 'It's front on, Ruth, see, you can see the bars on the visor.'

'How many bars?' gasped Miss Eliza.

'Five, I think. Miss Dot, what do you think?' Ruth appealed for help.

'Five, certainly,' agreed Dot. 'And plumes, very pretty.'

'A helmet, argent, five bars, full face?'

'That's it,' said Dot. 'Miss Eliza, what's wrong?'

'The helmet signifies rank,' explained Miss Eliza, who had paled to the colour of milk. 'A duke or marquess has a silver helmet with five bars, full face. An earl, viscount or baron has silver with four bars, in profile.'

'I never knew there was so much information in a coat of arms,' marvelled Jane.

'I think it's meant to tell you a lot,' said Ruth. 'So that when you meet the person you know what rank they are and you don't make a mistake in addressing them. So this belonged to a marquess or a duke, and he had a quartered shield with a star, a couple of chevrons and a snake, though I bet they didn't call it a snake.'

'A serpent coiled to strike, or,' said Miss Eliza. 'Oh, dear Lord. What shall I do?'

'Tell us all about it, that's what,' said Dot. 'A trouble shared is a trouble halved—or maybe quartered. I'll ask Mr B for some strong coffee and then you can tell us all about it.'

Dot did not need to ring the bell. There was a whisking noise and Mr Butler appeared with the coffee tray, setting it down on the table without disturbing a grain of the coloured coffee sugar pyramid.

'I wish I knew how he did that,' said Jane thoughtfully.

'Miss Thomas says that only saints bilocate,' Ruth reminded her sister.

'She hasn't met Mr Butler,' Jane told her.

They were bantering to give Miss Eliza time to recover her nerve. For a moment Dot feared that she was about to start crying again, but Miss Eliza stiffened her upper lip, gulped a cup of scalding coffee and began to explain.

'I told you about Lady Alice Harborough, whom I knew in London? She is a marquess's daughter. Her family crest is two quarters a field sable with chevron argent, one quarter a field gules with a mullet of six points, or, and one quarter a field azure with a serpent, coiled to strike, or. The helmet is correct for her rank and the supporters are dolphins, like these here.'

Jane and Ruth inspected the odd, roly-poly animals and agreed that they were indeed what had been tattooed on the dead man's arm.

'What shall I tell her?'

'Well, there isn't a lot to tell so far,' said Dot practically. 'It's so long ago. Did her grandad lose a gardener or someone, about seventy years ago?'

'Not a gardener,' said Eliza, taking more coffee. 'An heir.'

In the fifteenth year of the reign of the glorious Emperor Lord of the Dragon Throne Kwong Sui of the Ching Dynasty, Great Heat, sixth month, third day.

To the illustrious and well-beloved nephew Sung Ma from his uncle. It is my sad duty to tell you that your mother, our sister Tan, is very ill and calling for you. The priests say that she will not last long. Come and share our mourning. You have duties here and your sister is distressed at your absence. She presented her husband with a baby boy, born almost at New Year, and lacks only your presence to be as happy as can be expected.

Heaven frowns on excess, nephew. You have found enough gold and the Lin family have reported well of you. Come home, Sung Ma. Your disgrace is forgotten. Your place is waiting for you and I have begun negotiations for your wife.

CHAPTER ELEVEN

How can you pass such days of quiet and calm
When human life is sore beset with ills?

Su Tungpo, translated by Lin Yutang

Lin Chung had expected gales of laughter to greet his arrival at the farm in such an exotic costume, but only old Uncle Lin Tao reacted. The old man helped Lin out of the car, boggled a little, then nodded.

'Very wise, cousin Chung. We hear that you need to talk to the ghosts, and in that garb, they will at least not spit at you. Come in, please, we are all awaiting your honoured arrival. We have heard that you are taking over from your honoured and revered grandmother, and we are eager to account to you for our work.'

This was, of course, not true. No one could be pleased at the sudden advent of a new boss, who might be more captious and difficult than the old lady herself. But it was courteous of the old man and Lin allowed himself to be conducted inside.

It was an old-fashioned Australian farmhouse with verandahs all around, but while Australians grew happy wanderer or potato vine, Chinese grew passionfruit, jasmine and grapes. The boards were newly painted, though not suspiciously new, the paths were swept and the house breathed cooking and jasmine flowers. The whole household of twenty-two was gathered in a large room with a table running its whole length.

Lin was introduced to a number of previously unknown cousins and second cousins, all of whom murmured polite greetings and some of whom were very pretty girls. Lin approved of pretty girls. He was conducted to a throne-like chair, carved from blackwood and undoubtedly an heirloom. A ceremonial cup of tea was brought to him by the old man. Acceptance of it meant that Lin Chung was now ruler of his family and this household.

He accepted it with some trepidation. Lin was not yet comfortable with the idea of being head of the family. But it was good, strong, Jasmine-flavoured tea. Power, he reflected, tasted sweet.

He would be shown the accounts and given a guided tour of the farm later. Now he would have to endure a banquet, and massive umbrage would be taken if he did not at least taste every dish. Lin family gossip was still busy with the Sin of Uncle Tan, a knockabout elderly uncle who spent most of his time as a drover and boundary rider. He had not only rejected several dishes with contumely, but had flung a piece of roasted pork with special Szechuan sauce—to his dog!

Poor old Uncle Tan, thought Lin as he was handed a pair of gold-tipped chopsticks. Not that it bothered Uncle overmuch. He had just belched politely, patted a few small heads, tipped his hat, and ridden off, his dog running behind him. A life which gained in attractiveness as the feast wore on and more and more superlative dishes were brought forth from the kitchen. The youngest beans, the crispest water chestnuts, the finest chickens, quail, turkey, duck, pork, something which tasted like beef, bean curd, fish, shellfish, yabby, crab, multitudinous fruits and combinations salted, pickled, stir-fried, marinated and cleverly enclosed in pastry of four separate types were spread forth.

Lin adopted a tactic which he had seen his grandmother use. He called forth the children and began to feed them tidbits. They opened their mouths like little birds and he found himself moved by their trust. He now understood Old Lady Lin's uncharacteristic generosity. The children were small, well plaited and charmingly dressed little gluttons and they disposed of a heroic amount of food.

Just when even the stoutest little boy was beginning to flag and turn green, the soup arrived and the end of the meal was announced. The children flopped quietly into the garden and lay under bushes, breathing heavily. They were very happy. And their Cousin Lin, instead of the monster they had been expecting, had turned out to be a Very Good Cousin indeed.

Due to his grandmother's cunning, Lin was still able to move as he was conducted around the holding. Water from the Campbells Creek provided for a string of fish ponds, in which golden carp swam lazily, on which lotus flowers floated, and near which water-loving plants flourished. The first tomatoes were ripening on the vine, along with pumpkins, melons and cucumbers. Lin nodded at a swathe of green salad vegetables growing alongside tilled rows of root vegetables. Several of the small children were installed to throw pebbles at intruding birds. Grapes ran eagerly along their wires. Soy beans flourished.

'We make the best vinegar,' observed Lin Tao. 'Both red

wine and all varieties of soy sauces and pickles. I have always thought that we should consider selling it on a broader market.' He looked sidelong at Lin Chung. Old Lady Lin would never hear of this idea but he might as well test it on the young master and see if he had an open mind.

'Where?' asked Lin.

'America,' said Lin Tao. 'Freight prices are lower now and we make a most superior product. If we could, say, send out samples to the best Chinese restaurants in San Francisco . . .'

'Do so,' said Lin. 'And try Darwin and Broome. The expense will be trifling and if it succeeds we will have another market. If it does not succeed we have lost little. This is a most well-ordered and attractive farm, Cousin. I congratulate you.'

Lin Tao muttered his thanks, looking down modestly.

'The stone fruit crop this year will be poor,' he confessed. 'And I fear that the codlin moth has got into the apples. This damp humid air encourages the insects. But we expect excellent results in the vine fruits and our flowers sell very well in Melbourne.'

'Expect a suitable bonus,' Lin told him. 'Now tell me, Cousin, about the establishment of this farm. How long have we been here?'

Pausing only to draw the young master's attention to an unusually beautiful cluster of wisteria against the dark, heavy drystone of the boundary wall, Lin Tao racked his brains for the farm's history as told to him by his own grandfather. Who would have thought the new master would want to know about history? Old Lady Lin only wanted to know about profit.

'I believe that it was about 1854, sir, when the goldfields were established. Our venerable ancestor purchased this land when the gold had been extracted, hoping to get enough water from the damaged bed of the Campbells Creek to nurture his vegetables for the summer, which here is very hot and dry, with north winds like a dragon's breath. Our ancestor was patient. The Lins have always been good farmers. He watched the seasons for a whole year before he began planting. Then he began with the easiest crops—cabbages and spinach. They grew well. Then he tried potatoes, onions and carrots. Suitably manured, they also grew well and he began to sell them to the miners in Castlemaine. Since then, we have been here, altering our crops to suit the climate and the change of fashions. When bad seasons came we had water, when crops were damaged by insects we found suitable sprays, and when fire came we fought the fire and then rebuilt and replanted. Since the Lin family was arranging for the education of our children, fewer of us stayed on the land and we have had to employ some local labour. This has had . . . difficulties,' said Lin Tao. Lin could imagine. 'But some of the children come home, and mostly we are self-sufficient. Now, master, if you have seen enough, perhaps we could return to the house.'

'Oh? Why?' asked Lin idly, hoping that food would not be mentioned to him again for a long time.

'Why, for the family council's judgments,' said Lin Tao. 'It has been a year since anyone came from Melbourne.'

'Of course,' agreed Lin, panicking inwardly. Family council? Who held family councils any more? He wasn't prepared for the weight of judgment to fall on his unworthy shoulders.

Then again, how bad could the sins of the Lin family be? It was unlikely to entail anything really scandalous, because such things would have been quietly dealt with by Uncle Tao and the formidable Great Aunt Wing. It was unlikely that any real problems would be left for the master's judgment. Not telling things to the master which might upset him was the bedrock of the Chinese family system.

So Lin mounted his throne again in the large, scented room, having offered suitable incense to the ancestral tablets, and received a bundle of accounts for perusal. He read through them. Neat. Well kept. No sign of any peculation and the farm was making a modest profit, which was astounding considering the liberal way in which it supplied the Lin family restaurants with fresh produce. The fancy goldfish were doing well though the market for lotus flowers meant that few lotus seeds were being packaged for sale. Lin asked a couple of questions, listened to the answers, and marked the accounts with his personal seal. There was no betraying sigh of relief from Uncle Tao. The accounts were fine.

Then a few defaulters were brought for his judgment. Great Aunt Wing, a haggard woman who had personally delivered, fed, dosed, instructed and spanked most of those present, clipped a small boy over the back of the head as she drove him forward. The child knelt. It was the small stout boy and he was still too full of banquet to be really daunted.

'Inattentive to his studies!' Great Aunt Wing denounced. 'Out every day watching birds!'

'Who speaks for the boy?' asked Lin, trying to remember the procedure.

Uncle Tao stepped forward. 'Knows all the birds by their songs,' he said. 'The ducks follow him. Hatched out pheasants' eggs under a broody hen, which everyone said could not be done. Looks after the quails. Just doesn't like books,' concluded Uncle Tao.

'I can have books about birds sent from the city,' said Lin. 'If I do that, will you read them?'

'Yes, honourable Cousin,' the boy whispered.

'And if you read the bird books then you will also read other books,' Lin said as magisterially as possible. 'Then you may be learned enough to write a book of your own. About birds.'

'Yes, honourable Cousin!' exclaimed the boy, who had never thought of education as being about anything important. 'I will!'

'See that you do,' said Lin, and waved the boy away.

'Idle, useless layabout called Fuchsia!' Great Aunt Wing ushered in one of the pretty girls. 'Won't wash dishes because it will dirty her hands! Won't go out into the sun because of her complexion! Thinks only of her appearance!'

'Who speaks for her?' asked Lin. The girl looked insolent and frightened. Pushed too far, Fuchsia might run for Melbourne, and what would happen to an unprotected Chinese girl in the city did not bear thinking about.

'She is gentle,' said Uncle Tao. 'She cares for the sick very carefully. She reads to me very fluently and knows a lot of poems by heart.'

'I may have a task for her,' said Lin. 'Let her stand by the door. If she suits, then she will have a profession and will be paid a salary and she can spend it on cosmetics if that is what she wishes.'

'Wants to marry a ghost!' snarled Great Aunt Wing, dragging a young man forward by his collar. She hit him over the back of the head so hard that she drove him to his knees. The young man looked up and stared straight into Lin's face, a breach of protocol.

'Who speaks for him?' asked Lin.

Uncle Tao was silent. No one, it appeared, spoke for this unfortunate young Lin.

'Speak for yourself, then,' said Lin. 'What is this about?'

'Maisie,' said the young man, sullenly. 'She wants to marry me and I want to marry her but they won't let me.'

'How old are you?'

'Twenty-two, Cousin.'

'We cannot stop you from marrying whoever you wish,' Lin said gently.

'But I am owed a share of the profits,' objected the young man. 'After all, it's not the first time this has happened. Remember Hu Ky, who became Annie Reilly!'

'Hu Ky?' asked Lin. Someone had said that name to him. Yes, that frightful Hu grandmother. Liely, she had said. Reilly to her Cantonese ear would be Liely. Lin shivered a little. What a woman. What a family. But he should not keep this young man on his knees so long.

'Come and sit at the table and we will talk privately. What is your name?'

'They call me Tommy,' said the young man reluctantly.

'And I am Lin Chung. Everyone else can go back to their duties,' said Lin, waving a dismissive hand. 'Except you, Miss Fuchsia. Sit down in that chair and wait for me, if you please.'

Great Aunt Wing scowled but collected the others and everyone left, closing the door.

'Tell me about Maisie,' said Lin quietly.

'Her father has a horse stud down on the Campbells Creek,' said Tommy, readily enough. 'She's his third daughter and he doesn't care much for her. His son is just about ready to take over the run when his father retires at the end of the year. The old man is going to his sister's at Shepparton. There won't be room for Maisie at her brother's house. His new wife can't stand her. She's a good girl,' protested Tommy passionately.

'I'm sure she is,' said Lin. 'Why not marry her and bring her here?'

'Because Great Aunt Wing would make her life hell,' said Tommy dispassionately. 'I've been working here all my life with the fish. If I could buy a bit of land down on the flats, I could

172

make ponds and breed trout. Good market for trout. And yabbies. Build a little house. I could get the land and the water rights for next to nothing.'

'How close to nothing?' asked Lin Chung.

'I reckon twenty pounds would do it. Maybe thirty for some building materials. We wouldn't want much to start with, Maisie knows that. I got the licence. We could get married tomorrow.'

'That,' said Lin, 'is an idea. Very well. I will personally advance you fifty pounds. This is not family money, you understand, but my own. If your Maisie is still of the same mind, you shall marry her tomorrow and bring her here to begin with, so that she may learn some Chinese ways and please you. You may have family labour to dig your ponds and that will give you enough capital to build a little house. In return for your past labour you shall have provisions from the farm for five years, free of charge. I will undertake to explain the situation to Great Aunt and she will not make trouble.'

'You're a braver man than I am,' said Tommy, tongue loosened by shock.

'I trained on Grandmother,' said Lin. 'Now, tell me all about Hu Ky and Mr Reilly.'

'Honoured Cousin, after such a generous gift I will tell you anything you like. But the Venerable Ones know more about it than me.'

The boy was clearly itching to get away to his Maisie and it would be cruel to keep him.

'Off you go,' said Lin. He was getting the hang of the dismissive gesture. 'Send in Great Aunt Wing and ask for some tea and salted pine nuts.'

'And me, Cousin?' asked Fuchsia, from her footstool by the door.

173

'I will find you something to do which will not soil your hands,' said Lin. 'Stay out of Great Aunt's way, and when she has left this room, you come back.'

Fuchsia squeaked her thanks and escaped as Great Aunt Wing came in, escorting a boy with tea.

Lin waited until the old woman was seated and said slowly, 'I have solved your problem with Tommy. I will finance his venture with the trout personally. He will not be a drain on the farm's finances and I think a little exile might be good for him. And did not the ancients say that "nothing must come between a man and his wife"?'

Great Aunt made a complicated movement which might have been a sitting-down flounce, but said nothing. Lin felt a little dizzy. So far, he was getting away with this.

'And Fuchsia will be well occupied and will certainly work hard in the profession I have in mind. Now, Great Aunt, tell me all about Hu Ky and Mr Reilly.'

'It was long ago,' said Great Aunt. 'During the Gold Rush. The respectable daughter of a respectable merchant was given in marriage—proper marriage, mind, not concubinage—to a Mr Reilly who came here as a miner. He found gold and was comfortable and able to support a wife. And he spoke Cantonese, having been a sailor. Alice's father deemed him appropriate and his descendants are still here. Why?'

'Old Mrs Hu mentioned a sister and I wondered if perhaps there was a connection. The Hu family didn't steal that gold, Great Aunt. I did a settlement with Mr Hu and it wasn't them. Therefore I am searching, very late in the day, for four hundred ounces of gold which went missing in 1857 and I also need to discover the fate of the couriers. There were four, led by someone called Sung, or so Great Great Uncle said.'

'I never did think it was the Hu family,' exclaimed Great

Aunt Wing, slapping her brocaded knee. 'I was friends with some of the Hu girls before they left for Melbourne and they all said that their ancestors hadn't stolen it, that they also had searched and no one knew what became of it, or of the bearers. What a mystery!' Great Aunt Wing appeared to have forgotten about Tommy, which was all to the good. 'There were four couriers, so they say, led by a scholar turned herbalist called Sung Ma. If it wasn't the Hu family, then the Ah camp was closest to the Moonlight road. I wonder if any of them are still alive? Well, Great Nephew, we will help as we can. Should we recover that much gold I am sure that you will allow us a reasonable sum for new pig pens.'

'You shall have pig pens which will be the envy of the neighbourhood,' promised Lin. 'I am taking the wagon into Castlemaine tomorrow morning and Fuchsia will come with me. Now, how much notice will you need for Tommy's marriage feast? And I am sure that, since the girl is a stranger and will not be staying in your domain, you will treat Tommy's Maisie as you would an honoured guest,' he said without emphasis.

There was a nerve-wracking pause during which Great Aunt Wing stared straight into Lin Chung's eyes. He did not blink. Then she gave a resigned nod.

'The feast will be ordered as you wish for tomorrow night, Great Nephew,' she said quietly. 'The young woman will not be able to complain of her treatment here. And if you are really intending to travel in the wagon tomorrow, it must be cleansed. Its last load was horse dung. I will send Fuchsia to you instantly,' she added, making it perfectly clear that she knew what he had arranged with the young Miss. The ability to know exactly what skulduggery was being concocted under her roof was a sixth sense of all old Chinese ladies, Lin knew. He took a sip of tea and nodded in return. He was unexpectedly weary. Being head of a family was exhausting. He arranged that Fuchsia would accompany him on the morrow, fending off the young woman's questions. He allowed a small cousin to conduct him to the seldom used, elaborate guest house, availed himself of a mineral water bath, and went to sleep, along with the rest of the farm, as the sun went down.

Phryne caught herself as she was falling asleep into her glass of wine. Old Bill Gaskin was sweeping the floor with short, stabbing strokes. His broom whispered, unlike Mr Harrison's voice. The bar was closed, but as a bona fide traveller, Phryne could sit there all night and before Mr Harrison got to anything like a peroration it might well be dawn. She forced her concentration to a point and was rewarded at once.

'Then there was doctors—well, they called themselves doctors—they were a bodgy lot! There was old Doctor Andersen, he was locked up because he took some bit of some poor kid's stomach and kept it—kept it in a jar! Then there was a bloke called Beecham who guaranteed to embalm a body so that it would never rot, not never. They called him the Egyptian Professor because he was always talking about the old Gyppoes. Dad said he was as mad as a cut snake.'

Phryne dared not interrupt. Tempting as it was to take this ruffian by the throat and squeeze gently until he told her everything she needed to know, this would probably mean that he would lose his place in his reminiscences and not for anything would Phryne agree to listen to them all again. She was making a mental note to address the League of Nations on the subject of including 'listening to Mr Harrison for more than ten seconds' as cruel and unusual punishment under their Geneva Convention when at last he concluded his sentence and told her what she wanted to know.

'Doc Mercer took over from the Professor when he died suddenly in 1858. He told my dad that there were all sorts of stuffed things in the house, all meant to be willed to some university somewhere, but the old Prof never made a will. So Doc Mercer knocked them down to a travelling show for a few shillings. Even the stuffed crocodile. Dunno what they wanted with that.'

'And the name of the show . . .?' insinuated Phryne, a delicate whisper which the addled old person might decide had come from his own mind, if he had one.

'Carter's, they had the bushranger. Said he was Black Douglas but he wasn't. Reason I know was, Black Douglas escaped from jail and started a little sheep farm out Mansfield way. So their Wild Colonial Boy wasn't Douglas. I always thought it was a fake anyway. It was shiny. Corpses ain't shiny as a rule. But we had bushrangers in them days! We had Mad Dog Morgan—he was a brutal sort of bloke. Only time he wasn't thinking of murder was when he was asleep, and then he was dreamin' of it.'

Young Billy Gaskin brought Mr Harrison another beer and Miss Fisher more coffee, another bottle of wine, a sympathetic smile and a selection of grapes, biscuits and several small cheeses, compliments of the kitchen, which was now closing.

'How fascinating,' lied Phryne. 'Doctors . . .' she allowed the phrase to trail away.

'Doctor Beamish said there'd be hell to pay,' blurred Mr Harrison. 'If it got into the general population.'

'What?' asked Phryne, her lips close to his ear.

'Leprosy,' exclaimed Mr Harrison. 'That was it! Beamish said that there was leprosy in those dirty Chinese. He set up a lepers' camp. There weren't many, he said, but it was another reason to get them off the fields. Drive 'em over the Murray! Filthy devils!'

Fairly soon, Phryne knew, the rein on her temper was going to break and she was not sure what she was going to do. It would, she knew, be worth watching.

'Murder . . .' she insinuated again.

'They was dangerous places, the goldfields. They used to have a cartload of bodies some nights, especially Sat'd'y night. No work on Sunday so every man Jack got stinking drunk. The beer was good here even then, you see! And no one to say what happened or who woodened 'em over the bonce with a shovel. All sorts of fights to watch if you liked fights, the lascars and the Jamaicans, the proddy and the bog Irish, even the Chinks fought each other a couple of times. Don't know what about, some Chink reason. That How Qua Ah Kim, the interpreter, he told my dad that one lot were from the five provinces and the other lot from the four provinces and they hated each other. Laugh? The old man nearly died to watch 'em tearing each other's pigtails off.'

Phryne spared a moment to be exceedingly glad that Old Mr Harrison was no longer with us. She was confident that he was burning in hell.

'Then the unclaimed bodies used to go to Prof Beecham to be embalmed, you know, in case someone could come and identify them, but after he died, Doc Mercer sent them into the undertakers in Bendigo. They did a very nice corpse, I have to say. Not dry and shiny like the Professor's.'

'Well, Mister Harrison, it has been very kind of you to talk to me so long,' said Phryne, seeing that the old blighter's glass was at last empty. He grabbed for her arm, missed, and tried again. Old Bill Gaskin stopped sweeping and undid Mr Harrison's fingers.

'Wait, I haven't told you about the Stockade,' he protested.

'That's enough for tonight,' said Bill. 'You could talk the leg off an iron pot, you could.'

'My dad was there! He saw them build the fence out of logs and hoist the Eureka flag! Every man took an oath of loyalty to the Southern Cross.'

'Yair, and betrayed it. Your dad run like a rabbit as soon as the soldiers came,' observed Bill Gaskin dispassionately. 'You run your forge as a non union shop and you squeeze your workers till the pips squeak. Eureka, my arse,' said Bill. 'Beg pardon, Miss. And as for them poor bloody Chinese, Madge's hubby's grandpa said they was nice quiet people and he always camped next to them because they wouldn't cut his throat and pinch his gold while he slept. Unlike your brave Eurekas. Come on, you old pest, give the lady's ears a rest.'

'It was the most glorious moment in Australia's history!'

'Very nice,' said Phryne. 'But that is well known. Good night, Mr Harrison. Billy? Can you and your admirable dad see Mr Harrison home?'

'Sure thing,' said Young Billy, who read a lot of Sexton Blake. He helped the old man to his feet and Bill Gaskin led him away, still mumbling about the Eureka Stockade. As he reached the door his voice was raised in song.

'Over the border to rife and to plunder

'Over the border with Morgan the bold!

'Over the border, a terrible blunder

'For over the border poor Morgan lies cold.'

The last line was almost a sob, and was followed by a light curse as Mr Harrison tripped over the step on the way out.

The pathos was undeniable, and hardhearted Phryne laughed into her final glass of wine for the evening. She was about to rise and put herself to bed when the hair on the back of her neck rose instead. She had the strongest feeling of being watched. She looked around and saw only a couple of young men, one fair and built like a wrestler, and the other smaller and darker. But young men usually looked at Phryne.

She went to bed in the rose-patterned room and slept like a baby with nothing on its conscience.

Random Thoughts of the Vagrant Weed Sung Ma.

Five hates four
Four hates five
Neither wants
the other alive.

CHAPTER TWELVE

*When you see a rich man's wife shaking her head
over the thriftlessness of the poor because they
do not save, pity the lady's ignorance; but do
not irritate the poor by repeating her nonsense
to them.*

George Bernard Shaw
*The Intelligent Woman's Guide
to Socialism and Capitalism*

Second Cousin Kong took up the reins. Fuchsia was lifted up
beside him. Lin sat on the end of the bench seat and the horse,
Little Flower, glanced back and sneered. Lin had only seen an
expression like that on a camel. Little Flower presumably lacked
the camel's power to spit a half-digested glob of grass into a
human's face, but she looked as if that was her dearest wish.
She was a big, raw-boned, wall-eyed, chestnut beast, awkward-
ness on hairy hooves.

'Why this horse?' asked Lin as they jogged into the road.

'Because she is strong but no one would ever steal her,'
said Fuchsia. 'What do you have in mind for me, Cousin?'

'Nothing which need concern you,' said Lin absently.
'I must examine three blazed trees. I need to find the Imperial
Hotel, where we are leaving a message, and then I need to

visit the Chinese people who still live in Castlemaine.'

'That means Union Street,' said Second Cousin Kong, rumbling into life. 'There's still a temple there, and a priest, and a few old people.'

'Good. We have the parcels?'

'Yes, Cousin.' Second Cousin Kong was the strongest man on the farm. His mother said that the gods who had given him all that muscle had economised on brain, but he was the only man who could lift a cast sow back onto her trotters and he usually rode with the market cart, in case of any trouble. With Fuchsia aboard there might well be trouble. The young woman was wearing her best summer dress and a wide-brimmed straw hat, but her charms were not extinguished under it. Fuchsia was loaded with what Phryne would call 'it', and in Castlemaine she was a total exotic. The young woman needed an occupation that would take her off the farm and into a relatively lively place, without too much danger into which her inexperience of the Big Bad World would conduct her. Second Cousin Kong would at least see that any errors of judgment didn't turn into disasters.

Lin looked at the landscape as they bounced and tottered into the Moonlight road. Three eucalyptus trees. Standing alone. He got down and ran his fingers over the marks. They certainly were characters in the old script. He was sure about the first, the ideogram for 'pig'. The next tree appeared to be called 'salt', and the third 'black'. Cryptic. He got back into the cart and Second Cousin Kong flicked a rein at Little Flower, who grunted but began to move. This was a beautiful place, thought Lin as they lurched ahead.

Then he decided that the Lin family could do with a new cart, one, perhaps, with four matching and, above all, circular wheels. A rich place, he thought. Lush, deep soil, well watered by the many creeks and springs. Truly an earthly paradise. Where was its snake?

Phryne arose betimes, dressed soberly and went down to breakfast in the Imperial's breakfast room. In an attempt to lighten the mood of the morning-after breakfaster, it had been simply decorated with whitewash above the panelling and there were flowers on each table, a little handful of pansies or grape hyacinths. Nothing strongly scented or too bright. Beautiful.

Phryne collected a large breakfast from the buffet: local bacon, eggs from contented hens scrambled with cream and chives, grilled tomatoes, toast and a pot of tea. She longed for coffee and wondered where she might find some which wasn't out of a bottle with a djinn on the front, and resolved to go for a walk later. Perhaps the coffee palace made good coffee.

To sum up, she thought, forking in sublime scrambled eggs: the body seems to have been one left unclaimed on the goldfields, which produced a reasonable number of unclaimed bodies. The fact that he had been shot indicated a murder, but that did not seem like an uncommon occurrence either, what with bushrangers, quarrels, and what Mr Harrison called 'Sat'd'y night'. The corpse was then mummified by the eccentric Professor Beecham using Egyptian methods and then sold as unclaimed goods along with the stuffed crocodile when the Professor died suddenly; this placed the murder before 1858, when the Professor ceased operations. There was every reason to believe that the mummy was Carter's Travelling Miracles and Marvels Show's Wild Colonial Boy. And he was not, according to Mr Harrison's dad, the bushranger Black Douglas, because he had retired after his escape from prison and devoted his remaining years to good works and the cultivation of sheep at Mansfield.

So, who had he been?

A good question to which Dot might have some more answers. The body had then been sold to Luna Park after Carter's had gone bust. Then it had hung unnoticed in the Ghost Train until a foolish woman had grabbed its foot. And someone to whom that corpse was important was in Australia, actively trying to discourage Phryne from investigating it. Important enough to send whizbangs by mail and try to run Dot down.

Phryne finished her breakfast and decided to find a telephone. She left a sixpence under her plate, gathered her handbag and light coat, and went toward the desk, where she noticed an elegant figure. A young Chinese man in a cassock. He was handing over a message and asking the clerk to be sure to give it to the Hon. Miss Fisher as soon as possible.

Phryne leaned against the wall and fanned herself against a wave of heat. That was Lin Chung in that long black gown. Better she should not greet him, since he was clearly in disguise. Every adolescent yearning she had ever had towards curates rushed through her. Lin was leaving, his body willowy and slender under the strict geometry of the robe. What was he doing in disguise?

Phryne fished out a handkerchief and mopped her brow. Tonight, she promised herself, tonight she needed to get her hands on Lin Chung, or she might actually melt like a chocolate bar left in the sun.

She shook herself into order. Stern daughter of the voice of God, Duty, she reminded herself. First, the telephone, and then the note.

Annie, the desk clerk, pointed out the panelled alcove in which the Imperial hid its public telephone and gave Phryne a folded piece of handmade paper.

'A Chinese Father left this for you, my lady,' she said, so overcome that her film magazine lay unregarded on the desk and her toffee had dislodged from her palate. 'He's from a mission in Canton and he's here to see after the old Chinks in Union Street. He's very dreamy!'

'And a very virtuous person,' said Phryne repressively. The clerk blushed. Phryne walked into the telephone cubicle and prepared for the arduous task of persuading a partially deaf and obtuse operator that she really did mean to stay in this close, airless confinement until she, Phryne, was connected with her, Phryne's, house in St Kilda, even though it would mean that the operator had to bend and even if she had just filed her nails.

The operator in Castlemaine was a brisk young woman with a singsong delivery and commendable efficiency. The Melbourne operator was of the old school and considerable time and pennies were wasted in persuading her to pull out some plugs and stick in some others. All the time Phryne's mind was running on steamily carnal lines and she was rather relieved when Mr Butler's magisterial tones echoed through the apparatus.

'Castlemaine calling,' said the brisk young woman, with a relieved note in her voice. 'Your Melbourne connection, caller!'

Phryne waited until the operator had clicked out of the line. Listening in to phone calls was a recognised perk of the profession.

'Mr Butler, how are you? Any trouble?'

'One suspicious parcel, Miss Fisher, which on Mr Li's advice we put into a bucket of water. When the bubbles subsided we found it contained a couple of fireworks, a trigger made of a fulminate cap and another note requiring us to desist from our investigation.'

'Well done, Mr B.'

'Miss Dot has some news for you, Miss. If you would wait just one moment . . .?'

'Miss?' Dot distrusted telephones and tended to shout. After all, Miss Phryne was seventy-eight miles away. 'Are you all right?'

'Certainly, though my ears have been grossly abused by a lot of very long stories. Have you got any more news for me?'

'Yes, Miss. That Roderick who's pursuing your sister, he's a blond bloke who looks like a wrestler and he's not a nice person, Miss, but we haven't seen him. And we worked out the tattoo, you know, on the poor fellow's arm? Miss Eliza is real good at heraldry.' Dot was proud of her new word and used it again. 'The heraldic crest says he was a marquess and Miss Eliza says it's the coat of arms of her friend Lady Alice Harborough. They had an ancestor who went to the goldfields and never came back and Miss Eliza thinks it's him. He was the heir.'

'Who succeeded to the title?' asked Phryne.

'It fell into . . .' Dot was consulting a note, Phryne heard the rustle. 'Desuetude. The distant heir who succeeded was Lady Alice's great grandfather.'

'Who went with this poor boy to the goldfields, Dot? Or did he go alone?'

'Don't know. Miss Eliza is trying to find out. She's going to the State Library today to look at Debrett. Or was it Burke? Anyway, if you call back tonight, we might know more.'

'Very good, Dot. Do we know the young man's name?'

'Thomas Beaconsfield,' said Dot.

'Oh,' said Phryne, abruptly enlightened. Mr Harrison's dad's friends. Thomas Beaconsfield and a bloke called Chumley, who had left the field one night without a farewell, leaving Mr Harrison senior and his mate Duncan with a good find in their abandoned claim. Well, well. This was the point in a problem when all the answers started dropping down like manna from heaven.

'That's very interesting, Dot. Tell Eliza to keep digging and I'll call again tonight.'

Phryne hung up. So. The plot, instead of thickening, had thinned. And about time too, she thought ungratefully. The young aristocrat who had vanished one night with his dearest friend Chumley had been murdered, shot between the eyes at close range. Possibly by a stranger, possibly by his best mate, who then presumably went back to England, Home and Beauty with the gold. Because the quarrel would have been over the gold. The two Englishmen dug and dug, said Mr Harrison, but only a bit of colour, and then when they were gone, his dad and Duncan had struck it rich in their abandoned trench.

Of course, perhaps Mr Harrison senior and his fellow miner had done away with both of these young men, and only Thomas Beaconsfield had been found and mummified. It was not as though there weren't a lot of nice pre-dug graves on that goldfield. And after the gold was gone and the landscape had been allowed to return to cultivation, the holes would have been filled in and ploughed over and all trace of them obliterated.

A perfect murder, and then Miss Fisher had to poke her nose into it.

Both Lady Alice, whom Eliza had been sure she had seen at Luna Park, and Roderick the Wrestler were prime candidates for the bomb maker. Phryne had no doubt that a well brought up, literate socialist who worked in the East End would be able to find some freedom-loving anarchist who would teach her how to make a bomb. And Roderick doubtless had friends amongst engineers, and the sort of sense of humour that puts fireworks into the letterboxes of the elderly and timid. But which one? Eliza loathed the brute boy and loved the lady, but Eliza's was not a reliable judgment . . . time and further research would have to tell.

Phryne unfolded her note. The paper had been hand-pressed and was scented with jasmine.

'Silver Lady, I have yearned to see you. I will call at midnight. At your window.'

That was enterprising of Lin Chung. Phryne would watch his future progress, hopefully to her window, with great interest.

Meanwhile, coffee, and a visit to the newspaper office. The *Mount Alexander Mail* had been operating at the time when the brave policeman Thomas Cooke had stopped the riot at Golden Point. Presumably, it had archives.

They might even know where they were. Mostyn Street ho, thought Phryne.

Lin Chung alighted outside four tumbledown houses in Union Street and brushed falling peppercorns off his cassock. Second Cousin Kong knocked at the first door and it sagged open, missing a hinge.

It was dark within. Lin called out 'Hello?' in Cantonese and heard something stirring. Second Cousin Kong found a curtain and drew it aside.

The room was bare of any comfort. The house was a badly built bark shack off which most of the bark had peeled. The floor was of beaten earth. The roof had holes in several places and slimy pools showed where the rain had fallen. Lin gestured and Second Cousin Kong reached down and lifted an old, old Chinese lady and hefted her without effort into the light.

His reward was a feeble blow across the nose and a faint scream of outrage.

'Who are you?'

'I am Lin Chung,' said Lin. 'Adoptive Grandmother, I am here to find you a better place to live.'

'Why?' The old eyes were pearled.

'Because it is my wish,' said Lin Chung. This seemed to comfort the old lady and she relaxed in Second Cousin Kong's embrace.

'Try the next house,' ordered Lin, and Fuchsia pushed at the door. This one opened and revealed a bare, swept room where an old man was drinking tea and reading a scroll book. Scriptures of some kind, Lin assumed. Behind him, against the far wall, was an altar with the usual deities and a meagre single joss stick burning in a brass bowl. Kwan Yin smiled blandly on this tiny offering. Under the stand for the incense was a large box in which the little scrolls with wishes on them were placed. It was almost full and must have been there for many years. The old man looked up in surprise, allowing his scroll to roll up under his lifted hand.

'Adoptive Grandfather, may I lay this woman in your room while I arrange for her future? I am Lin Chung, and I have funds to disburse for better housing and care.'

'You have managed to get her out of her hovel!' The old man leapt to his feet. 'More than I could do, Adoptive Grandson. Though I never tried using an ox,' he added, sighting up the slopes of Second Cousin Kong.

'Oxen are useful,' rumbled Kong, laying the old woman in her wrappings down on a clean patch of floor.

'Are you the priest?' asked Lin. The old man bowed.

'I am Ching Ta, at your service. A Follower of the Five Forbiddens. With our state of extreme poverty, this has not been too onerous.'

'Are there other Chinese people in this street?'

'The Ah sisters in the next house,' said the old man, eyeing the bundles which Second Cousin Kong was carrying into the temple. 'Old Man Lo and his wife and brother next to them. We are the last. When they are all dead I shall pack up this temple and go to Bendigo, where I have relatives. Do I smell lacquered duck?'

'You do. Come with me to these other people and give me the benefit of your advice. Would it be better to buy a new house and have the people live together, or shall I have these houses repaired? Rebuilt, in the case of the old lady's shack.'

'They would not be happy living together,' opined the old man. 'The old woman on my floor, Old Lady Chang, she was a concubine—well, that's putting it politely. The Ah sisters detest her. She can't stand Old Man Lo, because he was once her . . . well. Better to repair and provide some care for them. The Sam Yup Benevolent Society sends us sacks of rice and we still have some money to buy vegetables and sometimes a little meat.'

'So you are Sam Yup? The Lin family are Sze Yup, the four provinces,' said Lin. 'We are by way of being hereditary enemies, Adoptive Grandfather.'

'Yes, so better you just pass as Father Chung, don't you think?' Ching Ta was not going to allow a few centuries of feud to get between him and that lacquered duck. Not to mention allowing this benevolent enemy to acquire merit by improving the lives of the indigent. 'What we don't have is money for medicine or new clothes. The Ah sisters haven't been out of the house since July because they tore their only good dress.'

'That can be amended. I shall speak to a builder today, and also arrange for new clothes to be bought and repairs to be done. You could also do with some furniture,' added Lin. 'A carpenter shall make some for you.'

'No need,' said the priest. 'If we have funds, then the ox, the cart and the young lady can go and buy ready-made at Niebuhr's General Merchants. We can at least get Old Lady Chang a bed of her own. I've been trying to get her to leave that shack and come and sleep, at least, in the temple, but she accused me of having designs on her person and said that she had quarrelled with all the gods and wasn't going to sleep with any of them unless they paid her.'

'I am sure that conversation with such a witty lady will be improving,' said Lin politely. 'Miss Fuchsia, if you please, come here. These people are now in your care. I will hire cleaners and a cook; you are not a housekeeper. You will purchase suitable furniture and clothes, serve tea, and read aloud. You will help with tasks like embroidery and you will listen to tales of the old days and I will pay you five shillings a week. Will you accept this task?'

Fuchsia thought about it. She would have to come into Castlemaine, that haven of forbidden delights, every day. She would have money to spend and a position of her own. Lin could hear her contrasting this with a lifetime of having her arms up to the elbow in washing-up water, confined to the farm under Great Aunt Wing's disapproving eye. She made her decision. It was no contest, really.

'You do me too much honour, Cousin,' she murmured, casting down her eyes in the proper fashion. Ching Ta beamed.

'A very virtuous maiden,' he decided. 'Old Man Lo will be delighted. He loves poetry and he can't read now that his eyes are so bad. Come and meet the others,' he said, and Lin and Fuchsia followed him.

Three of the little houses were basically sound, Lin decided, needing only a few bits of carpentry and the odd new window latch or door knob. They had been kept as clean as possible but they were bare and sad, lacking even the calendar picture of a smiling girl which enlivened even the garages of the west. He could send a selection of cheap scroll pictures for the walls, once they had been made sound and freshly whitewashed. He had a box of them in the silk shop, to be given away free with large purchases. Two days' work would make these little houses very comfortable, he thought. Old Lady Chang would need a new house, and that would have to be built with all speed as he did not know how long Ching Ta would be able to cope with her. He mentioned the problem to Fuchsia.

'Take her back to Great Aunt,' suggested Fuchsia sweetly. 'Until her new house is ready.'

Her tone suggested a certain underlying glee. Lin decided to take no official notice of it. It was a good solution.

The Ah sisters would not come out, telling the good Father Chung from behind the door that they were delighted to see him and would welcome him suitably if they could. Old Man Lo grumbled about how long it had taken the Sam Yup Society to send any help but was mollified by the promise of poetry.

Then Fuchsia, Lin Chung and Second Cousin Kong rode into Castlemaine proper to purchase a few households' worth of goods.

Only ten minutes into their negotiations with Niebuhr's, Home Furnishings, Lin was very glad that he had picked Fuchsia. She knew exactly what she wanted, was not daunted by the size of the task, and was not going to take no for an answer. Niebuhr's clerk had never met anyone like her and fell in with her every wish, enunciated in her clear little voice from under the shady hat.

There was more to a household than a few beds and chairs, Lin found. There were also buckets and pots and cups and saucers and bowls and cutlery and rush mats and linen and tablecloths and sheets and mattresses and curtains. There was also soap and towels and embroidery silks and powder and hairpins. Two loads went back to the little houses before Fuchsia was satisfied. Lin did wonder why she had insisted on a trestle table and a lot of cheap folding chairs, but assumed that inside that glossy black head resided the same organising genius shared by Great Aunt Wing and Grandmama Lin.

Lin loitered outside M'Creery and Hopkin, the drapers, as Fuchsia worked her magic on the astounded Miss Lobban. It was amazing. Yesterday she had been an insolent, frightened, rebellious girl. Now she was a competent woman. Remarkable what power and responsibility can do, Lin thought, considering what it had done for him. His thoughts returned to the words of the aged and unpleasant Old Lady Hu. Look for the couriers by the third blazed tree on the Moonlight road, she had said. That was very close to where the Lin farm was now. Perhaps the solution was near at hand. That still did not explain how the scholar-herbalist Sung Ma, who must have been trusted, and three other servants had vanished without a trace.

He saw himself reflected in the window. The cassock suited him. It was very close to a Chinese scholar's gown, which he had never worn. A hand on his shoulder made him turn around.

'Good morning!' exclaimed a stout, well-dressed gentleman in identical dress. 'I noticed you from across the road and I believe that you are taking charge of those poor Chinese people in Union Street. Father John,' he introduced himself. 'From Saint Michael's.'

'Chung,' said Lin, praying to a variety of gods for guidance and protection. 'From Canton.'

'I don't know any of the mission people,' said Father John. Lin thanked his lucky stars. 'But they say that the situation in China is very bad now.'

'So bad that my little mission was dissolved and I was sent home,' said Lin. 'I am attached to Saint Saviour's in Brunswick. I am travelling around, tending to the remnant Chinese people.'

'But, Father Chung, I have some doubts about those people,' said Father John, leaning closer. He was scented with pipe smoke and starch. 'I believe that some of them cling stubbornly to their pagan ways.'

'They are very old,' said Lin gently. 'As old people go back to the language they spoke as children, they also go back to old superstitions. We must care for their bodies,' said Lin, remembering sermons from a hundred school chapels. 'God will find a safe place for their souls.'

'I believe that you are a good man,' said Father John. He had made up his mind. 'If there is anything which we can provide, ask for it. You will find me in the church,' he said over his shoulder as he strode away. 'Tea every day at four for the schoolchildren whose parents are working. And you might like to come to Sung Eucharist at ten on Sunday.'

And there goes another good man, thought Lin, watching the straight back and determined stride. If the devil came to Castlemaine, he would get such a belting with that vicar's umbrella that he'd think himself back in hell.

Fuchsia emerged in a flurry with an extraordinary number of bags.

'Cousin, that was the vicar!' she exclaimed. 'He stopped to talk to you!'

'And we had a nice conversation about souls,' said Lin. 'Have you finished the shopping?'

'Yes, for the moment,' she answered. 'I need some real green tea and medicines from the Health and Harmony Medicine and Tea Import Company in Bendigo. That's where

Great Aunt Wing gets her tea, herbs and pearl pills from. Miss Lobban allowed me to telephone an order to them and they will put the parcel on the ten twenty-five. I have used your credit freely, Cousin. I hope all is as you wish.'

'You are doing beautifully,' Lin reassured her. 'I want to talk to the old people about the old days, and I want to find out some secrets which they may know. How do you suggest that we arrange this?'

Fuchsia blushed with pleasure. No one had ever consulted her opinion before. She thought before she answered.

'Presenting all these new things will please the old people, but it will also upset their day,' she said. 'The rest of the morning will have to be spent in arranging and rearranging the new furniture and then in washing and arraying themselves in their new clothes. We will need Second Cousin Kong to move heavy things around. Perhaps we might put on Little Flower's nosebag and put her behind the houses so that she will be out of the way and doesn't get a chance to kick anyone. The space under the pepper trees in front of the houses is very suitable for what I have in mind. If you would like to go away for four hours, most admired and generous Cousin Chung, I think I can arrange a sight for you which will please your eyes and meet your purposes.'

'I shall go to the art gallery,' said Lin. 'And cultivate my taste for beauty.'

He bowed and walked away.

In the sixteenth year of the reign of the glorious Emperor Lord of the Dragon Throne Kwong Sui of the Ching Dynasty, Cold Dew, ninth month, sixteenth day.

. . .

To the respected Uncle from the errant nephew Sung Ma, greetings in haste. I have been given one more task to perform, Uncle, and because it is for the Lin family who have been so good to me, I shall perform it. Then I shall return for your welcome. Bid my young sister Mai expect me at her husband's residence in Canton before the end of the summer. I have already booked my passage on the SS Annabel Wilson, *leaving Melbourne on the 29th of July 1857, solar calendar.*

The one whose strength is no longer bitter, Sung Ma.

CHAPTER THIRTEEN

Despite ten years' exile and isolation
The sight of a dimple caught him unawares
Nothing should be more feared than this
    damnation
How many lives are wrecked by women's snare?

Chu Shi, translated by Lin Yutang

Phryne occupied her morning with a saunter and a cup of coffee at the Midland Hotel. It was reasonable coffee, though not the dangerous inky beverage which her caffeine-addicted body really required. She mused on Thomas Beaconsfield and his strange fate. If Phryne at Luna Park had not grabbed the boot of what she thought was a carnival dummy, a thing she had never done before, the lost heir to the marquisate of Harborough would have remained forever lost.

And that was what someone had in mind. And the question was, why?

What did it matter? Even if one of the great grandparents of one of the noble families had proved to be a murderer, this was not a bar to acceptability in polite society. Phryne recalled several titled people positively revelling in the appalling things their ancestors had done during the Hundred Years' War or, even more recently, reciting the Dirty Doings at the Crimea starring Sir Francis Bingham, later Lord Lucan, which she had had inflicted on her by one of Cardigan's relatives, was it? She regretted that she had not paid more attention to ancestral gossip while she had been living in a miasma of it. As far as Phryne could remember, every family had a least one black sheep of whom they were secretly rather proud, whether it was for worshipping Satan in the Hellfire Club, losing all the family property at vingt-et-un, debauching dairymaids or marrying Gaiety girls. She supposed that the General Earl Haig could not be considered a black sheep. He was just an ordinary monster who killed all those young men . . . The aristocracy would forgive each other anything except shooting a fox.

So why bother about dead—very dead—Thomas Beaconsfield now? Who cared if someone killed him in 1857?

Where, as Jack Robinson would say, was the money? Cui bono?

Phryne ordered another cup, asking the server to treble the amount of coffee and heat the water until it was really boiling and she would happily pay a sixpence.

There were three possibilities, she decided. An inheritance, an insurance claim or a bet. It should be possible to find out about the will of the late Thomas Beaconsfield, assuming he had made one and assuming that it was on record. St Katherine's House in London would have it and someone could find it for Phryne for the fee of one shilling. If there had been an insurance policy then Lady Alice Harborough would possibly know. Phryne had a vague feeling that some scandal attached to that name. No, it was the Marchioness, presumably Lady Alice's mother, who had—

done something. Run away with the chauffeur? No, worse. She had sold her jewellery and joined a mission. She had gone to Africa to nurse lepers and her husband, the Marquess of Harborough, had filed for divorce. A passion for good causes clearly ran in the female line of the Harboroughs.

Which was entirely unrelated to what Phryne was supposed to be considering. If the bone of contention or benefit of some sort had been a bet, it would seem to be safely locked in the past except, again, there must be some reason why a living person was trying to block Phryne's research. Didn't they put bets on the book at White's? And how could one gain access to it? No, she struck that idea from her mental notepad. It was too silly. Inheritance or insurance. Both would need research which could not be done in Castlemaine.

And why should she search for old newspapers when that policeman—was his name Laurence?—was supposed to be doing it for her? It was far too nice a day to sit in an archive. Most of which, in Phryne's experience, were under the ground and had not been dusted since the declaration of the Boer War.

Phryne braved the Imperial's imprisoned telephone again with a fresh purse of pennies and persisted until she gained not only Russell Street Police Station itself but her old friend Detective Inspector 'call me Jack' Robinson.

'Miss Fisher,' he said gloomily. Phryne could envisage his unremarkable countenance and smell the dank scent of police station tea, which in other places would have been classified as 'drain cleaner' or 'tar derivative'.

'Jack dear,' Phryne began. 'I'm in Castlemaine. Just wondered if anything had turned up on that bit of newspaper found in the mummy.'

'Oh, yes, Miss Fisher, it was the *Mount Alexander Mail* all right.'

'Good. The man's name is, in all probability, the Lord Thomas Beaconsfield, son of the Marquess of Harborough. He vanished one night in 1857 from the goldfields along with his mate. All I know about the mate is that he was a pink-faced lad called Chumley.'

'And you found this by . . .?' he trailed the question. She could hear him making notes. Jack Robinson was always supplied with at least a dozen very sharp pencils.

'Listening for half the night to an amazing local bore. I have, however, his dad's reminiscences of the goldfields, which contain, among other things, this information. The dad in question, one Jim Harrison, moved into the abandoned Beaconsfield claim and struck it moderately rich.'

'How did Beaconsfield end up as an Egyptian mummy?' asked Jack Robinson, reflecting that it was a question he had never asked before in a lifetime of asking questions.

'One Professor Beecham, who embalmed unclaimed corpses, seems to have done it, and then the body was sold with his effects to Carter's Travelling Miracles and Marvels Show. He became the Wild Colonial Boy, to be sold later to Luna Park as a rather unconvincing cowboy. Come to think of it, the original moleskins had TB embroidered inside the waistband. You can check.'

'Good. Now, why is anyone interested in him in 1928?'
Phryne sighed.

'A very good question, and one to which I do not have the answer.'

'Hmm,' said Robinson.

'However, it is probable that a relative, Lady Alice Harborough, is in Australia. And also that Roderick Cholmondeley, heir of the Duke of Dunstable, may be the person sending my household surprise packages.'

'I'll look into that,' said Robinson. 'Already found out a bit about the Roderick boy. He's been making enquiries up and down about an Amelia Gascoigne, who kept a boarding house in Port. Hired a private detective, who mentioned it to one of our blokes. Been looking up birth certificates, he has. Says it's a change from lurking outside hotel rooms. Ran advertisements in all the papers. Cholmondeley is staying at Scott's and we are keeping an eye on him. Luna Park wants to talk to him about sabotaging their mermaid to deliver bad fortunes. Funny sense of humour, the nobility. We found the owner of that motor-cycle which nearly ran Miss Dot down. It was a hired bike. The hirer was described as a thin, darkish bloke with no identifying marks who might have been English. He paid a pound for a week's hire and brought it back after one day. Gave an address in Station Street, Port Melbourne which does not exist. According to the owner of the bike he gave his name as Thomas Atkins.'

'Oh, very funny,' said Phryne flatly.

'Might be a clue. He might have been a soldier. You staying in Castlemaine?'

'For the present. I'm at the Imperial. You can call me here and leave a message.'

'Very well, Miss Fisher. Nice little town. You can't get into too much trouble in Castlemaine.'

'I devoutly hope not,' Phryne told him, and hung up. She had just seen Lin Chung walk past and strolled out to fall in behind him.

He walked slowly, enjoying the air, and turned at the corner to go into the art gallery, housed in the post office until the splendid new gallery could be built. Since the arguments about it had gone on since 1913, and would probably continue, the paintings were safe enough where they were, in this staid stone building on the corner of Lyttleton and Barker Streets. There was something satisfying about a building with a bell tower. Especially when it was crammed with paintings.

'I have always thought Elioth Gruner underappreciated,' she remarked quietly to the elegant figure in the cassock. 'Australia is so suited to post impressionism.'

'The quality of the light,' agreed Lin, not looking around from his perusal of *In the Orchard*. 'This McCubbin is particularly fine. You can feel the settling, peaceful chill as the sun goes down and the man returns to family and dinner and firelight.'

'I always thought of him as a swaggie, hoping for a bed in the cowshed and a handout,' said Phryne.

Lin smiled and did not reply.

'How are you getting on with your puzzle?' asked Phryne.

'I think I shall have some more pieces of the jigsaw in a few hours,' he said. 'I have been playing the bountiful young master and it is surprisingly pleasant. You?'

'I've got the mummy's name and when he died and who embalmed him and why, and how he got to Luna Park,' she said. 'But why someone is pursuing me now—not the faintest. This is a good collection, isn't it? Someone must have bought up bundles of post impressionists when the place still had some gold left over.'

'This has always been a prosperous place,' replied Lin. 'It has that comfortably wealthy feeling about it, as though it hasn't starved or been seriously threatened for a long time. Very hard to stay alert. Ah! Here is a map of the diggings.'

'What a mess,' said Phryne. 'Holes everywhere. I see that they closed the camp and made everyone move into their nice, well laid out town. A good idea. Did you find your Chinese people?'

'Yes, in Union Street. They are terribly poor. I have just bought a lot of furniture and goods and talked to Tonks about sending a builder to repair three of the cottages and build another one, demolishing a bark shack in which a very old prostitute was lying on the floor . . . but I have done better than just buying them presents. I have brought them Miss Fuchsia.'

He explained about Fuchsia. Phryne was impressed.

'I suppose she was restless and discontented because she had no scope to show what she could do,' she remarked, moving to look at a fine Rupert Bunny painting of a woman and child at the beach. 'She's probably another Grandmother Lin in training.'

'That is a frightening thought,' said Lin gravely. 'And you are probably right.'

'Do you think,' said Phryne, 'that someone would go to all this trouble, bombs and assaults and so on, just for the honour of their family?'

'It is possible,' Lin replied. 'We would be looking for a very young, idealistic person to whom their family was very important, though. I don't know how many of them there are in this modern world.'

'Hmm,' she said. 'I believe that there may be one. But better I should look for a baser motive, I think.'

'Always wise,' agreed Lin. 'One can always rely on base motives.'

'Have a cup of coffee with me?'

'I had better get back to Union Street. But I will see you tonight,' said Lin. They were standing shoulder to shoulder, considering the Rupert Bunny, and Lin's hand moved very gently to touch the back of Phryne's hand. A thrill ran right through her, grounding in the base of her spine.

'Tonight,' she said.

In a nearby mirror she watched his slim back as he walked out of the post office. She sighed and continued her perusal of the gallery's collection.

When Lin returned to Union Street it had been transformed. The bark hut had been felled—one touch would have done it, Lin decided—and the remains removed, and a taciturn man and a boy in a straw hat were measuring for foundations. The space under the pepper trees had been swept and sprinkled with water to lay the dust, and the trestle table had been erected. On it was a red tablecloth, for celebration, and all of the food which he had brought from Melbourne, with the addition of mounds of rice. He saw new dishes, chopsticks, plates, cups, and each setting had its own teapot. These were not new. They were clearly old and valued companions. A Chinese household may be bare of every comfort and down to its last brush and sewing needle, but it always has a teapot.

The residents, too, had been transformed. At one end of the table sat the priest, Ching Ta, his beard freshly combed, wearing a new shirt. Next to him were two very old ladies wearing art silk dresses patterned with hibiscus flowers; one blue, one yellow. Two old men, which must have been Mr Lo and his brother, were wearing their own clothes, and the third lady, Mrs Lo, had the red version of the hibiscus dress.

The greatest transformation of all was to be found in an old woman who had clearly once been very beautiful. Her abundant white hair had been washed and dressed in a chignon with a high comb. Old Lady Chang was dressed in an elaborate embroidered gown. She had been propped up with several pillows and while she might not have been able to endure sitting up for long, she was magnificent for the moment. Lin bowed to the table in general.

'Adoptive relatives,' he said, deciding that extreme formality would please them, 'I have provided a small and unpalatable dinner for you. Will it please you to taste it?'

'It pleases, Adoptive Grandson,' said Ching Ta, reaching for the lacquered duck. Ching Ta's view was that if you are going to break vows, you should break them hard and repent afterwards. 'And while we are eating, perhaps you will tell us what brings such a munificent benefactor to our unimportant hovels?'

Fuchsia served tea, rice and then holiday treats to the old people. She was neat, unobtrusive and properly deferential; she behaved not as though she was a servant, but as though she was a favoured daughter of the household demonstrating her respect.

'I am trying to find out what happened to the couriers of a certain amount of gold,' said Lin. 'This goes to the honour of my family. I need to know where they went on the twenty-first of July 1857, when they fell out of history. Their leader was a scholar called Sung Ma.'

'So long ago,' sighed a Miss Ah. 'We will have to think about this, Adoptive Grandson.'

'No need to think,' cackled Old Lady Chang. 'I was eighteen that year. You were sixteen, Annie. Sung Ma saw me once, just once, and fell in love with me.'

'A carnal love,' scoffed Miss Ah.

'There is no other kind,' snapped Old Lady Chang.

'In your experience,' sneered the other Miss Ah.

'Be civil, women!' snarled Old Man Lo with his mouth full. 'If you spoil the first good dinner I have had in twenty years, I will strangle all of you and sell your carcasses to the cat food man. Not that he'd have you,' he added. 'The kind adoptive grandson is asking you a polite question. Answer politely.'

'Sung Ma was my lover,' said Old Lady Chang. She paused for a challenge, but none came. 'One night he came to me with tears in his eyes and said that he was going home and begged me to come with him. He said he would take me as his first wife. He said that he had adequate means and that his family would accept me. I said yes, but only if we take the Lin gold. The Lins are Sze Yup, I said, our enemies. Steal their gold and we shall make merry on it in Canton.'

'And what did Sung Ma reply?' asked Fuchsia, interested.

'That he'd not betray his trust. That he was shocked that I could suggest such a thing. He left me . . . yes, he left me. I was angry.'

The lines of the old face, blurred with age, were still fine. She must have been bewitching when young, thought Lin. As beautiful as a goddess, with the internal ethics of a demon. A fox-spirit.

Fuchsia flicked a finger and Second Cousin Kong lifted Old Lady Chang up in her nest of pillows as she coughed. Each cough shook her frail body, from the elaborate coiffure down to the lily feet. Lin wondered if it would shake her apart.

The rest of the diners returned their attention to their food. Lin wished he had brought three lacquered ducks. It was amazing how much these wispy little people, so thin that sunlight ought to go right through them, could eat. He hoped that Fuchsia had bought pills to prevent indigestion, though he was sure that that thorough young woman would have added them to the order for the Health and Harmony tea company.

Mr Lo's brother offered an observation. 'It was all the fault of her worthless brother,' he said, nodding to Fuchsia as she refilled his tea cup. 'Chang Gao was a big, strong, lazy ruffian and decided, once their father died, that his sister would earn his living for him. She could not refuse. She could not even walk far without help. She could not scrub or cook or muster sheep, could she?'

'More virtuous women could sew,' said Miss Annie severely. 'And did, until our eyes were ruined and our fingers bled. More virtuous women made shoes and paper fans. I and my sister made artificial flowers.'

'Artificial flowers won't bring in enough to suit a bully like Chang Gao,' said Mr Lo.

Mrs Lo gave Mr Lo a look which would have scorched paper. He subsided.

Miss Chang had recovered and Fuchsia gave her some wine. A little colour came into her chalk-white face. She looked at Lin Chung and tapped two fingers on the back of his hand, a flirtatious gesture which made the Misses Ah bridle and hiss.

'My brother found out when the gold was to be transported,' she said. 'He told me he would hunt the couriers and steal the gold. I was angry with Sung Ma. He looked at me as though . . . he looked at me . . .' she was fading. Fuchsia gave her more wine. 'Elder Brother went out on that day in July that you said. He was to find the couriers and beat them and take the gold. He never came back. Never. Neither did Sung Ma. I had to take what lovers I could. Crude men. They did not understand the Chinese custom of concubinage. They thought I was a . . . a . . .'

'Whore,' snarled Miss Annie. 'And so you were.'

Miss Chang screamed an epithet at Miss Annie and then collapsed.

At a signal from Fuchsia, Second Cousin Kong picked up the fainting Miss Chang and bore her into the priest's house. Fuchsia went with him, taking a selection of dainties and all the pillows. Lin paused to wonder how Great Aunt Wing, a woman of ferocious virtue, was going to cope with Miss Chang. Perhaps Great Aunt Wing would welcome a challenge.

'Does anyone else know any more of the story?' he asked the diners.

'They passed my house and I sold them tea,' said Miss Annie. 'Three men, led by Sung Ma—he was very good-looking, sister, do you remember? So refined, for all that he called himself a coolie. Old Lady Loong told me that she saw them heading towards the Moonlight road. If that scoundrel Chang Gao was following, then he would have met them around where the Lin farm is now.'

'Something else,' said Old Man Lo. 'I was a boy at the time. I met Sung Ma alone, later that day, when the riot happened. He was out of breath. He had been running and there was blood on his shirt. He was trying to get back to Golden Point but he couldn't get there because of the miners. He gave me a letter.'

'And did you deliver it?'

Old Man Lo looked surprised at Lin's ignorance.

'No, of course I couldn't. It was to the Lin family. I couldn't go into Sze Yup territory or they would have beaten me. And there was the riot, I was frightened. I gave it to the priest.'

'And what did he do with it?' asked Lin, trying to keep his voice steady.

'I don't know,' said Old Man Lo. 'I haven't thought about it from that day to this. We all had to move, you see, and we came into Castlemaine to get away from the camp. My father bought this plot of land and built houses for us. And the temple, of course.'

'Father Chung,' said Ching Ta, dabbing his lips with a napkin. 'I believe that I can assist you. If you will come into the temple?'

Lin bowed to the diners and suggested that there was still ample if plain fare if they would do him the honour of eating it. In the temple, Ching Ta stepped past the recumbent old lady and spilled the box of offering scrolls onto the floor.

'Right at the bottom,' he said. 'We may find something useful.'

Lin gathered an armload of the paper spills and sat down on the priest's new bed to read them. The oldest ones were fragile and turned to confetti in his fingers. Prayers to the gods, prayers for a good voyage, prayers for a son, prayers for recovery from illness, prayers to Lan Ts'ai-ho, patron of singers, and Ts'ao Kuo-ch'iu, patron of actors. Hundreds of prayers to Kwan Yin, Goddess of Mercy, and Tou Mou, the Mother of Stars. Hundreds more to the God of Wealth. The little scrolls crumbled and fell as he unrolled them until one met his touch which was folded, not rolled, and heavier than the little temple offerings. He opened it very carefully on Ching Ta's table and weighted the end with his inkstone.

It was written in fluent, eager calligraphy in a scholar's hand. Lin read it aloud.

'Esteemed patron, I have been hunted by the Sam Yup and have committed murder in self defence. I have hidden the gold in a place we know of and I am leaving with my fellows to take ship for Canton. I fear our journey was betrayed and this was my own most grievous fault. Spring betrays even virtuous men. I pray to the goddess Nu Kua for your future success and prosperity. The unworthy scholar Sung Ma bids farewell to the Second Gold Mountain.'

'You'll never find it now,' croaked old Lady Chang from the floor. 'That bastard Sung Ma must have killed my brother Gao! That's why he never came home to me! My sweet Elder Brother! Sung Ma murdered you!'

Old Lady Chang began to cry. Fuchsia patted away her tears. Lin and Ching Ta faced each other across the table.

'We say nothing of this,' suggested Lin.

'What is there to say?' shrugged Ching Ta. 'Old Lady Chang must live here with us. Why outrage the virtuous with the deeds of the wicked? She will be judged soon enough.'

'Indeed,' said Lin warmly.

'And your generosity will not go unacknowledged by heaven,' said Ching Ta.

Lin knew what this meant. He was now committed to care for these people until they died. They had told him all he needed to know about the fate of the couriers. And the Lin family would save on offerings at the Feast of Hungry Ghosts. Sung Ma and the unrelated couriers had not died on Lin family business. They had fled, and their funerary arrangements could properly be returned to their own families.

Lin presided over the rest of the feast and then inspected and approved of Fuchsia's arrangements. Each little house now had rush mats on the floor, a bed per person, a cupboard for cutlery and crockery, and various comforts. Each person now had at least three changes of clothes and new linen and blankets. Ching Ta was engaged in writing, in his best calligraphy, the four blessings of health, long life, wealth and many children on red paper for each lintel.

Lin reflected how much power mere money had. Lying in the purse it was just coins. Let loose from confinement, it was blankets against the cold, and candied chestnuts. It was an old lady clad in a new dress with hibiscus flowers on it.

Now it was time to load up Old Lady Chang and introduce her to Great Aunt Wing. It was likely to be an instructive meeting. Lin folded Sung Ma's letter and pocketed it. He needed to read it again and consider it. A scholar like Sung Ma would not risk a plain declaration of the hiding place of the gold, but neither would he omit it. There were many perils in the world. The Lin to whom the letter was addressed—Lin Chiang, probably—might have died or forgotten and then the gold would be lost. There was a clue in the letter, and Lin Chung must find it. And there were the blazed trees. Something itched at the back of his mind. What connected salt, pig, and black? Another list, chanted by his tutor, from *The Yellow Emperor's Classic of Medicine*. Of course. The element of water, he remembered. Its season is winter. Its star is mercury. Its flavour is rotten. Its weather is cold. Its cereal is bean, its sound is moaning, its animal is the pig, its colour is black, its mineral is salt, its direction is . . . north. North of the blazed trees Sung Ma had hidden the gold.

But now to return to the farm and—Lord, he had nearly forgotten—attend Tommy's wedding feast. And then to take the car into Castlemaine, to see if Miss Fisher was interested in Anglican priests at all.

In the festival of Pure Brightness on the day of Sweeping the Graves. From Magistrate Li of the third quarter of the city of Canton to his esteemed father-in-law Sung.

May your house be forever prosperous. I have the honour to report that your nephew and my brother-in-law Sung Ma has arrived safely in this city, to your niece's great delight. My dear wife Mai was beside herself with joy to see her much loved brother return from such a perilous voyage. He is still weak from his journey and a fever he suffered on board ship, so he is staying here and will celebrate my son's first birthday with us. This is for your eyes only, venerable Father-in-Law. Sung Ma showed me his poems and it is to be feared that he suffered a disappointment, even a betrayal, in love while in the Second Gold Mountain. But he professes himself happy to entertain your choice as to a wife, asking only that she not be beautiful. He wishes for a kind and generous girl of some education and does not mind if she is plain or even crippled as long as her heart is good. Meanwhile we will feed him well and he is already recovered enough to play the poetic couplets game with us after dinner. He is a very fine poet. I am sorry to hear of your quarrel with the Lin family. I had meant to write to them to ask about Sung Ma. But I believe that we can soothe his mind here. He loves the courtyard with the peach trees and is sitting there now, drinking a little wine and talking to his sister. I believe that you will see him recovered within three months, and returned to your house to meet his new wife. The son-in-law bows respectfully.

CHAPTER FOURTEEN

And what of the daughters? Their business was to get married: and I can remember the time when there was no other hopeful opening in life for them.

George Bernard Shaw
*The Intelligent Woman's Guide
to Socialism and Capitalism*

Mr Butler came into the garden with a card on his much-prized and personally polished silver salver.

'A Lady Harborough to see you, Miss Eliza.'

'Alice?' Eliza leapt up, spilling Ember from her lap. He fell neatly, landed with all paws in position, and stalked away to the end of the garden, thoroughly miffed. Dot put down her sewing. 'Show her out here, Mr Butler, and bring some cool drinks. Or perhaps tea. Whichever she would prefer.'

Mr Butler vanished, reappeared with a small plump woman in a flowered hat, booked his orders for tea and cooling drinks and dematerialised. Lady Alice took the chair which was offered, removed the hat and shook out her hair. Dot was unimpressed. Lady Alice was a short, plain woman with brown eyes and straggly brownish hair, out of breath and running to fat. Marquess's daughters ought to look more tailored, Dot considered, if not beautiful. But her voice was very sweet, though her manner was distracted.

'Oh, my dear,' she said in a voice which strove for a social tone and failed. 'How very nice—oh, how very nice to see you again!'

Eliza embraced her. As the two faces touched, Dot discovered what Miss Eliza was not telling Miss Phryne, wondered if Phryne had already guessed, and expected that she had. No wonder Miss Eliza had turned down two eligible marriages! Even the prettiest young man in the world would not meet Miss Eliza's requirements in a mate. They held each other close for nearly a minute while Dot sought out Ember and soothed his ruffled feelings. She found him behind the chicken run, one of his favourite sulking places. Dot always suspected that he liked the way the chickens panicked when he yawned casually in their general direction. Dot was not surprised to find Li Pen there, standing as silently as a young tree. He nodded at her and she went back to the table.

Returning, she saw that Lady Alice was holding a glass of Pimms Number One Cup and was sipping it absent-mindedly. Dot was introduced. Lady Alice gave Dot her hand and smiled without, Dot was convinced, seeing her at all.

'I came because I feared for your safety,' said Lady Alice abruptly, taking Eliza's hand. 'I've got myself embroiled, and I've embroiled you, in the most frightful mess, Beth, and I really can't tell you how sorry I am, or how foolish I've been.'

How curious, thought Dot, that Miss Eliza's passionate friend calls her by the same name as her sister did when she was a child.

'You can tell me,' said Eliza. 'I don't care how foolish you have been now that I've got you with me again. You will stay? Tell me that you will stay,' she pleaded.

'Yes, dear, I will stay, if somehow we can extricate ourselves from this pickle. I never wanted to let you go to Australia without me,' said Lady Alice. 'But I could not afford the ticket on my own and my father, as you know, has practically disowned me, especially since he has formed a new attachment now that mother is divorced. His new prospective wife is twelve years younger than me and . . . well, we would not suit. She calls me a dowdy old bitch and I call her a tart, and there is a chance that we are both right.'

'Ally, you mustn't say that!' protested Eliza, hugging her friend again.

'What seems to be the trouble, Lady Alice?' asked Dot firmly. If these two got onto billing and cooing it could be months before Dot found out the facts. Ally and Beth had a billing and cooing deficit at least two months long. Lady Alice blinked at the brisk tone.

'I had better explain it to your sister as well, Beth. Where is she?'

'Castlemaine,' said Dot. 'Tell us instead and we'll tell her.'

'Castlemaine? Then she's in terrible danger!' exclaimed Lady Alice. 'That's where he's gone!'

Phryne Fisher viewed the note with quiet scorn. It was a piece of cheap Woolworth's lined paper and written on it in wobbly capitals were the instructions 'Meet me at the stables and you will hear something to your advantage. Tell no one. Bring this note with you. At seven o'clock tonight.'

'Really,' said Phryne. She had idled away the day, wondering what more she could do in Castlemaine, and was about to climb the stairs in pursuit of a nice bath and something cool to wear to dinner. 'You have been reading too many Gothic novels, my dear anonymous sir or madam. I am not going to put on a pair of high-heeled shoes and a low-necked nightgown, tell no one and walk trustingly into that nice dark partly ruined building at seven o'clock tonight, bringing the note so that it can be destroyed and I can vanish without a trace. I may have been born in Collingwood but it wasn't yesterday. A small consultation with Bill is indicated, I believe. The people who are pursuing me are here, which is a blessing, not back in Melbourne, harassing my family, and that is good. And nothing is going to stop me meeting Lin Chung tonight—nothing. It is still light enough to canvass the stables,' said Phryne to herself, and went to find Bill Gaskin.

Lin Chung was very pleased. Dealing with Miss Chang, thoroughly exhausted and exigent after a bumpy cart journey, had taken Great Aunt Wing's attention away from her household, who had therefore relaxed and stopped dropping things. Tommy was there with his newly married Maisie, who had been carried off by attentive Chinese girls, fascinated with her shiny golden hair and her blue eyes. Lin knew they were in the bridal chamber, trying on different garments and cosmetics, and giggling. Tommy was allowed to go away and commune with his fish until it was time for him to get dressed. Cousin Tan had stabled Little Flower too casually and was having a bite on his arm dressed by Aunt Tilly. Lin had bathed in his admirable spring-fed bath, adopted a proper Chinese gown for the marriage ceremony, and was sitting on the west verandah, a lantern and a glass of wine on the table beside him, rereading Sung Ma's last letter to Lin Chiang and breathing in the scent of jasmine flowers.

The letter must contain a clue. There was nothing now discernible painted or scratched into the surface of the paper. There were no words to be got from scrambling the letters or reading it backwards. The message was in the text, so he needed to analyse the text. 'Esteemed patron'—the usual form of address of a scholar in a hurry. Otherwise he would have put the name and all the titles. 'I have been hunted by the Sam Yup and have committed murder in self defence'. Plain narrative. The murder would be the accidental killing of the ruffian Chang Gao, whose fox-spirit sister would have told him of the timing of the gold shipment. Only Miss Chang could ever miss Chang Gao. The enmity between Sze Yup and Sam Yup had already caused a couple of riots on the goldfields by 1857 and doubtless would have caused more, as in those unenlightened days each side considered the other brutish, uneducated and greedy. Sam Yup would have loved to rob Sze Yup, and vice versa. Chang Gao must have forgotten that scholars are taught to fight, and that Sung Ma was an honourable person who had refused his sister's proposition. 'I have hidden the gold in a place we know of and I am leaving with my fellows to take ship for Canton'. More narrative. Lin tried the phrase 'a place we know of' several times in different dialects to see if it was suggestive of anything, but it wasn't. He sighed, sipped, and read on.

'I fear our journey was betrayed and this was my own most grievous fault'. Certainly was. But Miss Chang must have been utterly adorable when young. How was poor Sung Ma to know she was a fox-spirit? 'Spring betrays even virtuous men'. By which he meant the emotions of spring—love or lust. 'I pray to the goddess Nu Kua for your future success and prosperity'. Just a moment.

Lin sat up. He was not entirely familiar with the complete pantheon of Chinese gods. Nu Kua was not one of whom he knew. She was not one of the pure ones, the beneficent deities. She was some sort of land goddess, wasn't she? He forced his mind back to the long lists he had learned when he was a child. His tutor's singsong voice came back into his mind. She was, in fact, the goddess of . . .

Lin Chung picked up the lantern and strode into the house, calling for Uncle Tao, Second Cousin Kong, a sledgehammer and a sack.

'Tell me about the wall,' said Lin as he hiked his embroidered hem to his knees and hurried Uncle Tao across the onion field.

'It's very old,' said Tao, running to keep up. 'It's the first wall, made by the ancestor. He built it double, to be strong. That's all I know, Cousin.'

'Imagine the scene,' said Lin, inspecting the wall. It was five feet high and three feet wide. 'There is a riot. The Lin couriers are ambushed and run for the farm, even though there is no one here as they are all hiding or at the diggings. Or they may have been ambushed here. The attacker is killed and they know that they are in trouble. If the law catches them they will hang. Sung Ma sees the half-built wall. He drops the gold in between the two walls and pulls some capping across so that it is hidden. Then he and his fellows run for Canton. But he leaves a message, though it never got delivered. He blazes three trees with the message "north". And in the letter, he commends Lin Chiang to the protection of Nu Kua, the goddess . . .'

'. . . of walls,' said Uncle Tao. 'Where should we strike?'

'I don't know.'

'Oldest bit,' rumbled Second Cousin Kong. 'You always build a wall from the road back to the house. Here?'

'Try,' said Lin.

It was a still, quiet, peaceful evening. Outside the chatter and rush of the wedding night house it was silent, except for the cooing of pigeons and a couple of kookaburras laughing. Whenever he had been in any difficulty in the bush, Lin remembered, he had noticed kookaburras falling off their branch laughing at the human, who, as it might be, had just fallen over a log, skinned his knee, picked up a hot frying pan, or hammered a tent peg into his foot. Lin did not consider that kookaburras were birds of good omen. But they would have to do.

The sledgehammer made a satisfying smash as Second Cousin Kong limbered up a few muscles and hit the wall. It boomed.

'So it is hollow,' said Uncle Tao.

A stone moved, slid, took another stone with it. A section of wall collapsed and they leapt back out of the way. No gleam of gold. Nothing but old sticks and rags. Or were they sticks? They had snapped like sticks . . .

Lin stirred the dusty mass with his foot, drawing back his silken hem in distaste. A skull rolled and showed him empty eye sockets.

'We have found Chang Gao, I suspect. Try again, Second Cousin.'

'Here?' asked Second Cousin Kong. He struck. A stone groaned. Kong struck again, then stood, hammer raised, dumbfounded.

The drystone fence fountained gold.

Kong's hammer had split one rock in half, and through the hole, onto the grass, gold nuggets no larger than grains of rice poured like sand. Uncle Tao shoved the sack underneath. The grains of gold whispered as they flowed. Kong, Lin Chung and Uncle Tao stood, amazed, and listened to the noise. Finally it died away. The sack was half full and too heavy for Lin to lift. The kookaburras had stopped laughing.

Uncle Tao said consideringly, 'He thought fast, that Sung Ma, hiding the body as well as the gold. But he gave the gold an uneasy guardian. We stayed away from this place for six months, until it had all calmed down. By then he was fallen away to bones and didn't smell any more.'

'And then we finished the fence and never looked inside. Well, Uncle, that's our mystery solved. Second Cousin, if you would be so kind, go and get some more sacks. We can gather up Chang Gao and have him properly buried. And we should sieve this part of the wall, tomorrow, for any leftover gold. Thank you very much for your assistance, Second Cousin Kong. I have already promised your farm new pigsties. What can I give you? A new horse, perhaps?'

'No,' said Kong. 'I like Little Flower. She never bites me. Let me take Fuchsia into town every day, Cousin. She is too pretty to be out alone. She needs someone to protect her.'

'Exactly my thought,' said Lin, hoping that Fuchsia wouldn't be too unkind to Second Cousin Kong's boyish heart. 'And you are the man to look after her.'

Second Cousin Kong swung the sack of gold into his embrace and grinned.

'They will be starting the ceremony soon,' said Uncle Tao. 'We must hurry.'

Leaving Second Cousin Kong to gather up Chang Gao's remains and dispose of them respectfully for the moment, Lin and Uncle Tao traversed the field as it began to get dark.

'To think it was there all along,' sighed Uncle Tao.

'The ways of heaven are most peculiar,' agreed Lin.

His mission was accomplished. The Lin gold was found at the cost of some merit-acquiring charity, a new wall and new pigsty. Only a few hours and a wedding feast stood between him and Miss Phryne Fisher, and he was full of the emotions of spring.

The family Sung wishes to announce that scholar Sung Ma, recently returned from the Second Gold Mountain, will marry Tsao Pan, daughter of retired scholar Tsao Mai-te. The wedding will take place at the home of Uncle Sung on the first auspicious day of the third month in the next year, as Sung Ma then completes his mourning for his mother.

CHAPTER FIFTEEN

For a short parting, I can bear it well,
But for a long parting, tears wet my breast.

Su Tungpo, translated by Lin Yutang

It wasn't hard to find Bill Gaskin because he was looking for
Phryne. As she strolled into the stable yard in the late afternoon
sunlight he beckoned her into his shed and closed the door.

'Sorry to stop you, Miss, but I heard that you know
something about Thomas Beaconsfield.'

Phryne leaned against the edge of a scarred workbench and
stared at this gnarled and sooty member of the working classes.
Bill Gaskin reminded Phryne of that headline about sons of toil
buried beneath tons of soil.

'Yes, I do,' she said. 'How on earth did you hear that?'

'Young Billy was passing by the phone cabinet,' said Bill,
mumbling a little. 'And he meant no harm, Miss, but he heard
the name, and then, well, he listened.'

'All right,' said Phryne. 'I'll tell you all I know and then you can tell me why you know the name. I was in the Ghost Train at Luna Park,' she began. As the story progressed she noted that Bill Gaskin was becoming more and more emotional. Finally, when she had wound down to the reminiscences of Jim Harrison and the bombs in the post, he rummaged under some sacks, produced a bottle of rum and a cash box. He gulped some of the spirit and then opened the cash box. It was full of letters.

'I dunno what to do,' he said.

'Start by telling me all,' suggested Phryne, waving away the offer of the bottle.

'My mum died this year,' said Bill.

'I'm sorry,' began Phryne, but he waved at her to stop.

'She wasn't, so you needn't be. My dad died years before, I can hardly remember him, and my stepfather was a good bloke. Mum kept a boarding house in Port, which she'd had from Dad's mother, old Mrs Gascoigne. We shortened the name a bit to make it sound less foreign. We knew there was some sort of mystery about Dad. Grandma Gascoigne said things like 'If only they knew . . .' about him and hinted that he had rich relatives in England which, if it weren't for her pride, she could have got money off. I never paid much attention and, anyway, she died not long after Dad.'

'With you so far,' said Phryne encouragingly, as Bill seemed to be drying up. He refreshed himself with another swig.

'I don't usually drink during the day,' he said, looking at the bottle. 'Well, when Mum died we were cleaning out her house. Me and Young Billy like it here in Castlemaine and we were going to sell it. Mum kept everything. All of Grandma's stuff and all her own—it took days. We sold the furniture and then Young Billy has to go fiddling with a desk and popped a secret drawer, and this was inside.'

'So you opened it,' said Phryne.

'So we opened it and there was a will. Made by this Thomas Beaconsfield, leaving everything to his beloved wife Amelia Gascoigne. There was a marriage certificate too. Didn't mean a thing to me but it's a legal document, and I thought there might be a quid in it even though it's so old. There was a letter marked "to be opened in the event of my untimely death". I didn't know what to make of it so we took it to a lawyer chap that the union said was a good bloke. He got all excited.'

'I bet he did,' said Phryne. Inheritance. She had been right. But why chase Phryne rather than the heir, which would be this grimy stableman and his son Young Billy? Possibly because the assailant was confident that Phryne would lead him or her to the heir?

And she had too. She just had. Damn.

'The lawyer said that we had a claim to be a marquess. And what's more, this Thomas Beaconsfield chap had left an accusation against his mate, one Cholmondeley, saying that if he turned up dead then this Cholmondeley bloke would have done it.'

'Chumley,' said Phryne absently. 'It's pronounced Chumley. That matches with what Mr Harrison's father said too. They both vanished one night and he and his mate took over the claim. Thomas was shot and later embalmed by Professor Beecham. But the body remained unclaimed. So why didn't Amelia come looking for him?'

'I've got her letters here, to her sister. They explain what happened. Apparently they had a fight and she stormed off to Melbourne with half the gold and told him to come looking for her there if he wanted her. He didn't know she was expecting. She built a big house in Port and took in boarders. She got all the papers for safekeeping, I expect, or took them with her when she flounced off. Then Thomas didn't turn up and I suppose she thought . . .'

'That he'd gone back to England and forgotten her. Instead he was lying in a carnival show as the Wild Colonial Boy. Poor woman!'

'She was a proud woman,' Bill told Phryne. 'Never married again. Brought up her son to be a good man. My mum married again, after Dad died, said she'd never find another like him but she'd settle for some company. Stepdad and her got on all right and I really liked him. I've got two half-sisters. Mum and old Grandma Gascoigne got on like a house afire. My wife died a few years ago and we came to Castlemaine to live with my sister Madge. Got this job here, easy job, and Young Billy has the makings of a hotel manager. That's what he wants to do. I never wanted all the . . . the . . . outmoded trappings of a corrupt aristocracy to fall on me!'

'Hardly seems fair,' agreed Phryne. 'What did the lawyer do with these documents?'

'He had a search made in London and found out that Thomas was the heir of this marquessate, or whatever the bloody thing is, and that the title had gone to a collateral branch of the family when Thomas didn't come home. But he said that if we could prove that we were the legitimate direct descendants of the heir, we could still claim the title. There might be a great fortune, he said.'

'And what did you say?' asked Phryne, agog.

'That I wouldn't have it as a gift,' spat Bill Gaskin, kicking at an inoffensive passing woodlouse. 'I told him to forget about it, but he said he'd keep the documents in his safe and I should go away and think about it. Talked it over with Young Billy. He said he didn't want a bar of it either, they probably wouldn't let him run a hotel if he was a lord. We've got the money from

Mum's house and we've both got a job. To buggery with the whole thing, I said. I was going to write a letter and tell the lawyer to send me my papers back and then I'll burn the bloody things. Sorry, shouldn't swear in front of a lady.'

'Bravo!' said Phryne. 'The right decision. You would not like the weather and you would certainly not like the company.'

'Sorry, Miss, you're one of 'em. I shouldn't have said that.'

'I'm not one of them,' said Phryne firmly. 'I never have been. Now, that being settled, I need your help. Have a look at this note. I suspect that it was sent by one of your distant relatives. This is a trap. Set presumably for me. However, in all probability, my dear Bill, you are in serious danger until you can tell someone that you do not want this . . . er . . . unwelcome honour. People have come to Australia to find you and either buy you out, or . . .'

'Kill me?' said Bill calmly. 'And Young Billy as well? We'll see about that.'

'I thought I could rely on you,' said Phryne. 'They were after me to dissuade me from continuing my investigation into the identity of the mummy. Not much point in continuing with that now, of course, but they don't know that. We need to get their attention. What I would like to do, Bill dear, is this . . .'

'I am so sorry,' repeated Lady Alice.

'What are you sorry for?' demanded Dot, who had supplied a clean handkerchief and some of Mrs Butler's Nervine and was about to resort to the good cognac if Lady Alice didn't start making sense soon.

'Father got a letter a few months ago which said that enquiries were being made by a Melbourne lawyer about the descent of the title to Grandfather. We were only a collateral branch of the Harboroughs, you know, before Thomas Beaconsfield vanished and was presumed to have died without issue in Australia. Grandfather inherited and he built a new house next to Dunstable. They were great friends. I believe they also had some secret in common. They used to get drunk together and behave badly—shooting out windows in passing railway trains, for instance. That one got them into court, and they had to pay heavy compensation. And my father told me that I was destined to marry Roderick Cholmondeley because of my grandfather and his grandfather making some sort of pact. I never heard of such a thing and I refused immediately. Father was very angry but I took my little property and went off to London. I have a small income from a trust fund, you know, quite enough to live on. Especially when one considers the East End, eh, Beth?'

'Indeed,' murmured Eliza, who had not let her friend out of touching range since she had arrived.

'Anyway, this Melbourne lawyer said that Thomas Beaconsfield had married in Castlemaine in a private house and his wife had borne him a son. This son had a son of his own who was living. Therefore the whole inheritance of the Harboroughs belonged to this unknown Beaconsfield. Except that he wasn't a Beaconsfield, his name was Gascoigne, his mother's name. Father swore that it was some imposture but he was so furious that I knew he wasn't sure. He offered me a ticket to Australia if I helped Roderick Cholmondeley in his enquiries—Roddy is almost illiterate and his idea of solving a problem is to hit someone until they solve it for him. Dunstable still hopes one of us will marry Roddy, you know, Beth dear.'

'As if we would,' said Eliza.

'Well, someone has to, this is Dunstable's view, because he won't cope in the world without someone to look after him and tame his wilder impulses,' said Lady Alice.

'The only way you could tame Roderick Cholmondeley is to geld him,' said Eliza indelicately. 'And I'm sure his father would not allow that since his primary use is to breed an heir—ugh, what a thought. I've seen your Roddy drunk at a Hunt Ball and he was beastlier than any beast. He bit the head off a chicken. It was disgusting. Even the county thinks he is too unstable for matrimony. Not even the most pushing of mothers is pushing her daughter onto Roddy.'

'Which is why he has come down to two such biddies as us, eh, Beth?' chuckled Lady Alice. 'Anyway, he has someone to look after him. His batman, before he was asked to leave the regiment. Thin, dark man. Wallace? Yes, Wallace, I think. He seems perfectly all right, but the fact that he has chosen to be a friend to Roddy puts a black mark against his sanity too. Anyway, I agreed, so that I could see you again. I took the ticket and came over on the *Orient* and stayed in my cabin most of the voyage to avoid those two. Then I found the lawyer's office for them and found them a private enquiry agent to conduct the searches and put advertisements in all the newspapers.'

'I saw them,' said Dot. 'Seemed to be in every paper I picked up. Must have cost a good deal.'

'That was irrelevant if the title was in question. Then—of all unlucky things! I told them that I was going to Luna Park—you know how I love such places, Beth—and they insisted on coming too. They were suspicious of me. They were right! But that put us in the right place at the right time to . . .'

'See Miss Phryne find the mummy,' said Dot. 'They must have seen the crest on the forearm and known it instantly. For an idiot, your Roderick thinks real fast! Or p'raps it was this Wallace bloke. And since then they have been trying to frighten Miss Phryne off.'

'And to find the descendants of Amelia Gascoigne,' said Lady Alice. 'And they have, and he's living in Castlemaine, and they've burgled the lawyer's safe and burned the documents, and gone to buy him off or to frighten him off or even . . . but surely even Roddy would not go that far . . . and your sister is there as well.'

'Miss Phryne is clever,' said Dot. 'And she's very hard to catch off guard. But I'll phone right away. What are you going to do now, Lady Alice?'

'Well, since I am not going to be welcome back in England, and since I am now just plain Miss Beaconsfield, I think I'll stay here,' said Lady Alice comfortably. 'I was never happy with being titled anyway. I'll have my small income and get a room somewhere cheap and continue with my work. Will you join me, Beth?'

'You know I will,' sobbed Eliza and fell into Miss Beaconsfield's arms.

Dot went to the phone. Li Pen went with her.

Phryne listened carefully to the whole sorry tale.

'Well, that explains Eliza,' she commented. 'I can just imagine what Father would think of a Sapphic in the family. Better he has his apoplexy out of spitting distance from us. That only leaves Thos, our little brother, and Thos has always been a perfect little thug. I'm sure he will marry and breed. Very good-looking, Thos. Once he gets past the pimples and puppy-fat stage he'll be gorgeous, and Eton is teaching him to conceal the essential unpleasant banality of his character. Go on, Dot dear.'

'Miss Phryne, that Roderick is in Castlemaine and Lady Alice says he's dangerous,' Dot yelled.

'So am I,' said Phryne, holding the earpiece a little further away. 'But he can't get up to too much in the stable yard of a respectable hotel. At least, I expect not. But I shall take care. I've talked to our Tichborne Claimant, Mr Bill Gaskin. He doesn't want the title. He's a socialist. The place is positively rife with socialists lately. And I've got an assignation later. This matter has taken up far too much of my holiday time. But at least I'll be able to bury the poor mummy properly, as I promised Sister Elizabeth. And under his own name. Call Jack Robinson for me, will you, Dot, and ask him to alert the local cops to anything odd happening to me. This Roddy and his valet Wallace sound unsightly and essentially harmless, but you never know. Never trust a man who bites the heads off chickens is probably a good sound rule of practice.'

'Mr Li wants to ask if Mr Lin is all right.' Dot gave up trying to tell Phryne to be careful.

'Perfectly, if a little overfed. He has every hope of finding the gold and he's been spreading good cheer amongst some old Chinese people here. He also looks gorgeous in a cassock, though Li Pen might not appreciate that comment, so don't tell him. I'll call you tomorrow, Dot dear. Not early. If anything happens, you can find me here.'

Phryne rang off, biting her lip. This Roderick Cholmondeley sounded like a dangerously unstable little petal. Even for a Hunt Ball, where perfectly respectable men performed a dance called 'the cocking of the legs' and exclaimed 'Och, aye!' while doing so without public reproof, mutilating animals—even chickens— was extreme. No wonder he was having trouble finding a titled wife. Mothers with daughters to sell might be desperate after the second unsuccessful season, but probably not that desperate. Someone had married Lord Greystoke, admittedly, but he was just a large ape, and Phryne had seen behaviour in Belgravia which would have drawn pursed lips and adverse comment in the worst conducted of baboon cages at the zoo.

Perhaps this was not such a good idea after all.

Still, the idiot Roderick had to be faced, and he had to be informed that Gaskins never never would be aristos, and how else was she going to catch him? If he was the pink-cheeked muscle man in the Imperial dining room last night, blond hair cut unbecomingly en brosse like a prize fighter, she might just catch him at dinner and tell him it was all off and he could go home. If he dined early.

And would he believe her?

Phryne went upstairs for her bath, lay for a long time dreamily splashing Floris Tea Rose bath oil with her fingers, and emerged boiled pink and strongly scented. She dressed carefully, including her petticoat pocket and her small gun in its garter holster, just in case. She had once been dropped into a deep pit by persons who were afterward very, very sorry, and the presence of that petticoat pocket, an invention of her grandmother's time, had meant that she had not been without matches to make light or a soothing smoke while contemplating escape.

Thus accoutred, she went down to the dining room at seven, but the large young man and his dark-haired friend were not apparent. Drat. That means we will have to do this the hard way, thought Phryne, and went into the stable yard.

It was getting towards dusk. Bill Gaskin, cleaned up to meet his new neighbour, was waiting for her in the shed. He was wearing a clean shirt and had combed his hair and Phryne saw with approval that he had that good solid Australian face, knobbly around the nose with a chin you could break flints on. A face, she had thought, which had died out in Gallipoli and Passchendaele. And here it was, cleaned of cinders and very personable too, not to mention historic. He approved of her low-heeled shoes.

'Difficult walking in that old ruin,' he commented. 'Missus is about to have it pulled down so she can build a proper garage. Almost no one has horses any more.'

'What, even here? It's time, Bill. Come along,' said Phryne, and walked into the darkness. 'We need to tell them loudly that you don't want their title. That will defuse them.'

She shut her eyes and when she opened them she could see. The late sun shot golden bolts of light through the holes in the galvanised iron roof. Not a creature was stirring, not even a passing rat, and she was about to speak when a lot of things happened at once.

She was grabbed in arms which felt like they were made of iron, bound and wrapped in something like a sack, before she had time to react. A shout of dismay near her ear made her aware that Bill had been similarly treated. A huge engine roared. Phryne was lifted and flung, landing painfully on someone's knee or elbow. The car or truck roared and took the road at a dangerous speed. There was a shriek of tortured metal which told Phryne that part of the Imperial's decorative wrought iron gate had come too.

Around a corner, slung against the knobby projections, around another corner, slung the other way. Phryne was dazed. First thing to do: think. Roddy had better have his wits about him when Phryne got out of this sack. She was seriously displeased.

The thing she was lying on was struggling. Phryne wriggled, trying to guess which end of this bundle was his head. 'Lie still!' she shrieked at what she thought might be a face. 'Try and get your hands free!'

Her only answer was an inarticulate growl which informed her that her guess was correct. That was the head end. Phryne sneezed. This sack had contained flour. Her nose started to run and she fought to get a hand free from the enclosing material. This never happens to Sexton Blake, she reflected, managing to slide a hand up inside the bag and scratch her nose. Bliss. Now to release the rest of her.

She could detect a change of light through the bag. The world appeared to be getting darker. Out of the street lights of Castlemaine into the gathering night. Where were they taking them? Towards Melbourne? Towards Bendigo? And what on earth did this Roderick think he was doing?

Probably not murder. Not in the first instance. If he had meant to murder both of them he could have shot them down in the stable where they stood artlessly outlined against the dusk. Phryne spent a useful minute castigating herself for breaking her own cardinal rules, viz, assume everyone is dangerous until proven otherwise and expect the unexpected. Then she forgave herself because she needed to think and plan, and kicking oneself is difficult inside a tight-fitting sack.

She had left notes and people would be looking for her. It was just a matter of surviving until rescued.

Phryne hated the idea of being rescued, but from the depths of her sack it had its attractions. The car swerved, turned, went around what was apparently a very tight corner on one wheel, squealed and fishtailed back onto the road again and drove on.

Breathing was not easy inside the bag and every time she took a breath she got a lungful of flour. Bill had ceased struggling and was making the complex, rhythmical movements of a man trying to work one hand out from underneath when he is stuffed down beside a car seat and is being lain upon by a small but inconvenient woman.

How long was this blighted journey going to take? Think, Phryne told herself. The journey will end somewhere and you have to be prepared. What is the best tactic to use on a bone-headed son of the nobility? What, in fact, did Roderick Cholmondeley know about women?

Probably not a lot, if he thought that tricks with chickens were going to make the girls agog at his strength and skill. Boys' school, space of time with the regiment—I wonder why he was asked to leave? Those regiments usually have quite strong stomachs; Roddy must be a cad as well, or that most damning of judgments, 'not quite a gentleman', even though he was quite definitely a lord.

Phryne was aware that the restricted air supply was making her woozy. She tried to focus. Pay attention, she told herself, breathe through the nose, you get less flour that way. How to tackle Roddy, that's the question. The batman may be the brains of the outfit, of course. But then, Roddy had spent a lot of his time slaughtering the beasts of the field and the pursuit of deer taught one patience. And exactly how heavy a fully grown stag is when you have had the good fortune to kill it, which would have built up the muscle, of course. Mind wandering again. Another howling turn. This must be a high-powered car. Probably a Bentley or one of the new Rolls Royces.

Now, he would only have met officers' wives and daughters, the available daughters of the aristocracy, and probably a few whores. The officers' wives would not have approved of this wild young subaltern, and the daughters would have been kept well away from him. The Misses of the season would have snubbed him, especially after the chicken incident, which would have taken fully ten minutes to run from mouth to ear the length and breadth of Polite Circles. That left only whores, and they were what their clients wanted. Roddy would know about whores, and so would his batman. That might be a useful piece of information.

A screech and the car shuddered to a halt. On, by the sound of it, gravel. Off the beaten track, then. Not that there were a lot of beaten tracks around here anyway. Hands were laid ungently on Phryne. She decided to collapse. With any luck she might give her captor a nice hernia. She was slung over someone's shoulder and carried ten paces into a house. She was dropped unceremoniously on a hard floor. She allowed herself to roll a little, getting her free hand on her garter and thus almost on her gun when she heard the footsteps coming back and relapsed into immobility. Let Roddy make the first move, so she could find out what he was planning.

Adrenalin poured into her bloodstream. In the sack, she bared her teeth.

The Elder Brother Sung Ma to the younger sister Li Mai, affectionate greetings.

I have been here in my own village for six months now. I have been setting up our jewellery workshop. We already have several commissions and I have secured the services of a famous enameller. Venerable Uncle has been very helpful. He assures me that my prospective wife is a pleasant person. I have seen some of her paintings, which are quite in the antique style, and her calligraphy is also very good. I cannot marry until my year's mourning for our mother is passed. But when I do I am convinced that I shall be much happier than I deserve to be.

The Elder Brother sends some poor poems which might amuse the younger sister.

CHAPTER SIXTEEN

Thank you for sweeping the grass from my grave.

The Peony Pavilion

Lin Chung enjoyed the wedding feast. The ceremony had been utterly foreign to the young bride, who had stood through the whole thing without understanding one word, looking at Tommy with an expression of lamb-like adoration which had even softened Great Aunt Wing (already much mollified by a strong exchange of views on morality with Old Lady Chang. Observers put the honours at about even). And Lin supposed that the earlier ceremony had been just as incomprehensible. Who amongst most congregations understood the Latin ceremony? Tommy said that he had had to . . . well, not exactly lie, since he was not really of any religion, but sign something which said that his children were to be brought up Catholic. Might as well, reflected Lin Chung, handing over his present of money, wrapped in red paper.

The local priest would doubtless instruct them and any religion was better than none for the very young. It was a pity that Maisie's relatives had not attended, disgusted that she was marrying a Chinaman, but Tommy had every chance of success and even adamant families usually came round in time.

He wondered how Phryne was whiling away her evening. Waiting for him.

He shifted a little and turned his attention to the feast. He had eaten more feasts in the last few days than in the whole of his rather austere life. Although he did not live on rice and vegetables like Li Pen, he usually ate sparingly. He listlessly took up a hundred year old egg, its white as translucently black as Vegemite and its yolk a sulphurous yellow. He really couldn't eat any more and put it down in his bowl again. A duck egg, if he was any judge, a product of that band of sleepy quackers in the shed outside. He recalled watching two very important small children, armed with long wands made of rushes, drive the ducks into their sleeping quarters. They had been charming, and he was getting sleepy.

He refused another refill of wine and went back to drinking tea. Tonight, Lin Chung did not mean to sleep.

Tommy was feeding Maisie from his own bowl. For a girl who had never tasted Chinese food before, she was managing well. They looked very happy.

At long last the young men of the household took Tommy away, and the girls claimed Maisie. Massed giggling announced that she had been stripped of her red wedding dress, dressed in her trousseau nightgown, combed, patted, kissed by all available children and put to bed. Shouts and gongs announced the arrival of Tommy, who was finally able to break free from his boisterous well-wishers and get through the bedroom door and it was, finally, shut and the revellers went away.

That was not the end of the feast, of course. The formal part was concluded and now everyone relaxed, nibbled more of their favourite delicacies and gossiped freely, not having to translate. Jokes, particularly, just didn't translate. Or, at least, they didn't translate into anything funny. Lin listened idly. He liked the sound of his own language, the flutter of syllables across various tones, not the high-pitched chirping of Mandarin. His ancestors had done well. He honoured them now as he had not before this journey into the past. They had braved a terrible sea voyage with hatred at the end of it; cruel weather and hard work had bent their backs. But they had persevered and prospered. They were still here. They were still Chinese.

Cousin Tan began to sing the closing aria from *The Peony Pavilion*, a tale of a scholar who marries a beautiful ghost. A Taoist nun brings the bride back to life, the lovers have to flee and are separated; and then the scholar wins fame at his examinations and they live happily ever after. Lin liked happy endings. He applauded and demanded another song.

The house rocked to the sound of the drunken poems of Li Po, and Maisie and Tommy ignored them all.

At half past eleven the household was going to bed and Lin went onto the verandah to look at the night. It was dark and still, moist, presaging rain.

'You are going out tonight?' asked Uncle Tao, coming out to enjoy the cool night air. The moon was full and as bright as a coin, casting faint blue shadows.

'Yes, into Castlemaine.'

'Be careful, Cousin. I heard a car driven down the Moonlight road screeching its tyres early in the evening. That usually means that the young men are abroad. When they are drunk they are unpleasant.'

Lin smiled. 'I will avoid them. It is not a young man I am going to see.'

'I guessed that,' said Uncle Tao reminiscently. 'One only has a few fragrant nights of spring. Store your memories for when you are old. You will enjoy them again under such a moon as this.'

'I will,' said Lin. He went back to his room to resume his cassock, got into the car and drove carefully to Castlemaine. The Imperial, he had ascertained, had a fire escape which was beautifully sited for access to Miss Fisher's room.

He did not have a chance to test it. When the big car swept around the corner into Lyttleton Street he was stopped by a sweating policeman.

'Sorry, Father, we're looking for a lady. Can I search the car?'

The policeman was so overwrought he did not even react to Lin Chung's Chinese face.

'A lady? Yes, of course, search all you like. Which lady?'

The policeman leaned in at the window, opened the back door, checked the boot and returned, touching his uniform helmet.

'Terrible thing. Lady kidnapped in the stable yard about seven, and Old Bill Gaskin as well, though what they wanted with Old Bill I can't imagine. Hang on! You wouldn't be called Lin, would you, Father?'

'Yes, I am Lin Chung,' said Lin, beginning to be seriously concerned.

'Go on to the Imperial, will you, Father? See my sergeant. There's a letter for you.'

Lin drove to the Imperial where a harassed porter tried to stop him, saw that he was a religious person, and allowed him to leave the car.

'Park it somewhere,' said Lin. 'Who is in charge of this investigation?'

Chinese was one thing but effortless authority was another and, adding the cassock to the equation, the door porter thought it best to allow Lin into the bar, where a worried owner was wringing his hands. A uniformed policeman was making notes in a notebook with one of those pencils which he had to keep licking, and Annie of Reception was crying like a fountain. Even the Imperial's guard dog was sitting in a corner, tail between its legs, whimpering occasionally.

'Excuse me,' said Lin. 'The policeman at the corner said that I should come here and speak to the sergeant. Is that you, sir?' he asked.

'You're Lin Chung?' demanded the policeman. 'Good! I'm Sergeant Hammond. Sit down, Father, here's the letter. We can't make head or tail of it.'

'The lady who was kidnapped, what is her name?' asked Lin urgently.

'Lady Phryne Fisher, and she was snatched in the stable yard about seven. They took off down the road like bats out of hell and we've not seen hide nor hair of them. Just this arvo I got a phone call from Jack Robinson in Melbourne asking me to take special care of her and now look what's happened. He's going to have me back pounding a beat before the night's out if I can't find her quick. Now, sir, can you tell me what this Lady Fisher means?'

Lin unfolded the letter. It was written in Phryne's fluid, italic hand with her very favourite black ink and the fountain pen he had given her. It smelt faintly of roses.

'Lin dear, if you are reading this it has all gone wrong. Call Dot for the whole story and lay hands, very quickly, on Roderick Cholmondeley and his mate Wallace. Bill Gaskin is the Beaconsfield heir. Also find Young Billy and keep him safe.'

'It is clear,' said Lin. A hollow was forming inside him.

240

'She had a meeting with these two men and they have kidnapped her. If you can find me a telephone I will get you more information. Detective Inspector Robinson has been looking for these two criminals for some time. They tried to murder a young lady in Melbourne. They are dangerous.'

'Bloody wonderful,' said the sergeant. 'No one of that name staying in the hotel.'

'We will get a description,' said Lin. 'Let me telephone.'

'Have to send young Annie here over to work the exchange. It's closed.'

Annie looked at the imploring eyes of the dreamy young priest. She rose to the occasion, wiped her eyes, claimed a porter as escort, and went off to open the telephone exchange.

Lin rubbed his palms over his face. This was not the evening he had been expecting. Phryne must have been taken entirely off guard. It must have been a sudden, brutal, unexpected assault. She might have been injured, concussed, dying at this moment. Time was ticking past with all the dancing alacrity of an ice age. How long did it take to get to the telephone exchange, for God's sake? It was practically next door!

He became aware that his hands were clenched together so tightly that his knuckles were white. He released them. He might need his hands.

After what seemed like years he managed to get Dot on the telephone, and then gave it to Sergeant Hammond. Soon information was pouring into his receptive ear. He made notes. He shouted orders. He demanded the register. And he found one Thomas Atkins and his friend Joseph Smith. Neither of whom were in their well-sprung beds enjoying the country peace. And their car, a sleek new Bentley, was also missing. This galvanised the sergeant, who at last knew what to search for. He sent minions into the night, shouting some more.

Lin recaptured the instrument.

'Miss Dot?' he asked gently. 'It is Lin Chung.'

'Oh, Mr Lin!' wailed Dot. 'Shall I send Mr Li?'

'Yes,' said Lin. 'Put him on the first train and tell him that I shall be here, at this hotel. Do not distress yourself,' he said. 'I am sure that Phryne will be all right. She is very clever.'

'But this bloke bites the heads off chickens!' cried Dot, on whom this story had had a strong effect.

'Even so. I have to go now. I will call you as soon as I know anything. Good night,' he said, and heard the connection break on a sob. As he did so, he recalled Uncle Tao saying that a car had screamed up the Moonlight road earlier in the evening. Returning to give this piece of information to the distracted Sergeant Hammond, he found him bellowing at the door porter.

'What do you mean you can't find Young Billy?' he demanded.

The door porter had had enough of being yelled at as though he was deaf or stupid or both.

'Can't find what isn't there! Madge Johnson, his aunt's here, creating. Says Old Bill never came home nor Young Billy neither.'

'So they have both of the Beaconsfield heirs,' said Lin Chung heavily.

Phryne listened hard. She heard the door slam and two sets of feet come into the house. She was lying on a wooden floor; it vibrated to the rhythm. She heard a chair being scraped back and someone dumped into it; Bill—she heard him groan.

Then she was hauled up, carried, divested of her sack and allowed to sit. A loop of rope was slung around her arms and torso before she could move and tied tightly behind her.

She shook her head, clearing her eyes of flour and dust. She was tied to an old kitchen chair in the single room of what was apparently the Old Bark Hut of the song. The inside walls had been lined with illustrated newspapers. A pack of wolves chased a sleigh across the snow. A little girl served tea to her dolly. It seemed that Mafeking had been relieved. If she was here for any time she could while away the hours reading the walls. Otherwise the room contained a table, Bill Gaskin in another chair, a fireplace with a small bright fire burning and a few odds and ends. And, of all things, a picnic basket.

Then a man came into view. Well, well. So this was Roderick. He was big, well-fed and full of righteous indignation. A pink-faced King Boar with big hands and huge physical assurance, not to mention bulging muscles. Phryne could not take this one on in single combat and survive. Strategy was going to be needed.

'Now, my good man,' he addressed a dishevelled Bill Gaskin in an upper class English tone guaranteed to raise every hackle this son of toil possessed. 'I'm here to clear up this bloody stupid nonsense about the succession. There's nothing you can do to interrupt it. You make up your mind to that.'

'Yair?' drawled Bill.

'Yes. I am the rightful heir to the Cholmondeley honour and I am going to marry Lady Alice Harborough. Pater has decided on her, since I can't get the old paws on the Fisher millions. Pater and old Harborough are bosom friends, y'know. She's an old frump but she'll do. Won't have m'wife reduced in rank.'

Phryne, filthy, untidy and struggling to breathe in her tight lashings, had a terrible urge to laugh. But the situation was not funny. Roddy was a giant and the darkish man in the background, hair ruffled from contact with the prisoners, should not be discounted either. There was a gleam of intelligence in the dark eyes which was lacking in Roderick's. Also, he had a gun. And she was tied up. She hated being tied up. No one seemed to be looking at her so she tried a slow, gentle wriggle. The ropes were tight. What would Roddy do when disabused of his delusions? Burned certificates could be replaced. Any reputable lawyer would have had copies made and certified. What did Roddy think he was going to be able to make Bill Gaskin, heir of the Harboroughs, do? He didn't want the honour anyway.

Roddy laid out a document on the table and said, 'You've got to sign this.'

'What is it?'

'Repudiation of the title. I had a lawyer chappie draw it up in London. He assures me it's watertight.'

'And then?' grated Bill Gaskin.

'Then we'll let you go,' said Roderick.

There was a long pause. Phryne wriggled a little more and felt some tightness go out of the ropes. They had not tied her hands, which might prove to be a mistake. She hoped so.

'And if I don't?' demanded Bill Gaskin.

'Then I'll hurt you,' replied Roddy. A pink tongue flicked out and licked his pink lips. And you'll enjoy it, thought Phryne, making another unobtrusive move toward her gun. She couldn't quite reach it, even with the tips of her fingers.

'Well, I can't sign nothing with me hands tied like this,' said Bill. Phryne saw his shoulder muscles tensing. Bill was about to take action.

Wallace forestalled him. He held a very large, sharp fishing knife to Bill Gaskin's throat, just close enough to bring one bright bead of blood from the skin as Roddy undid the ropes on his hands. Bill picked up the fountain pen.

'Sign here,' said Roddy.

Bill Gaskin spat in his face.

'You stupid bastard,' he snarled. 'I was ready to burn those papers and forget all about it. I was happy where I was and I didn't need no fortune, nor no title neither. Where do you get off, you bloated capitalist, kidnapping an honest working man and a lady, when all you had to do was ask? I was going to forget the whole thing, but to buggery with that. I'm not gonna sign your bloody paper, you bludger. I don't care how big you bloody are.'

Roderick slapped him so hard that his head snapped back.

'And you ain't gonna let me go,' added Bill, spitting blood. 'Or her. You want me to sign that paper and then you'll kill us. Go on, you bastard, admit it!'

'That was the plan,' said Wallace, speaking for the first time. He had a light, classless accent and a tenor voice. 'We need your authentic signature, you see, and we couldn't bribe anything out of the hotel which had your signature on it, or we wouldn't be going through all this folderol, we would have just thrown you down the hole to start with.'

'What hole?' asked Bill.

'Oh, an abandoned mine shaft. There are hundreds of them around here, very careless of the miners not to fill them in,' Wallace told him airily. 'We've picked a nice deep one just for you. If you are ever discovered, you will have all the broken bones you require to prove how hard you fell. It's at least thirty feet deep.'

'But we thought that you might be difficult,' said Roderick. 'So we got some insurance. Go get the boy, Wally.'

Wallace opened the door, turning his back on Phryne. Roderick was watching Gaskin. Phryne wriggled hard and managed to get some of the ropes to loosen. She still couldn't reach her gun. Should she speak, and thus attract attention to herself and risk being searched and disarmed? No. Better to watch for another opening when all the pieces were on the board. They couldn't kill Bill Gaskin until he signed. And he didn't seem likely to sign. The fools, thought Phryne. I don't like the idea of being killed by fools. I shall have to ensure that this does not happen. Rain began to fall outside with a soft whoosh. Wally came back inside, shaking raindrops off his face. The Boar and the Weasel, thought Phryne. What a strange partnership.

He put down a bundle wrapped in canvas and began to unfold it. Someone was inside. Phryne caught sight of a thin bare shin and a wrist in a too-short shirtsleeve. Then Young Billy emerged, cock's crest flattened by contact with his wrappings. He coughed. More flour sacks, Phryne diagnosed.

'Here,' said Roderick, 'is our bargaining chip. What will you give me for your boy, you upjumped colonial?'

'You all right, son?' asked Bill Gaskin roughly.

'I'm all right, Dad,' said Young Billy. His voice was shaking. He was trying to rub some life back into his wrists and ankles. 'They told me you were hurt and they'd take me to you so I got in the car after lunch and they bagged me. I'm sorry, Dad.'

'What'll I give yer?' demanded Bill Gaskin. 'I'll give yer anything if yer let the boy walk out of here.'

'No,' said Roderick.

'No deal,' snapped Bill Gaskin.

Roderick hit him again. Young Billy bit his lip. He was dazed and a little concussed. He knew this situation. It happened in almost every Western. The bad guys had the good guy tied up and were going to torture him until he signed over the deeds to the property that the railroad was going through. There ought to be a distressed maiden too. He looked around and saw Phryne tied to her chair. Ah. There she was. Now all they had to do was wait for either the Texas Rangers, the Seventh Cavalry or the man with no name to rescue them.

They were taking their time. It must be almost morning by now. Young Billy yawned. Dad swore. Roderick Cholmondeley yelled at Wallace: 'Think of something!'

Lin Chung stayed the night at the Imperial. He occupied Miss Fisher's room at his request. He lay surrounded by reminders of Phryne: her scent, her nightdress laid out on the bed, the book she was reading open on the bedside table. He cursed himself for not asking more about her investigation when he had seen her in the art gallery. There might have been some clue as to where the abductors had taken her, though police roadblocks on all the roads out of Castlemaine had not caught anyone. Sergeant Hammond thought that she had been taken to Melbourne. Lin's instincts said that she was still close by. The abductors had packed all their belongings and gone (adding robbing the Imperial of their bill to their account, a piece of meanness typical of their class) but unless they had elaborate means for disposal of the bodies, they would need the amenities which Castlemaine and environs would provide.

Perhaps. For some reason he was convinced that this was true. As soon as Li Pen arrived in the morning, he would start hunting his own trails. Someone must have spoken to Thomas Atkins, née Cholmondeley. He didn't know the area. He had only arrived a day before Phryne. One of the habitués of the Imperial bar would know where Roderick had gone. And then Li Pen would find her.

He did not sleep. Across his closed eyelids enchanting memories of spring danced and flickered. He groaned.

Roderick and Wallace had gone into a huddle. They were between a rock and a hard place, Phryne thought. They had painted themselves into a corner. Bill Gaskin wouldn't sign until he knew that Young Billy was safe. They weren't going to let Young Billy go until Bill signed (or at all, Phryne considered). It was a stalemate. Unless they could find some way of applying more pressure to Bill, they could either kill him or not kill him but he wasn't going to sign.

Phryne hoped that they wouldn't reach the realistic conclusion that they might as well kill them all anyway, because with the heir and the heir's son dead, the document didn't matter a straw. She was banking on Roddy's magnificent stupidity and his sadism. He was not going to let go of a torturable victim so easily.

Which, now she thought of it, included Phryne. Possibly it was time to bring herself to their attention. She wasn't going to get out of these ropes and, if not skilfully misdirected, Roddy might just decide to kill them all anyway.

Then Roddy snarled, 'I'm going to leave you here to think about it, you peasant!' He stalked out into the rain, leaving Wallace on guard.

'Hello,' said Phryne to Wallace. 'Could you perhaps wipe some of this flour off my face?'

'You have a slippery reputation, Miss Fisher,' replied the Weasel. 'I'm quite comfortable where I am, thank you.'

'You don't look it,' said Phryne candidly. 'You know that our dear Roddy is mad, don't you? Lady Alice isn't going to marry him.'

'She'll do as her father says,' replied Wallace.

'I don't think so,' said Phryne. 'She's a Sapphic. She's in love with my sister. Even if Roddy resorts to what used to be called marriage by capture, she isn't going to be overcome by his physique, you know. She'll just lay a complaint of rape. And they hang you for rape in Australia, even if you are a lord. Also for being an accessory, I believe.'

'Shut up,' said Wallace.

'They also hang you for murder,' said Phryne quietly.

'I said shut up!' Wallace came close enough to slap Phryne across the face. At least it got rid of some of the flour. The slap rocked the chair back on its back legs. It made a heartening cracking noise. Phryne tried to make it thump down hard on one leg, which creaked. Excellent. If she couldn't get the ropes off perhaps she could demolish the chair.

'That's enough of that, my man!' snapped Phryne, using the accents which Wallace had obeyed all his life. He backed off, returning to his place by the fire.

'Historic little hut,' remarked Phryne after a few moments of listening to the rain. 'Where are we?'

'Why should I tell you that?'

'Because I am asking civilly,' she said, using the same tone.

'Hasn't got a name,' said Wallace. 'Close to the Moonlight road. Bloke in the pub told us about it. Hunters use it.'

'And it has a nice deep mine shaft. Did the bloke in the pub tell you about that too?' asked Phryne encouragingly. Wallace found he was having a conversation.

'No, it was a stroke of luck. Rod almost fell down it. We dropped a plummet and it's at least thirty feet and water at the bottom. Perfect.'

'How very useful. Every convenience. They will take you away to the court, Wallace. An old man with a black cap on his wig will sentence you to death and ask God to have mercy on your soul. Then you'll wait awhile, imagining what it is going to be like. Then they'll come in the morning, they'll march you up the wooden stairs. They'll put a bag over your head and a hemp rope around your neck. Eight turns in the hangman's rope, Wallace. Then they'll drop you through the trap and into eternity. If they've been careful, it will break your neck almost instantly. If they've been careless, and they are not highly paid men, then you'll strangle slowly, kicking, or the drop will tear your head off. All this if you stay with Roddy and his insane plans. All this will come to pass.'

Her voice was soft, hypnotic. Wallace took some time before he snarled, 'I told you to shut up!' and hit Phryne again. The chair back snapped, but he did not notice.

'We ain't gonna get out of this, son,' said Bill Gaskin to Young Billy.

'Don't say that, Dad!' protested the dazed boy. 'We just have to hold on until the cavalry arrives.'

The door burst open. It wasn't the cavalry. Roderick had come back.

Poems of a Vagrant Weed

I call for another pot of wine
And me and the moon drink together
She never takes more than a sip
So there's lots left for me.

The spring wind blows harshly
And tears the blossoms from the tree.
Spring has dealt so harshly with me
That all my flowers are blown.

Sweet songs the oriole sings;
Spring songs. I shut the blind.
I wish no songs of spring in my house
Where learning is my mistress.

It is so warm and gentle a day
The sun pools heavily in my upturned palms.
One would never have thought
That blood once filled my hands with red
Also warm; also alive.

CHAPTER SEVENTEEN

Oh, hush the night, each minute an ounce of gold
While faintly floats the music of flute and song.
So fragrant the air, so cool the midnight courtyard,
While darkly glides the silent night along.

Su Tungpo, translated by Lin Yutang

Li Pen arrived after a slow journey on the early train and found his master buying drinks in the bar of the Imperial for the morning crowd. There was plenty to talk about and the pub was busy. Li Pen was about to utter a reproof when he realised that Lin Chung had one untouched glass of beer in front of him, while the rest of the pub was enjoying OP Queensland rum heart-starters. Lin was pale but composed and Li Pen decided not to comment; in fact, he would recommend a glass of brandy when Lin had ascertained whatever it was he was trying to find out.

'So you talked to this Atkins,' said Lin very gently, as if he was trying to coax a wild bird into his hand. 'And he was a great hunter?'

'Shot and fished all over the world,' said Mr Harrison.

'Knew a lot about it. Told some good stories. Aub told him about his croc. Said he wanted to do a bit of rough shooting and we said there's only rabbits round here, mate, and he said he didn't care.'

'And where did you suggest that he go for his rabbits?' asked Lin delicately. The bird was just stepping onto his palm.

'Up that way,' said Mr Harrison, pointing. 'Second turn on the right off the Moonlight road there's a big burnt stump. Turn off there and there's a bush hut about quarter of a mile. He said that'd be good-o.'

'Thank you,' said Lin, his timid bird in hand at last. He dropped some silver on the bar, drained one small glass of the OP rum, and collected Li Pen on the way out.

'I've been pumping those fools for half an hour,' he said to Li Pen a little defensively. 'That was my only drink.'

'I was about to suggest that you take one,' said Li Pen. 'You have not slept. You feel that the Silver Lady is in that hut?'

'Yes, or nearby. Cholmondeley hasn't had time to find a more elaborate hiding place. That is the only suitable one those morons in there told him about.'

'Then we should tell the police of your suspicions,' said Li Pen.

'I left a note,' said Lin. 'Sergeant Hammond is out harassing motorists. A young boy is missing also and the only reason he was wanted is because he is the final heir. They must be going to kill them, Li Pen. Nothing else makes sense.'

'Sense and nonsense are in the eye of the beholder,' said Li Pen. 'Let us go and try to sort out one from the other.'

The big car slid out through the roadblock.

The directions were no more difficult to follow than such directions usually are. After taking one wrong turn and digging the car out of a wallow, Lin Chung saw the hut and stopped the car.

'How shall we know that she is there?' asked Li Pen.

Lin pointed to a new, shiny, mud-spattered Bentley.

They closed the car doors very quietly. No window in the rude hut faced this gravel track. They approached the house, treading as light as leaves.

Roderick had reached the conclusion that Phryne had hoped he wouldn't.

'If we just kill them,' he told Wallace, 'then it doesn't matter about the damned paper.'

'You care a great deal about the honour of your family, don't you, Roddy?' asked Phryne in her English voice.

'Of course,' he responded automatically.

'The accusation of murder which Thomas Beaconsfield made against your great grandfather upset you, didn't it?' insinuated Phryne, leaning on the weak leg of her rickety chair. It had started to splinter very promisingly. 'Your family honour is your obsession.'

'The nerve of that hound, saying such things about a Cholmondeley!' said Roddy, looking at Phryne for the first time. Bill Gaskin and Young Billy didn't move, sensing that something was happening. 'I won't have such things—such lies—noised abroad.'

'And what are you going to do with Wallace?' asked Phryne in the same intimate tone, as though they were alone. 'Think of what he knows about you! Think of what he could tell the press! Think of waking up one morning to find the paper with a headline "Dunstable Dishonoured"!'

'You can't turn me against Wallace,' sneered Roddy. 'He's as loyal as a dog.'

'And you want him to pine to death on your grave, do you?' asked Phryne. 'Have you a nice, quiet death picked out for him? Over the side on the voyage home? They say that the South China Sea is full of sharks. They demolish a man in five minutes, nothing left to say who he was and why he followed a madman to destruction. There's an excuse for you, Roddy. You are quite obviously insane. And you are a lord, of course. That will always make a difference. At your trial, all you need to do is blame Wallace. He's clearly sane and he's a peasant— isn't that what you called Bill? A peasant? Isn't that what you think of him? No one who knows you will ever testify that you had the capacity to think of this on your own.'

'You aren't going to be able to twist my thoughts!' yelled Roderick, swelling and turning red. He shook Phryne until her chair broke completely. 'You won't turn me from my purpose with your clever voice!'

His face bore a look of utter astonishment as he found himself falling after the gun butt came down hard on his head.

'I wasn't trying to turn you,' spat Phryne. She heaved, shrugged off the ropes and the remains of the chair and added another scientific blow to the base of the neck with a lump of wood. She took the gun out of Wallace's hand and shoved it in her pocket. Then she went to Bill Gaskin. While she was struggling with the knots she said over her shoulder, 'Give me your knife, Wallace, and if I were you I'd leave. Quite fast. Before the cops get here.'

Wallace, who had felled Roderick under the spell of Phryne's voice, turned pale and handed over the knife.

'Where can I go? What shall I do?' he stammered.

'Pinch whatever Roddy's got and go while the going is good, is my advice. Your future career is up to you. Goodbye,' said Phryne, shoving him out of the door of the hut and dragging Bill Gaskin after her. He seemed dazed. 'Come on, Bill, make an effort. I need your ropes to secure the giant. Young Billy, can you walk?'

'Yes, Miss, I think so, Miss,' said Billy, who was not at all clear on the course of events. Except that the Seventh Cavalry hadn't arrived and he was somehow free. This was not in his mental script at all and he was already fuzzy with terror, thirst and the blow to his head.

'Then walk, Young Billy,' said Phryne. 'Take your dad with you. See if he can get the Bentley started. I am quite bored with this hut.' She knelt on the fallen Roderick, tying sheet bends around his wrists and ankles. He was awake, fuming impotently. Phryne dived a hand into her petticoat pocket and found that the packet was empty. She investigated the picnic basket. None there. Damn! She insinuated a hand into Roddy's breast pocket and brought out a cigarette case and a lighter. Thank the lord for that.

When Lin Chung came into the bark hut, he found Phryne Fisher, much dishevelled and corpse-white with flour, sitting on Roderick Cholmondeley's back and smoking luxuriously.

'Have one?' she said, smiling up at him. 'Turkish that side, Virginian this.'

Lin was torn between terror, fear, relief and astonishment. He did not know what to say. Though he had tried to comfort Dot, he was at a loss to explain how Phryne, who from the look of the weals on her arms had been tied to a chair the whole time, had managed to get the better of two strong, armed men.

He settled for a cigarette.

Phryne explained. 'I just had to find the sane one and convince him of the madness of the plan. I would be wasting my powder on Roddy, he is completely away with the pixies. So it had to be Wallace. I presume Li Pen is with you? So he probably has Wallace. I think we should let him go. He did save my life.'

'Only after endangering it,' said Lin severely. 'The ambush must have been his idea if Cholmondeley is as stupid as you say.'

'Probably. But by himself he is not dangerous.' Phryne was losing interest. She combed her hair with her fingers and took stock of herself. 'It's the rag bag for this dress,' she said. 'And I seem to have lost my hat. My stockings are ruined, though Dot can probably save the shoes. But there's nothing wrong with me which a little attention wouldn't cure.'

'Shall we go back to Castlemaine, then?' he asked, still amazed.

'We'd better take Bill Gaskin and Young Billy home. Young Billy has had a bang on the head and should see a doctor. And we have to hand over this menace to public order and see him confined in a nice safe cell. They can hold him on bilking the Imperial. I bet he didn't pay his account.'

Li Pen had secured Wallace and brought him into the hut.

'I really don't think letting him go is just,' said Lin. 'He is an accomplice, and I believe he was the man who tried to run Dot down.'

'It was Rod!' pleaded Wallace. 'He told me to!'

'You knew he was mad,' said Lin. 'You helped him.'

'He wasn't all that mad,' said Wallace. 'Not until today. Then he went cuckoo. Before that he was just determined.'

'You could tell us a lot about him,' said Lin.

Wallace struggled. 'Please, Father!' he said. 'I didn't do nothing!'

He was about to cry and Lin was revolted. He waved a hand, dismissing his objections. This was a pathetic creature. Li Pen had held the dark man without difficulty but released him on Phryne's order. He ran away through the trees without a word.

Then the Shaolin monk checked Roderick's bindings, approved of Phryne's knots and stowed him in the boot of the Bentley. Both cars' engines purred easily as the starting handles were employed.

'I'll drive this car,' said Phryne. 'You drive yours. You'll have to show me the way. I came here in a sack and I didn't notice any landmarks.'

The cars went soberly back into Castlemaine. The police cavalcade met them coming the other way. It was an exultant group who came into the town, blowing horns and cheering. The whole staff of the Imperial was on the front step. Annie was crying happy tears. Sergeant Hammond was looking as relieved as a man could be who was now no longer expecting instant demotion and who knew his bunions wouldn't stand walking the beat again. That was how he'd got the bunions in the first place.

Roderick was lodged in a small but well-appointed cell with locks straight out of *Little Dorrit*. He still had not spoken. Phryne, having bathed and changed, sat in the front bar (where women did not sit, ever, not even women of an unfortunate profession) eating breakfast and accepting champagne from the old French part of the cellar while chain-smoking Roddy's cigarettes. The guard dog sat at her feet, thumping the floor with his tail and accepting bacon rind. Old Bill Gaskin supped a beer, still disconcerted but of a mind to agree with his old mates Bert and Cec that this sheila was different from all other sheilas. After the doctor had diagnosed mild concussion, Young Billy had been taken home by his Aunt Madge to lie in a nice dark room and be fed lemonade. Lin and Li Pen joined the party. It had been such a prodigious day that the presence of a Chinese priest and his acolyte did not seem strange.

Phryne interrupted this to telephone home. It took her some time to calm Dot and longer for Dot to calm Miss Eliza, but eventually, she gathered, her household was going to sit down to a late breakfast, everyone having been too distraught to eat their early one, and then they were all going to have a little nap, especially Miss Eliza and Lady Alice, who had sat up listening for the phone all night. Then they were setting out on the train for Castlemaine and expected to be there for dinner.

After some hours of carousing, Phryne slid a hand onto Lin's cassock-clad knee. 'Is there somewhere we can go?' she asked. 'Or can you come to me?'

'Certainly,' said Lin. He stood up. 'Miss Fisher has asked me to escort her to her room. She is feeling a little overcome,' he announced in his suave priest's voice. No one in the public bar said a word.

Phryne waved as they left and climbed the stairs.

'I'm not the only one with a powerful voice,' she commented.

As soon as the door was locked, Phryne sprang on Lin Chung and tore at the buttons on his cassock, stripping off her own clothes as they came to hand. Lin felt an answering fire leap in his own breast. He shed the cassock and the shirt underneath tore as her clever fingers found more buttons and she rubbed her face against him like an amorous cat, growling in her throat.

She backed Lin until he fell across the well-sprung bed and then with a flash of smooth flanks she was on him and he wondered, as teeth closed on his throat, if this was how it felt to lie down under a tiger. The predator growled, stooped and pounced, and Lin cried out at the conjunction, a pure animal sound. She had him. He could not move. She could. She rose over him; the first thrust went deep enough to hurt.

The clutch of her internal muscles brought him almost to orgasm, and he groaned at the waste, but his captor was alert to the prey's every move. Twisting, she toppled them over so that he was lying on her breast, her legs wrapped around him, and they coupled like dragon and phoenix, so close that not a hair could come between the lithe body and the supple one and their black hair mingled on the pillow.

It was too intense to last. Phryne collapsed on Lin Chung and gasped as though she had been pulling a rickshaw. He held her carefully, in case she bit him again. He was astonished, gratified, and lightly bruised.

'The prospect of death makes one love life,' he said.

'I was so close,' she panted. 'So close to Death last night that I could smell his breath. But I'm alive. Lin, did I hurt you?'

'Nothing like as much as you pleased me,' he said. 'Come and I'll show you another way to defy death,' he said, and touched tiny, delicate caresses to all the pressure points along her back. When he reached the lowest one she convulsed.

'The theory is that each one of these points is a centre of ch'i,' he told her. 'That is, life force. Your ch'i has been disrupted by spending a lot of time tied to a chair in danger of being murdered,' he added.

Phryne laughed shakily. 'Yes, that can certainly disrupt a girl's ch'i energy,' she agreed.

'Then if we do this . . .' The clever fingers slid along her spine. 'And this . . .' They slipped sideways onto her breasts. 'We can regulate your breathing like that of a Shaolin master.'

The caresses were not slowing Phryne's heartbeat. She felt it pound. She reached and captured the hand.

'Or perhaps we could try this way,' she suggested, laying

one thigh over his hip, and drawing him gently back into conjunction with her again. Slowly, slowly; the sensation was so exquisite that she bit her lip, trying not to grab. They began to move, very quietly and circumspectly, then faster and faster.

The day wore on. Phryne woke from a light sleep to see that the square of sunlight from the window had moved from one side of the room to the other and was now shining directly into her eyes. It must be late afternoon.

Lin was asleep. Of course, he had had an interrupted night. Phryne rose and went to the bathroom. Returning, she sat down on the side of the bed and looked at her lover. Golden skin, cock's feather hair with a blue sheen, the black line of his eyelashes absurdly thick. He was utterly beautiful and very dear.

She became aware that he had opened his eyes and was looking at her with a similar expression to her own.

'I thought I'd lost you,' he said, cupping her cheek in his hand. Her freshly washed hair swung over his hand.

'And I thought I'd lost me,' she replied. 'It's getting late. Look, the sun has almost gone. Shall we bathe and dress and go down to dinner?'

'If we must,' he said. 'Oh, lord,' he said, raising himself on one elbow and looking at the mass of garments on the floor.

'What?' asked Phryne from the bathroom, over the roar of water.

'There are no buttons left on my cassock!' he said.

'There goes your reputation,' said Phryne.

As it happened, the party from Melbourne had just arrived, and Lin's cassock was rebuttoned by Dot, who had been sewing on buttons for little brothers since she could first hold a needle. She also repaired his shirt with fast, even stitches. Li Pen stood by the window as his master was rearrayed in his priestly disguise, which concealed the bite on his throat, and escorted him downstairs to reserve a table.

Everyone was coming to dinner.

Phryne was dressed in a new outfit which Dot had brought from St Kilda: a bright red crepe de Chine cocktail dress with red shoes to match and a trailing, slightly outrageous red ostrich feather panache for her hair. Dot herself, slightly weak with relief, wore her favourite terracotta and ochre evening dress and a rather nice bandeau with an orange geranium in it. Lady Alice and Eliza were in their own room and emerged as Phryne and Dot reached the stairs.

'So it's all over, Miss?' demanded Dot. She liked to be reassured.

'Absolutely all over. The bad man is in jail and I would say that he has gone over the edge. He is probably completely and incurably insane, and he is guilty of attempted murder. Twice. Of you and me. Therefore he will be held at His Majesty's Pleasure, and that will probably be for his whole life.'

'Good,' observed Lady Alice. She wore a faded but good dark blue silk dress which had been let out, inexpertly, at least twice as Lady Alice's corpulence increased. But around her neck was a chain of star sapphires and there were sapphires in her dark hair. Eliza wore a dusty rose damask dress with a small hat with more roses on it and the pearls her mother had given her before she fled to the lepers. Both women glowed with joy: they were pleasant to be near, like a wood fire.

'I've asked the Beaconsfield heir to dinner,' said Phryne. 'You'll like him. A good honest man.'

'Then I hope he just demands the money and doesn't go anywhere near Father,' said Lady Alice. 'That man could corrupt a monk.'

Dinner was laid out on several small tables pushed together. Soup was already on the table as the ladies came down and bottles of champagne popped. Old Bill Gaskin, in a new shirt which Annie had bought for him, looked uncomfortably at Lady Alice over the rim of his beer glass. Madge Johnson, his sister, escorting Young Billy, prepared to sniff and didn't. This looked like an ordinary woman, getting on for middle age, a bit plump, not some lady come to put on side. Lady Alice improved her opportunity by sitting down with the Gaskins and enquiring gently after Young Billy's poor head and telling them that she wasn't Lady Alice, just Alice Beaconsfield, and she was pleased to meet them and had to apologise for the appalling heir of Dunstable.

Madge Johnson let out her breath. 'He wasn't your fault, my lady . . . Miss,' she said. 'Neither was your ancestor. Nor the attack on Young Billy. He'll be all right.'

'He will,' said Bill Gaskin. 'Boy's head's as hard as teak, fortunately. Nice to meet you, Miss.'

At the other end of the table Sergeant Hammond was greeting Detective Inspector Robinson, who had come to relieve him of his prisoner and had decided to stay for dinner.

'He might have been sane before he came here,' Hammond said in answer to a question, 'but he's a fruitcake now. We've had to put him in a straitjacket and that wasn't an easy job, he's as strong as a bull. Nasty bump on the head might have slowed him down a bit.'

'Governor's Pleasure job, then, you reckon?' said Robinson, taking another spoonful of the soup, which was spring chicken and very good.

'You'll never get him to trial,' said Hammond. 'Keeps saying he's the king and we're all his subjects.'

'What about the other bloke, this Wallace?'

'Got away, Miss Fisher says. I don't know how she did that. She seems to have talked this Wallace into felling the prisoner.'

'She's a woman of uncanny powers,' said Robinson, slurping more soup. 'And fortunately, unique. See the grey hair at the side of my head? I call these my Miss Fisher hairs. But she got him,' he said. 'She uses methods which no Commissioner would ever countenance, but she always gets her man.'

'Too right,' said Sergeant Hammond.

'More bread? Certainly,' said Miss Eliza to Dot. 'I have to apologise for my previous behaviour at your house, Dorothy. I was unbearable. I was so unhappy and so angry and there didn't seem to be a chance that I'd extricate myself from the situation, or ever see my dear Alice again. But I shouldn't have been so odious. I'll be leaving soon, as soon as Alice and I can find a small house. We've got quite enough between us if I sell my pearls and she sells her sapphires. Where do you think we should live, to do the most good?'

'Well,' said Dot, 'there's the city itself, that's a sink of wickedness. St Kilda could do you some pretty good wickedness as well. Why not let me walk you around some of the likely places? The girls can come too,' she added.

Ruth and Jane, clad in their proper but just a bit spangly evening dresses, were being good, which was always a charming sight for as long as it lasted, Dot thought. They were drinking soup by the respectable but remarkably inefficient 'tilt the bowl away from you and scoop' method which they had been taught, which was nice of them, and they were doing it well. Jane was sitting next to Professor Ayers, quivering with questions. He took pity on her and began to talk. Jane, he had decided, was a scientific lusus naturae and therefore to be encouraged.

Dr Treasure had pleaded family commitments and had not come, but Mr Josiah Burton was there, enthroned in a hastily adapted chair and talking affably to Young Billy, who was wondering if he was actually talking to a dwarf or perhaps was not fully recovered from his concussion. Mr Harrison, who was not going to be excluded, sat beside him and sucked soup like a vacuum cleaner.

'We've got something to ask you, Miss Alice,' said Old Bill. 'I don't want this title, but I don't think a man ought to give way to tyranny, so I told that Roddy that I wouldn't sign. However, I'd like your advice. What do you think I should do?'

'You're asking the wrong person,' said Lady Alice. 'I'm not going back to England and I don't think you'd be comfortable there either. But there's no reason to allow Father to get away with this—outrageous, utterly outrageous scheme. I say, sting the old bastard for a small fortune in exchange for signing the repudiation. You should be compensated for your ordeal, for Billy's head, and for all that insult and inconvenience. Get the Melbourne lawyer to tell him so. Then you can use the money for good works, buy your own business or take a trip around the world . . .'

'Always wanted to do that,' said Bill Gaskin. 'On one of them cruise ships. Egypt. Ceylon. India. All the islands.' He made up his mind. 'Yair. I reckon that's a good idea, Lady Alice. I wouldn't be comfortable, taking anything away from a nice lady like you. And Madge works hard, she could do with some help in the house, eh, Madge? Send the laundry out? Girl to do the scrubbing? Bit of money'd be nice.'

Madge nodded. A devout reader of romances, she could not see Bill Gaskin as the newly discovered marquess of anywhere, not even Castlemaine. But help in the house would be lovely and would give her more time for her reading.

'Still,' said Bill Gaskin comfortably, aware of the joint of beef which had just been wheeled in and a prosperous future which certainly contained more beer, 'all's well that ends well, eh?'

'Is all ending well?' asked Phryne of Lin Chung. His hand found her knee under the table.

'We are not going to Melbourne with the others,' he whispered.

'No?' She raised an eyebrow.

'If you please, we are going to a Chinese farm, where there is a guesthouse of palatial magnificence, and no one will bother us for at least a week. I asked Dot to bring you enough clothes and things,' he said.

'Wonderful,' said Phryne.

She looked around the room. Everyone was present, happy, well fed and contented. Lady Alice and Eliza were holding hands under the table. Both Gaskins looked pleased. Mr Burton was delivering a blistering snub to Mr Harrison, who had not noticed. The policemen were deep in police shop. Dot was discussing a new house with Eliza, so she would be moving out. And Phryne was about to have free range over Lin Chung's admirable person for a week, without anyone trying to kill her, telephoning her or demanding that she solve some puzzle. She rose to her feet and proposed a toast. More champagne corks popped, one of the most festive sounds in the world.

'To happy endings!' she cried.

Everyone drank.

Castlemaine Post, Express edition, 12 January 1998

Heritage workers who were cutting the grass at the Old Bark Hut heritage site were alarmed when one of their mowers fell into an unmarked mine shaft on Saturday. They called in the local emergency services to retrieve the mower. At the bottom of the shaft, which was more than ten metres deep, shocked workers found the body of a man. Sergeant Hutton called in the local historical society when it became clear that the body had been there for at least fifty years. The man had been saponified, a condition which occurs when the stearates in body fat turn to a soapy substance called adipocere. This usually happens in cold water. He was very well preserved. From the papers in his pocket, the man seems to have been called Joseph Smith. (Continued on page 5 . . .)

AUTHOR'S NOTE

This is a work of fiction. I have used Castlemaine as a base for it but it is not, and cannot be, accurate to a centimetre. I have taken liberties with names and places. This is what a novel does. I have tried to be as accurate as I possibly could with the assistance of some very knowledgeable people. But if you find some small error and feel the need to tell me that I have got it wrong, please think again. Anyone else is welcome to email me on kgreenwood@netspace.net.au and if you would like to duplicate my research, here are my sources.

Bibliography

Adcock, WE, *Gold Rushes of the Fifties* Poppet Head Press, Glen Waverley, 1982

Bradfield, Raymond, *Castlemaine: A Golden Harvest* Lowden Printing Castlemaine Mail, Kilmore, 1972

——, *Campbells Creek* Castlemaine Mail, Castlemaine, not dated (privately published)

——, Unpublished Notes on the Chinese in Castlemaine, Castlemaine Historical Society archives

Cannon, Michael, *Who's Master? Who's Man? Australia in the Victorian Age: 1* Thomas Nelson Australia, Melbourne, 1971

Chang, Julie (ed.), *Chinese Cultures in the Diaspora* National Endowment for Culture and Arts, Taiwan, 1997

Disher, Garry, *Australia Then and Now* Oxford University Press, Melbourne, 1987

Evans, William (ed.), *Diary of a Welsh Swagman, 1869–1894* Sun Books, Melbourne, 1977

Fauchery, Antoine, *Letters from a Miner in Australia*, trans. AR Chisholm, Georgian House, Melbourne, 1965

Fawcett, Raymond, *How Did They Live?* Gawthorn Ltd, London, circa 1950

Filer, Joyce, *Disease* British Museum, London, 1995

Gerritsen, Rupert, *And Their Ghosts May Be Heard* Fremantle Arts Centre Press, Perth, 1994

Gittins, Jean, *The Diggers from China* Quartet Books, Melbourne, 1981

Goodman, David, *Gold Seeking Victoria and California in the 1850s* Allen & Unwin, Sydney, 1994

Hocking, Geoff, *Castlemaine from Camp to City, 1835–1900* Five Mile Press, Melbourne, 1994

Howitt, William, *Land, Labour and Gold* facsimile edition, Sydney University Press, Sydney, 1972

Joyce, Christopher and Stover, Eric, *Witnesses from the Grave* Grafton Press, London, 1993

Keesing, Nancy, *The Golden Dream* William Collins Australia, Sydney, 1974

—— (ed.), *Gold Fever* Angus & Robertson, Sydney, 1967

Kwan, Choi Wah, *The Right Word in Cantonese* The Commercial Press, Hong Kong, 1989

McMillan, AR, *The Pennyweight Kids* Castlemaine Mail, Castlemaine, 1988

Morris, Wendy, *A Guide to Maldon* Currency Productions, Melbourne, 1984

Ni, Maoshing, PhD translator of Suwen, Neijing, *The Yellow Emperor's Classic of Medicine* Shambala, Boston, 1995

O'Brien, Joanne and Kwok, Man Ho, *Chinese Myths and Legends* Arrow Books, London, 1990

Pearl, Cyril, *Wild Men of Sydney* WH Allen and Co, London, 1958

Roberts, Charlotte and Manchester, Keith, *The Archaeology of Disease* Cornell University Press, New York, 1983

Rolls, Eric, *Sojourners* University of Queensland Press, St Lucia, 1992

Sagazio, Celestina, *Tour of the Pennyweight Flat Cemetery and the Maldon Cemetery* National Trust, Melbourne, 1992

—— (ed.), *Cemeteries: Our Heritage* National Trust, Melbourne, 1992

Shaw, George Bernard, *The Intelligent Woman's Guide to Socialism and Capitalism* Constable and Co, London, 1928

Sherer, John, *The Gold-Finder of Australia* Colonial Facsimiles, Penguin, Melbourne, 1973

Siug, Jong Ah, *A Difficult Case*, trans. Ruth Moore and John Tully, Jim Crow Press, Daylesford, 2000

Tun, Li-Ch'en, *Annual Customs and Festivities in Peking*, trans. Derk Bodde, Hong Kong University Press, Hong Kong, 1965

Waley, Arthur, *Dear Monkey* Bobbs-Merril Co, New York, 1973

Wannan, Bill, *Tell 'Em I Died Game* Rigby Ltd, Sydney, 1963

Weir, David, *The Water Margin* WH Allen and Co, London, 1979

Yutang, Lin, *The Gay Genius* William Heinemann Ltd, London, 1948

——, *My Country and My People* William Heinemann Ltd, London, 1936

Maps and diagrams of Castlemaine and Melbourne
National Trust Guide to Castlemaine Market
Discovering the Mount Alexander Diggings, A Guidebook Mount Alexander Diggings Committee, 1999
Information for People Leaving Great Britain 1854 facsimile edition of the Colonization Circular issued by Her Majesty's Colonial Land and Emigration Commissioners in May 1854, Macbeth Genealogical Books, Sydney, 1990

Mr Butler's Considering Cocktail
1 part sweet vermouth
4 parts chilled orange juice
dash of angostura bitters
dash of lemon juice

Combine and shake with crushed ice. Decorate with a twist of lemon peel.

Murder in Montparnasse
Kerry Greenwood

The divine Phryne Fisher returns to lead another dance of intrigue.

Seven Australian soldiers, carousing in Paris in 1918, unknowingly witness a murder and their presence has devastating consequences. Ten years later, two are dead . . . under very suspicious circumstances.

Phryne's wharfie mates, Bert and Cec, appeal to her for help. They were part of this group of soldiers in 1918 and they fear for their lives and for those of the other three men. It's only as Phryne delves into the investigation that she, too, remembers being in Montparnasse on that very same day.

While Phryne is occupied with memories of Montparnasse past and the race to outpace the murderer, she finds troubles of a different kind at home. Her lover, Lin Chung, is about to be married. And the effect this is having on her own usually peaceful household is disastrous.

'Phryne Fisher is young, wealthy, beautiful, smart, confident and independently minded . . . and she has a knack for solving murders when she is not sipping a strengthening cocktail or planning another seduction.' —*Australian's Review of Books*

ISBN 1 86508 806 4

Away with the Fairies
Kerry Greenwood

Phryne Fisher — dangerous, passionate, kind, clever and seductive. She drinks cocktails, dances the tango, is the companion of wharfies, and is expert at conducting an elegant dalliance.

It's the 1920s in Melbourne and Phryne is asked to investigate the puzzling death of a famous author and illustrator of fairy stories. To do so, Phryne takes a job within the women's magazine that employed the victim and finds herself enmeshed in her colleagues' deceptions.

But while Phryne is learning the ins and outs of magazine publishing first hand, her personal life is thrown into chaos. Impatient for her lover Lin Chung's imminent return from a silk-buying expedition to China, she instead receives an unusual summons from Lin Chung's family followed by a series of mysterious assaults and warnings.

'Snappy one-liners and the ability to fight like a wildcat are appealing in a central character.' —*City Weekly*

ISBN 1 86508 489 1

Death Before Wicket
Kerry Greenwood

The sassy Phryne Fisher sets the seamy side of Sydney alight in her tenth adventure.

Phryne Fisher has plans for her Sydney sojourn — a few days at the Test cricket, a little sightseeing and the Artist's Ball with an up-and-coming young modernist. But these plans begin to go awry when Phryne's maid discovers her thoroughly respectable sister has left her family for the murky nightlife of the Cross. And Phryne is definitely not the woman to say 'no' when two delightful young men come to her on bended knees, begging for her help in finding their friend innocent of theft. Phryne's plans for a simple day or two of pleasure are postponed for good.

It all sounds simple enough as Phryne sets investigations into motion, but when greed and fear are the motivating factors, people become ruthless and Phryne finds herself enmeshed in blackmail, secrets, lies and the dangerous influences of deep magic.

'Pure indulgence . . . a 1920s heroine for the 90s . . . a fast and elegant read.' —*Who Weekly*

ISBN 1 74114 095 1

Raisins and Almonds
Kerry Greenwood

Super-sleuth Phryne Fisher steps, like an elegant cat, through this, her eighth adventure.

In investigating the poisoning of a young man in a bookshop at the Eastern market, and the wrongful arrest of one Miss Sylvia Lee, Phryne Fisher is plunged into a world of Jewish politics, alchemy, poison and chicken soup.

Stopping only for a brief, but intensely erotic, dalliance with the beautiful Simon Abrahams, Phryne picks her way through the mystery with help from the old faithfuls — Bert, Cec, Dot and Detective Inspector 'Call Me Jack' Robinson. But ultimately it is her stealth and wit which solve the crime — and all for the price of a song. . . .

'Phryne Fisher is gutsy and adventurous, and also well endowed with plenty of grey matter. She has it over Robicheaux and Poirot because she's drop-dead gorgeous.' —*West Australian*

ISBN 1 86508 880 3